PRAISE FOR

Children of the Edict

"*Children of the Edict* is an engrossing story describing the thirty-five-year-long toll on Chinese families under China's cruel one-child-per-family edict and how they coped. Millions of female infants, many torn from their mothers' arms, were 'disposed of' or outright killed as 'illegal babies.' Due to government-mandated education and brainwashing, most citizens accepted this as 'how things are,' and any dissidents were quickly punished. But some knew it was not right and were inspired by the memory of the Tiananmen Square students' courage in facing guns and tanks in the past. As public opinion and the gender imbalance caused by the inhumane one-child policy gained ground, the law was changed. Readers will find this book eye-opening, and it will inspire renewed empathy for citizens of countries governed by tyrants."

> —Sylvia Nickels, Author of *Lament for a Broken Girl,*
> thearborscribe.com

"Madelyn has conjured up an enticing mystery involving imposing government obfuscation, strong family bonds frequently stressed, and young lovers modifying current trends to honor elderly traditions, all intertwined with learning, teaching, and practicing the banned Christianity, thereby risking repercussions."

> —Carole Marks, Storytelling Guide, Positive Solutions Tours,
> Avid Reader

"A government edict by the Chinese communist party mandates that married couples are allowed only one child per family. For Heo Wong, this edict becomes personal and life changing as he uncovers family mysteries that will affect his life (and those around him) forevermore. Heo embarks on a journey plagued by epidemics, cruelty, and imprisonment. This book exposes twentieth-century Chinese history as you may have never seen it revealed.

"In *Children of the Edict*, families who give birth to a second child face severe penalties. If that child is a boy, he is sent to an orphanage and, hopefully, adopted by a loving family. Girls are not as fortunate; for the most part, they are unwanted and often murdered. As you read this book, you will feel the culpability, approval, and reconciliation of family affection, as well as the yearning for independence and eagerness for a changing China."

—Tony Dora, Author of *A Boy, an Orphanage, a Cuban Refugee: The Road to Freedom*, tonydorabooks.com

"Heo and his families, both adopted and biological, become a beautiful story amidst harsh Chinese government practices. This story reminds me of a jigsaw puzzle. When you first open the box and see the jumbled pieces, nothing looks like they will fit together. But gradually as you see a piece that goes with another, you continue on to discover a beautiful picture at the end. Chinese history, devastation, and sorrow intermingled with family, love, and hope makes this a must-read book. The author has created a riveting read."

—Victoria Fletcher, Author, Owner of Hoot Books Publishing

"This book was fascinating to read and learn about a time we have had so little understanding of."

—Pamela C. Miller, PhD, Founder and President of the Storytelling Resource Place, Author of *Cinderella: The Heroine with a Thousand Shoes*

"I found [this book] beautifully written, inspiring, and highly appropriate in terms of the faith content. I don't see anything to improve upon. The tension between the state-supported church and the underground church is well done. And the work of the Holy Spirit in the life of the man who was a soldier who was drawn to the real church was beautiful."

—Reverend Dr. Bradley Scott, Pastor, First United Methodist Church, Sweetwater, Tennessee

"This book is steeped in cultural chaos brought on by the one-child edict. Beautiful traditions and pageantry work to hide the ironclad hold the government of China has over its people. Rohrer takes the intertwining lives of individuals and draws families together in the search for truth. She takes us into the shadows where Christians have to exist just to practice their religion. In reading this book, you begin to understand that there is no privacy or 'rights,' and wrong words can cause a person to disappear into one of the prisons or work camps with no chance of a trial.

"Throughout the book, there are daunting scenarios . . . but there is always hope. There are some who are willing to be ostracized and hated to save children from the one-child edict. Reading this book brings the plight of many out into the open and gives us pause to really understand the value of human life. You are continuously pulled along by mysteries and emotions, but there are deeper messages. Give yourself time to reflect and understand the stories that are being told."

—Linda Poland, Jonesborough Tennessee's Resident Storyteller, Owner of Positive Solutions through Stories and Tours, Creator and Author of the "Positive Points" column of the Jonesborough *Herald & Tribune*, Director of Hidden Heroines of Northeast Tennessee, Founding Member of the Jonesborough Storytellers Guild

Children of The Edict

by Madelyn Rohrer

Published by

köehlerbooks™

3705 Shore Drive
Virginia Beach, VA 23455
800-435-4811
www.koehlerbooks.com

CHILDREN
of the
EDICT

MADELYN ROHRER

VIRGINIA BEACH
CAPE CHARLES

Table of Contents

Prologue

SOMEWHERE IN CHINA a woman cradles her newborn son for a couple of minutes before he is pulled away from her and whisked off to an orphanage. He is her second child—an illegal child. She cries but is comforted in knowing that he will be adopted by a childless couple who want a son to carry on their family lineage.

Another woman cradles her newborn daughter for a couple of minutes before she is pulled away from her and whisked off to an orphanage. She is her second child—an illegal child. She resists and cries deeply. There is no comfort, for she knows orphanages are filled with baby girls. Her daughter will probably not be adopted; she will most likely die there.

The cries of a woman in a small village pierce the darkness of night as her newborn daughter is taken away to be destroyed to teach her and her husband and other couples that illegal children will be dealt with severely. She does not know, and will never know, that her daughter's life is not being snuffed out; she is actually being saved by people willing to risk their own lives to save her. While the parents mourn, the child enters the *baby tunnel* to waiting parents in another country who will raise her in a loving home as their very own.

In the rural countryside, a woman cradles her newborn child—and keeps it. The child is cherished and hidden. It is her third child, maybe her fourth. Many children are needed in her family and village to work in the fields or businesses to help them survive. Her local government understands and looks the other way. Her child will grow up in a loving family but will never have a birth certificate. As far as the government is concerned, he or she does not exist, will not be entitled to medical care, government-run schooling, or a pension in old age.

In a larger city, a woman briefly holds her newborn daughter before giving her up willingly. It is her first child, but her husband wants a son in keeping with the centuries-old tradition of having a son to continue the family line. There are no tears. It is just a girl, a disposable child. They will try again for a son.

Different scenarios with common threads, tradition, and a government mandate. During the thirty-five years (1980 to 2015) of China's one-child-per-family edict, estimates are that more than four hundred million births were prevented by abortion, willingly or forced, disposal, or adopting out. Enforcement of the edict was often brutal.

This book is about the children who survived. They are the new generation of workers who are leading the world's largest Communist-run country into the future. Do they care about ancient traditions? Will they adhere to their country's tenets of government? Are they content to live with the policies of past regimes? Does any of this affect you and me? Yes. What happens in China does affect the rest of the world.

Chapter 1

DR. SHEN (2002)

DR. HEO WONG administered a sedative into the fragile arm of Dr. Shen, his elderly dying neighbor. "This should start working in a few minutes, Papa Shen. It will take away some of your pain and help you rest. Are you warm enough? Would you like another blanket?"

"Thank you, Heo," came the quiet answer in a shallow, raspy voice. "You are so kind. I just can't seem to get warm. Yes, another blanket would feel good. There is an extra one on top of the chest in the corner."

Heo walked over to the large trunk-like chest and reached for the blanket. He also picked up a framed picture sitting next to it and looked down into the smiling faces of two people who had been dear to him his entire life—his neighbors, Dr. and Mrs. Shen.

"Papa Shen, do you remember when this picture was taken?" Heo held it up for his neighbor to see. Dr. Shen's eyes opened, looking distant as he tried to focus on the picture. A faint smile of recognition told Heo he was cognizant but groggy. His eyes closed once again.

"Ah, yes. I certainly do. Your mother took that picture. She took many pictures that day. It was your graduation party from children's school. You and Jin were five years old and all you could talk about was that soon you would be going to the big children's school."

"That's right," Heo chuckled, "and I remember you carved out wooden badges for us with our names on them, and Mama Shen painted *Star Student* underneath our names. I still have mine, and Jin probably does, too."

The Shens were like adopted grandparents to Heo and his twin brother, Jin. He and Jin barely knew their real grandparents who lived two provinces away, but the Shens were right next door. And as much as the boys loved and respected their parents, they both had a special fondness for "Mama Shen" and "Papa Shen." Memories wafted through Heo's mind as he looked at the picture—memories of games, listening to folklore stories of China, and freshly baked rice cakes with honey. He remembered the sadness when Mama Shen passed away five years ago. Now Papa Shen would soon be joining her. The time was near when Heo would have to say goodbye to his special neighbor, friend, and mentor. He added the blanket to the others covering Dr. Shen from neck to toe and resumed his bedside vigil. He and his parents plus a visiting nurse were taking turns caring for him. After coming home from the university and having a quick evening meal, it was Heo's shift.

A recent graduate of medical school, Heo was continuing with clinical studies at the university, thanks in large part to the encouragement and tutelage of Dr. Shen, an esteemed doctor of general medicine. He never tired of answering Heo's medical questions and engaging in endless conversations that at times seemed like an inquisition. Heo always enjoyed being alone with Papa Shen when they could talk about diagnoses, medicines, and new procedures. Although tonight was not one of those medical question and answer times, it still felt special— just the two of them—tutor and student. Now it was Heo's turn to help his Papa Shen, blending his caregiving with homework when Dr. Shen was asleep.

Heo's father noticed earlier in the day that Dr. Shen's pain seemed to be increasing. "How is your pain level, my friend? Is there something Heo can give you to alleviate your pain when he gets here?" he had asked.

Dr. Shen agreed and specified the medicine he wanted, a small dose, enough to ease his pain but not enough to sedate him into a state of being unable to communicate. Heo was familiar with the medicine, of course, and procured it from the hospital.

Dr. Shen reopened his eyes just long enough to smile again at his young protégé. His breathing was sounding less labored, more relaxed. The medicine was starting to work.

"You and Jin have always been a source of joy to us," he said with a smile on his wrinkled face. "It's hard to imagine sometimes that you are now grown men. I remember the day your mother and father brought Jin home from the hospital and you arrived a day later with a nurse. Your parents were full of joy after waiting so long for a son. Now they had two."

What a strange thing to say, thought Heo. *Why would a nurse bring me home a day later?*

"Why didn't Jin and I both come home from the hospital at the same time, Papa Shen? Did I have some kind of medical issue when I was born? Why did a nurse bring me home a day later?"

"Oh, you were fine. Your brother came home from the hospital with your parents, but you didn't arrive until the next day from the orphanage."

What! Orphanage? Is Dr. Shen delusional? Heo knew that loss or distortion of memory was not a side effect of this medicine, although it could make people say things they might not say under ordinary circumstances.

"Papa Shen, how could I come from an orphanage if my brother and I are twins? Perhaps I came home later because I wasn't ready to leave the hospital for some reason and my brother was? Is that what you mean?" he asked again.

"No, you came from an orphanage. You and Jin are not twins, even though you were both born around the same time. Your parents had to say you were twins so they would be able to keep both of you."

Heo's reaction ranged between shock and rejection! *Certainly, this cannot be true. Jin is my twin brother! We have always been twins! Maybe Papa Shen's memory is blurred between reality here at home and what he has seen in the hospital. Yes, that has to be it—he is confused!*

Dr. Shen continued to speak quietly and with closed eyes, unaware that Heo was staring at him in disbelief.

"As you know, Heo, it is important for people in our country to have a son to carry on their family name. It is tradition, and your dear mother and father are no different. They already had an infant daughter and they loved her, so when they first heard about the one-child-per-family edict, they were devastated. It meant they were not allowed to have more children, and their desire was for two or three. The only way they could have a son to carry on their family line was to give their daughter up for adoption. Then they could try again for a son. They could have done that—turned her over to an orphanage—but the one-child-per-family rule came as such a surprise to the people of our country. There were rumors for a long time about limiting family size to control population, but they were only rumors. Then when it did happen, it was effective immediately."

Dr. Shen paused a moment to collect his thoughts and subdue his emotions.

"It was a difficult time for your parents, having to choose between keeping their daughter or giving her up with the hope of someday having a son. We felt so sorry for them, Mama Shen and I did. Your father left the decision to your mother, and I know he would have supported whatever she chose to do. She rocked her little girl to sleep every night, holding her so close. Her eyes were swollen from crying. She knew that having a son was important to your father and she had to do it, but it was many months before your mother was finally able to let her go."

Heo froze with the realization that Dr. Shen was *not* confused. He was *not* having a hallucinatory side effect. He was relaxed and lucid.

The medicine was doing what it was supposed to do, easing pain but also losing his inhibitions, revealing his innermost thoughts. And here they were, all spilling out in the form of a casual conversation.

Although it never affected him personally, Heo knew all about the one-child-per-household edict mandated twenty-two years earlier. It went into effect just before he was born. Some agreed with it, some hated it, others didn't care. It was a part of the history of China that, as an intern and now a doctor, he had to adhere to and enforce medically. It was never a part of his own private world, however—until now.

"After giving their daughter up and trying for almost a year to have another child," Dr. Shen continued, "your parents sadly assumed it was not going to happen. And even if it did, there was no guarantee it would be a son. So they decided to adopt. Male babies were becoming available for adoption because they were being taken away from parents who already had a child. But while they were waiting for an adopted son—you—they were surprised that they were going to have a child of their own. They were nervous, of course, as all parents were before the gender of their child was known, but your mother got tested. She learned they were going to have a son.

"During all this time, however, they never heard from the adoption people. They were so overwhelmed with joy that they actually forgot about the request they submitted, until they received a notice from an orphanage that a baby boy was available for them and would be delivered soon.

"Their first thought, of course, was to tell the authorities they were going to have a son of their own and that the adoption should be cancelled, but they didn't have time. That was when your brother decided to be born. The day your mother came home with Jin was the same day they were told that you would be delivered *tomorrow*. It all happened so fast. 'Twins!' It was the perfect opportunity to have two sons!"

The long explanation took an obvious toll on Dr. Shen's energy as he turned his head away and squirmed uneasily under his pile of blankets. Tears welled up in Heo's eyes as he looked down at the aged face on the pillow. As much as he wanted his friend to rest, he had more questions. Innately, he knew he had to ask now or forever let them go.

"Papa Shen, I do not question what you are saying, but this is a surprise. How did my parents keep Jin a secret when I was delivered to their home by a nurse and Jin was already there?"

"They brought Jin to our house before the nurse arrived with you," the quiet voice answered. "They were worried at first that the authorities would somehow find out and take you away again, but they wanted two children so badly that they were willing to take the chance. So we agreed to help them. It was a strange circumstance the way it happened, but we were the only ones who knew—until now. We pledged our secrecy to your parents. They told everyone they had twins and no one ever questioned it. Your parents loved you both."

Heo felt an almost out-of-body sensation sweeping over him as he internalized Dr. Shen's words. An image of Jin stared at him. *We are about the same height and the same build*, he admitted, *but other than that, there is no resemblance. But twins don't have to be identical. We have always been called fraternal twins.*

"And what happened to their daughter? Was she . . . was she adopted?" The second question caused him to swallow hard to even ask. He knew the fate of many baby girls in orphanages.

"Their daughter is Cha-Li."

Heo gasped at the name; it was their cousin!

Dr. Shen smiled faintly at the sound of surprise, but slowly continued. "It was arranged for her to be adopted by your mother's sister and her husband. They were a little older and had no children of their own. They also loved Cha-Li and were not concerned about tradition. It was all legal; my wife and I witnessed their signatures on the adoption papers. Cha-Li was only a little over a year old, so she doesn't remember. She spent a lot of time at her aunt and uncle's house as an infant anyway. It wasn't a big adjustment for her to simply start living there. So yes, your cousin Cha-Li is really Jin's biological sister. And in a way, your parents were still in their daughter's life. They were able to watch her grow up. It made your mother sad sometimes, but not as sad as she would have been if Cha-Li was given up for adoption to strangers or—" His voice drifted off. Heo knew what the *or* meant. Even before the one-child-per-family edict, it was acceptable to snuff out the life of a female child.

Giving in to one last nudge of doubt, Heo asked once more, "Papa Shen, do you think the medicine is making you feel strange, perhaps saying strange things?" The few seconds Heo waited for a response seemed like an eternity.

"Oh, I definitely feel strange, like I am floating above the earth somewhere. But are you forgetting that I, too, am a doctor? I am well aware of how the medicine is affecting me."

Heo suddenly felt foolish with the questions he had been asking Dr. Shen, his respected personal mentor. "I am sorry, Papa Shen. Of course, you know what the medicine is doing to you. I only hope someday that I may possess a fraction of your knowledge."

A slight smile confirmed the aging physician's forgiveness and affection. "Even though it was more than twenty years ago, Heo, your parents could still get in trouble. They didn't plan to deceive anyone. They just accepted an unexpected opportunity to have two sons. Remember, your father is career military with a respectable rank. He took a chance. Both of your parents did. Your mother considers you to be the answer to her prayers or, as she says, you are her *special* blessing."

There was silence for which Heo was thankful as his mind tried to fit all the pieces of this bizarre puzzle together. Then Dr. Shen continued.

"Even though it did make us uneasy at first to have this knowledge about you and Jin, and especially about playing a part in making it happen, it made us very happy to watch your parents enjoying their two beautiful sons year after year, and even their daughter when they could. Your family is dear to us."

"You and Mama Shen will always be dear to us too, Papa Shen. I am also happy to know that my mother considers me to be a blessing. She never said that to me."

"Did you know your mother is a Christian?"

Another surprise! "No, I did not. She never talked about religion. When Jin and I went to church, it was always with you and Father to the Three Self Church. I often wondered why mother never went with us. Now I know. The Three Self Church must only be Father's church."

"That is correct. It is the same with me. As a doctor and teacher, I am also mandated by our government to attend the Three Self Church. Mama Shen was a Christian and talked with your mother about her church. Then your mother became a believer in that religion, and they went to church together. Although your father and I could not participate, we agreed to respect our wives' choice of religion. It is another thing that cannot be discussed."

More silence. Heo knew it was time to stop talking. Even with the medicine, Dr. Shen was moving with increasing discomfort. He patted his neighbor's arm and gently rubbed his forehead. "Thank you for telling me these things, Papa Shen. I promise I will keep my parents' secrets." There was no response other than a deep sigh.

Later that night, Heo summoned his parents, Bin and Yan Wong. The time was near. With Bin, Yan, and Heo at his bedside, and as the sun inched up over the horizon, Dr. Shen peacefully left his earthly body.

Dr. Shen's only living relative, an elderly sister, was physically unable to travel from her distant home to attend her brother's funeral, as was anticipated. Consequently, the Wong family already had plans in place to take care of the funeral arrangements. It was a large gathering of neighbors, personal friends, and Dr. Shen's associates from the hospital. The only person missing was Jin. Bin Wong submitted a formal request to the prison work camp where Jin was incarcerated for his son to attend the funeral. It went unanswered.

Chapter 2

WHO AM I? WHO DO I WANT TO BE?

ALTHOUGH HEO WANTED to talk with his mother and father about Dr. Shen's final words, he couldn't bring himself to question the parents he held in high esteem his entire life. He felt it would be disrespectful, and he could only imagine the discomfort and sadness they would feel. Instead, he spent much time during the following days and weeks simply glancing unobtrusively at them, recalling family times, and thinking about Jin, Cha-Li, and his aunt and uncle. An endless volley of thoughts and questions filled his mind. He didn't doubt that what Papa Shen said was true, and he didn't doubt his parents' love for both him and Jin, but wanting to know more about his own past kept eating away at him.

Do I have sisters or brothers somewhere who were born before the edict? Was I a forbidden second child, or perhaps a third or fourth? Is that why they gave me up? Did my real parents go through the same anguish that my adoptive parents went through when giving up their daughter? Do my real parents ever think about me and wonder where I am or how I am? Why do I care? Why can't I just be happy knowing I am part of a family who wanted me and loves me and raised me as their own?

As much as he tried to push aside thoughts of the family he would never know, visuals filled Heo's mind, images of people somewhere in China that he might resemble. He looked in the mirror, especially at his hair. He had black wavy hair with a wide streak of white on the right side of his head. It grew in that way as a toddler. No one could explain why a child so young would have black hair with a streak of white. One theory was that he was dropped at a young age or something fell on his head that damaged hair follicles. His parents denied any such accident had occurred. Perhaps he *was* injured enroute from his birth home to the orphanage and then to his new home. *Perhaps I really was dropped or hurt*, he thought. Another theory, according to his barber, was genetics.

"Genes are attached to your hair as well as other parts of your body," his barber told him. "Does anyone else in your family have prematurely white hair or developed white hair around the temples at an early age?"

His brother Jin's hair was all black and straight, as was his mother's and father's.

Heo thought about Cha-Li. Yes, she and Jin did have some facial resemblance, he realized, plus her hair was all black and straight like Jin's. But just thinking about Cha-Li was annoying! She acted aloof, almost like she looked down on him, and he didn't know why. It wasn't always that way; they played together as cousins and friends when they were younger. It was only in the last few years that she had changed, about the same time Jin was arrested and sent to the laogai camp. *Does she blame me for what happened to Jin? I tried to stop him, but he wouldn't listen!*

But now, with all this new information from Papa Shen, there might be other reasons for Cha-Li's attitude. *Does she know about my being adopted? Does she know about herself? Is she angry knowing she was adopted out of the family, and I was adopted into it?*

Heo remembered their encounter at Papa Shen's funeral. She acknowledged his presence with a brief nod and then ignored him as usual for the rest of the time. It hurt. But again, Heo asked himself, *Why do I care? Why should I be concerned about what she thinks or what she knows? She's a cousin and not really mine.* He came to resent Cha-Li over time, an emotion that seemed even more justified on his part.

Months went by and Heo's longing for knowledge faded. He still had questions about who he was and where he came from, but his adoptive parents would most likely not know the answers. No one would, probably not even the orphanage, whichever one it was. Nothing was going to change by having a family discussion. Heo's past was erased. The only thing he knew for sure was that the one-child-per-family edict was now personal. Drawing on inner strength and adult reasoning, he decided to let it go. He couldn't live in the past and still look forward to his future as a physician.

What *did* bother him, however, was the part of his job involving gender identification of the unborn and "resolution." It was part of his curriculum as a med student and a continuing part of his duties at the clinic. No one really cared for it, but each intern and doctor had to take on gender ID assignments. Although there were occasional rumors of the tests being discontinued, it hadn't happened. There was still a continuous stream of couples or, in some cases, single women who were required by law to be tested simply because they were of child-bearing age. Month after month, Heo did what was required of him—until the day he met Li-Chou.

She was a sixteen-year-old, soon-to-be bride, obviously with child. The man in her life appeared to be considerably older, possibly twice her age, Heo guessed. Heo also realized that the gender of her child was key to their relationship. If it was a boy, they would be married. If it was a girl, it was to be aborted or the father would walk out of Li-Chou's life. As a minor, the girl's parents were also present. If it was determined that she was going to have a daughter and decided to keep her, the girl would be going home with them.

Although Heo had experienced many emotional moments in the

examining room, he felt conflicted today between Chinese tradition and determining the life or death of an unborn female. Secretly, he hoped Li-Chou's child was male, but that was not to be. X-rays revealed the child was female.

Heo tried to exhibit professionalism as he made the announcement and respectfully asked permission to perform the abortion. He expected sobs, disappointment, or at least indifference. There was nothing, just the sound of a whispered prayer as Li-Chou lay on the table, eyes closed, hands clasped together.

"Thank you, doctor," she announced calmly as she opened her eyes and sat up. "I do not want to abort my child. She is my daughter and I want to keep her."

There was nothing more to be said as far as the older man was concerned. He stood up and walked out of the room, presumably out of Li-Chou's life. Her parents went out to an adjoining waiting room.

Heo reached for the piece of paper that he was obligated to read to an unwed mother, outlining her options. It was something he had read and explained many times, but it seemed empty today. When he looked into the eyes of the trusting adolescent sitting before him, his human side won out over professionalism.

"You are an amazing young lady, Li-Chou," he smiled, "and very courageous, but I have to tell you what to expect if you choose to keep your child. Some of these things will affect you now and others will affect you in the future. First of all, unless you have a marriage certificate or a valid reproduction permit from the government, you will not be given a birth certificate and you will have to pay a social maintenance fee. It is a very expensive fee, usually about four times the income of an average working person. Do you have a job?"

"No."

"Second," Heo continued, "you will not be given a hukou. That is an official household registration. It will be as though your child does not exist. When it is time for her to go to school, you will have trouble getting her enrolled anywhere. You will most likely have to hire a private tutor or teach her yourself.

"Healthcare will be another obstacle. Because she is not a registered child, you will have difficulty obtaining healthcare for her. When she grows up, she will probably not be able to get healthcare for herself, even if she is married.

"As for yourself right now, an under-aged, unwed mother without a job, these expenses will have to be paid by your family and they will have to be willing to accept them. I do not know what your family's financial situation is, but these costs can be crushing. That is something you will need to discuss with them, and I will be happy to go over all these issues with them as well. Would you like to have some time alone to talk with them now?"

"No, doctor," she quietly replied. "There is nothing to discuss. I will undergo the abortion. As much as I want to keep my child, I cannot put this burden on my family. They have already given up much to keep me as their only child. I know they would have preferred a son but, as Christians, they taught me there is value in every person, whether male or female. I know I am here today because of that belief. I know they love me and would love my child, but I also know they will understand my decision under the circumstances."

Heo was taken by surprise once again with the word *Christian*. He made a mental note to find out more—probably from his mother.

"Would you consider marriage to the person who was here earlier?" he offered.

"No. I thought I loved him and that he loved me, but today I saw a different person. After listening to his words, they were cold – hurtful, and my feelings for him changed. If my child was going to be a boy, I probably would have married him for my child's sake and for my family's sake, but I would never feel the same about him. He says he is a Christian man, but he is not. It would not be a good marriage."

Tears of a broken relationship and an unwanted abortion spilled onto Li-Chou's cheeks. Heo sat on his chair in front of her and held her hand, his own eyes getting misty as he offered a box of tissues.

Li-Chou took a deep breath, dried her eyes, and sat up straighter. "Please forgive my tears, doctor. Thank you for taking the time to explain all these things to me. One more question. Do I have the option of letting my child be born and putting her up for adoption?"

"Unfortunately, no. I wish adoption was an option, but the orphanages are filled to capacity with female babies right now and there are very few adoptive parents within China wanting daughters. There are a small number of requests from outside our country, but not enough to give homes to all the girls needing them. There is just no room in the orphanages."

"Then I truly have no choice. Yes, I would like to have a few minutes with my parents so I can tell them why I have made this decision. I want to make sure they understand why it is necessary."

"Of course. Take all the time you need. I will ask them to come in."

Heo waited outside the room while Li-Chou talked with her parents. His hand shook as he held the vial of the life-ending drug. *If I was born a girl instead of a boy, this is how my own life would have ended before it ever had a chance to begin. I don't want to do this!*

"Doctor, we are ready," came the soft voice of Li-Chou's father.

As Heo prepared to administer the dose of medicine, he tried to avoid looking into Li-Chou's face. "I am so sorry," he told her as he hesitated, but she put her hand on his sleeve and looked at him.

"It's alright, doctor. I know I will meet my daughter someday in Heaven. She will know me, and I will know her. We believe that to be true. It is alright." She turned her face away as Heo injected the drug, vowing to himself that he would find a way to never have to do this again—*ever!*

He didn't have to wait long. A month later, gender testing for non-medical reasons was banned by the government to prevent further widening of the male-to-female imbalance. It meant doctors in hospitals no longer had to do forced testing and abortions, but the issue of wanting pre-birth identification persisted. While some embraced the new privacy as a step forward for women's rights, it caused a wave of outrage for thousands of other Chinese women. The one-child-per-family mandate was still very much in effect; now they were being denied the only way of identifying the sex of their child before birth. Having a son for an only child was still preferred. Consequently, a black-market for gender testing sprang up almost overnight in Hong Kong.

~⚜~

Christian. After his encounter with Li-Chou, the word resonated with Heo for a second time. The first was his conversation with Papa Shen and the disclosure that his own mother and Mama Shen were Christians. The importance of this strange religion was intriguing, especially the level of devotion it inspired. The word kept floating through his mind. Until now, Christianity meant nothing to him other than just another religion different from his own, although he did remember hearing someone describe the Three Self Church once as "a different form of Christianity." His personal religious knowledge, however, was limited to the teachings of the Three Self Church, which stood for self-governance, self-support, and self-propagation. It was government-run and the only government-sanctioned church in China. Consequently, it rejected interference from any other form of government or other religions. It was accepted by his father and Papa Shen, so Heo never had a reason to consider any other religion.

When he closed his eyes to sleep, he kept seeing Li-Chou's face. Her God was different from the god of the Three Self Church! Heo decided he wanted to know more about this Christian God. There was only one person he knew he could ask—his mother. Yes, that is what he would do, and wouldn't she be surprised! Just the thought of asking his mother for advice or if she had time to talk almost made him chuckle out loud. It was something he never did. He always looked to his father or Papa Shen for answers to anything serious.

Yan Wong was a quiet, fifty-something woman devoted to her family. When her husband brought guests home for dinner or a meeting, she was a perfect hostess. If she had opinions on anything political, religious, or military, she never expressed them—not to family and certainly not to guests.

To Heo and Jin, Yan Wong was a caring mother who was always there for them, as long as they behaved. On the rare occasions when they "pushed too many buttons," as she described it, and she felt it necessary to stop what she was doing and look squarely into their faces, it was too late. They were already in trouble. It was time to escape to Mama and Papa Shen's house if they could until Mother had time to cool down.

It was an hour after dinner when Heo had a chance to speak privately with his mother. She was at the counter in the kitchen preparing food for the next day. "Mother, do you have time to talk? I need your wisdom and advice."

Yan Wong stopped what she was doing and stood still for a moment. She put down her spoon, turned around, and faced her son, surprised at such a request. She was met with a slight smile, but a serious one. "Of course, I have time, Heo. What would you like to talk about?"

"I would like to know more about your Christian religion. Would you tell me what it is about? Or could I perhaps go to your church with you this week?"

Yan Wong's jaw dropped with this unfathomable request. As far as she knew, neither Heo nor Jin had any knowledge of her religious beliefs or of her church. It was never discussed in their home. And there was that scary look Heo remembered as a teenager—his mother's eyes staring squarely into his face.

"What do you know or think you know about my religious beliefs, Heo?" she asked firmly.

"It's alright, Mother," he offered quickly. "I know you and Mama Shen went to the Christian church together when Jin and I went with Father and Papa Shen to their church. Papa Shen told me so just before he died, and I know it was the truth because he was under the influence of a sedative. He did not intend to tell me things to be hurtful in any way. He just could not help himself. It was because of the medicine. I promised him I would keep our secrets."

"Secrets? Secrets?" she repeated with a slightly higher tone. "What other things did Papa Shen tell you?" She didn't wait for answers, which was a relief to Heo because he didn't have any.

Well, I guess we are going to have a family discussion, Heo realized, as his mother walked over to the door.

"Bin, you need to come in here."

"In a minute," came the answer from somewhere in the house. "I'm almost finished with my boots."

"You need to come in here NOW, Bin, and be involved in this conversation!"

Wiping the boot polish off his hands as he entered the room, he glanced at Heo before looking quizzically at his wife and selecting a chair between the two of them. The family discussion Heo wanted to have with his parents months ago but decided against was unexpectedly about to happen. In a way, he wanted it, but was afraid it would cause his parents pain. *Yes, the time has come,* he told himself again with trepidation.

Bin Wong was surprised at the suddenness of a command appearance, but not totally. He had sensed for quite a while that something was bothering Heo, assuming it had to do with the loss of Dr. Shen. But the look on his wife's face and that of his son's when he entered the room told him it might be something else.

Bin Wong decided to settle the prickly tension with a cautious approach. "My son, are you still saddened by the loss of Papa Shen? What is on your mind? How can we help?" he offered with a soothing smile.

But it was his wife who answered. "Your son wants to know about my church, Bin. He wants to go to *my* church this week. He learned about it from Papa Shen, along with other *secrets!*"

"Heo?" was all his father said as he looked at him.

So far, Heo hadn't said a word. It was the opportunity he initially wished for, to ask the questions that were on his troubled mind, but this wasn't the way he thought it would happen. He faced his parents and, clearing his throat, carefully considered his words—or tried to. He didn't know where to start. All the questions were a scrambled mess, trying to spill out in no particular order. *What's the most important thing?* He tried to reason methodically. *It's not only about religion anymore.* "Father, I—" He stopped, really not knowing what to say that would not cause hurt or make himself look weak or sound unappreciative to his adoptive parents.

Bin Wong pleaded, "Please tell us, Heo. Tell us what is bothering you. Whatever it is, we want to know."

With a deep breath, Heo pulled himself together. "When I was sitting with Papa Shen on his last night, and after I gave him a sedative for pain as he had asked, we spent some special time reminiscing about Mama Shen and then about days when Jin and I were young and some of the nice things they did for us. The conversation somehow shifted to the time Jin and I were born and . . . and came home on different days. Father . . ." he hesitated.

Bin's look changed from one of paternal comfort to one of sorrow with tears welling. He knew what was about to come from his son's mouth. "Tell us Papa Shen's words, son."

Heo glanced over at his mother; tears already flowing. "He couldn't help himself, Father, Mother. The medicine he requested was one that elicits tranquility and honesty of one's thoughts. I'm sure he was not expecting to talk about the things we did. He told me about Jin being born and how I unexpectedly came onto the scene as a surprise after you and mother applied for adoption and didn't have a chance to cancel the papers. He said I arrived a day after you brought Jin home, and I was delivered by a nurse from an orphanage and the decision for me to be Jin's twin."

There. The heaviest thing on his heart was out, but he regretted it as soon as he looked at his father's drawn face. "I am so sorry,

Father. I wouldn't hurt you or Mother for anything in the world. I had questions, so many questions, after Papa Shen died about who I really am and where I came from. I am so grateful to you both for accepting me as your own and treating me as an equal with Jin, and I feel so bad that your real son is in a prison camp somewhere and I, your adopted son, am still here. It should not have been this way. It must be pulling your hearts out and—"

"Whoa, Heo," his father interrupted. "You are both our sons equally! Of course, we love Jin. And yes, he is our flesh and blood. But your mother and I *chose* you to be our son and Jin's brother. The first time we held you in our arms, you were just as much a part of us as Jin. We decided to not tell you about how you came into our lives until such time as it was safe, not only for our own sake and yours, but for those of the Shens as well. I wish there could have been a time when we felt it was safe to tell you, but it is not so even now. We never thought you would find out by accident. There seemed to be no way that could happen. I am so sorry you had to find out the way you did and for the grief it has caused you. Let's talk about it now. But please remember the time we are living in. We are still under the government mandate. Nothing can be discussed outside of this room." He waited with a mixed look of sadness and anticipation for Heo's assurance.

"Of course, I will not talk about this to anyone, Father. I just don't want it to be hurtful for you or Mother. I do not want to cause either of you pain."

"It is alright, Heo," his mother added quietly. "It hurts my heart also that you had to find out these things the way you did. You have been a special blessing for us since the day you arrived and, for a long time, I was afraid someone would come back and say you were a mistake and take you away. Now I know better. You were meant to be here. You were meant to be our son."

"So, it sounds like you already know how you got here," his father continued. "Unfortunately, we know nothing about your biological family, so we cannot enlighten you. Jin was born on November 25. When you arrived on the twenty-sixth, we were handed a birth certificate showing you were born on November 19, 1980, and listing us as your parents. So realistically, you are older than Jin by a week. Where you came from, we don't know, but it took a week for you to get here," Bin Wong smiled.

"Your mother and I felt that no one would ever question the fact that you were twins or compare the dates on your birth certificates, but Dr. Shen took care of it anyway. He filled out a second birth certificate for you and filed it with the hospital. It indicated that yours was a 'home birth with complications,' a second unexpected child that didn't show up on the x-ray. Therefore, it indicated that your mother had to go to the hospital to deliver the second baby, which was Jin. So you actually have two birth certificates. Dr. Shen also made sure that the test results from the x-ray showing only one child quietly disappeared.

"So you see, Heo, there were four people who cared about you and loved you from the first day you arrived, and that has never changed. Please don't think for a moment that you are less important or less cared about than your brother.

"Now, what else did Papa Shen say that that you are concerned about? Religion? I'm not sure how the two of you got from birth to religion, but obviously you did. That is something we definitely need to talk about if you are thinking about going to your mother's church. I can explain your absence at my church if someone asks, but I know little about your mother's church. And as long as this is a time for truth, I want to confess that if I had my own way, I would be going to your mother's church as well. Unfortunately, I have no choice, but you do. Just be careful." He looked over at Yan for her to explain.

"The first thing you should know, Heo, is that my church is not in a big, beautiful building like the Three Self Church. Mine is called a house church and it is illegal in the eyes of our government. Our services are conducted privately in homes, different homes, or even in the back room of a store or a business. There are actually many religions in our country outside of the Three Self Church, not just my Christian one, and they are allowed to exist as long as they register with the government. That is where the problem comes in. By registering, it means we can hold services but are not allowed to teach our religion the way it is meant to be taught. It has to be modified. Everything has to be said and done in accordance with government regulations. Services are recorded on cameras and are often attended by military. If we want to practice our religion the way it is meant to be, we have to do it without registering. These are called *underground churches.* Whenever an underground church is discovered, there can be serious consequences for the members, but more so for the owners of the home or business, or for neighbors who did not report it. That is why Mama Shen and I never discussed our religion at home. Your father is a government employee and so was Papa Shen to some extent. Knowledge of our church had to be kept to ourselves so we didn't jeopardize their jobs—or worse. So, what I have told you today cannot be discussed with anyone . . . no one! You have to promise me that."

The *or worse* in his mother's words made Heo aware of the seriousness of religious dissidence. He knew there were government rules concerning religion, but it had never affected him as his knowledge was superficial. Now he knew. Going against the government guidelines on religion, like going against the one-child-per-family edict, was no longer something that only affected other people; it was personal and it was dangerous.

"I promise, Mother, of course."

"Now that you know these things, my son, do you still want to go to my church?"

"Yes."

"Very well. But please tell me, what ignited this interest in you? What made you want to know more?"

"It was a young girl at the hospital yesterday who was required to abort her child because she was an unwed mother, unless she intended to marry the man who was with her. Plus, her parents were there because she was a minor. We always try to make it sound to unwed mothers that they have a choice outside of marriage, but they don't, not really. Well, her x-ray showed she was going to have a girl and she decided she wanted to keep her child even if it meant being a single parent. She was willing to give up the security of marrying the father of the child who wanted only a son, and most likely having a comfortable life and a son at some time in the future, all for the sake of keeping her child. At that point, the man walked out, and I had to explain to her how everything was stacked against her, her parents, and the child if she chose to keep it. I did not give her the worst news, that if she didn't voluntarily decide to abort after knowing the personal and financial ramifications, then we would be going to the next step, which was a forced procedure. I have never had to do that, but some doctors have.

"Anyway, this young lady had a faith, a strength I never witnessed before. She prayed about it silently, but I knew she was praying. When she eventually realized that she didn't have a choice without bankrupting her parents, she agreed to the abortion. Her faith touched my heart, and then she actually comforted me! I really did not want to do the procedure. She was so young and trusting, so sincere in her Christian faith! She told me that as a Christian, she knew that all children were precious to God whether male or female. She also told me that she would meet her daughter someday in Heaven and that they would know each other and be together forever. She really believed that and so did her parents!

"So that's why I want to know more about this Christian God, Mother. He is obviously not driven by government or by politics or by anything other than caring about people and doing what is morally right. For some reason that I can't explain, even to myself, I sincerely want to know more. The fact that your Christian church is not sanctioned by our government does not surprise me. Your God is definitely different from the one I know."

"Very well, Heo," his mother agreed, her concerned look finally changing to a smile. "The best way I can tell you about the one true God who loves all people is to let you read my Bible. It is called The New Testament. Read as much of it as you have time for before we go to my church. Some of our members have to share Bibles, but Papa Shen gave me Mama Shen's Bible when she died. I will get it for you when we are finished."

"Is there anything else you wish to talk about, my son?" asked his father.

Heo hesitated. He thought about Cha-Li but decided against it. There was no way to talk about her without inflicting more pain on his mother. His father sensed Heo's hesitation.

"Heo. Tell us what else is on your mind. I feel you are keeping something else inside. Please, let's talk about it."

"No, Father. There's nothing more of any importance, but I appreciate all that you and Mother have shared with me. I just hope that someday I may repay even a small part of all the wonderful things you have done for me and still do for me every day. You are the best parents in the whole world. And you are right, Mother. It was meant for me to be here. I love and respect you both very much. By the way, where is your underground church? How far away is it?"

"Not far away this week. It is in my sister's house."

It took but a few seconds for Heo to realize that meant Cha-Li's house! *Oh, no! I don't even want to be in her presence, and now I have to be in her house? In her superior little world?* But it was too late, he couldn't back out now.

"Well, that is a surprise, Mother," he managed to comment with hopefully an unbiased tone. "Are my uncle and cousin Christians as well or just my aunt?"

"They all are."

"Wow. I never expected any of this in our family. Does Jin know about the Christians in our family, Mother? Does he know that we are not really twins?"

"No, I'm sure he doesn't know about the religious aspect. If he did suspect anything, he never mentioned it. He never talked with either of us about religion. He probably just assumed as you did that I stayed home while you were in church with your father and Papa Shen. And no, he does not know about you. I'm sure of it."

Bin Wong, who was silent during the whole part of the conversation about Christian churches, felt it was time to wrap up the conversation. "Heo, is there anything else we can tell you that you might have questions about? I am actually relieved that you know about these things now and maybe someday . . ." His voice trailed off. "Maybe someday when Jin gets home, we can talk some more."

It was another night without much sleep for Heo. Even though he still didn't know who he was, he did know who he wasn't. He wasn't Jin's twin brother. He wasn't Bin and Yan Wong's biological son. He wasn't Cha-Li's cousin, or brother, and for that he was grateful. He might have been an unwanted child when he was born but, right now, he knew for sure he was a wanted child of caring parents. His past was not important, he decided, only his future, and that may or may not be as a doctor. Even though he no longer had to do those disliked abortions, he was having second thoughts about his medical career.

Chapter 3

CHA-LI

"WHAT ARE YOU doing here?" Cha-Li exhorted icily as Heo walked in the door behind his mother.

Yan Wong was startled and annoyed at her niece's animosity toward her son. "He wants to know more about our religion, and I invited him to come to church with me today. Why do you ask in such a manner?"

"No reason. Sorry, Auntie Yan," she apologized. "I was just surprised to see him here. I was under the impression Heo was a strong supporter of the government church."

"Well obviously he is not."

Thanks, mother, Heo thought with relief. *Now I can ignore my obnoxious cousin and concentrate on what I'm really here for—to learn more about the Christian religion.* He had read the Books of Matthew and Mark and part of Luke after their family conversation and was particularly intrigued with Luke—the physician, the man of science. He didn't anticipate asking questions today, just listening and learning. There were a lot of unfamiliar words in his mother's Bible that he wanted to understand better.

After greeting his aunt and uncle and being introduced to the others in attendance, Heo settled back to hear the words of the leader. They were from the Book of Matthew, the story of the birth of the Baby Jesus who would become the Messiah. He remembered that there was also an account of the event in the Book of Luke. *What exactly is a Messiah?* Heo had pondered. It seemed odd at first why two different men would tell the same story, until he reread the beginnings of their books noting who they were and why they wrote as they did. Matthew's account, however, included the slaughter of children. The story weighed heavily on Heo's heart as he recalled his own experience a month earlier of another unwed mother. Both included governments dictating the deaths of children. He realized that the two-thousand-year-old story was still a part of modern culture! *How could that be? Are we destined to repeat the past?* There was one difference, he concluded—the killing two thousand years ago was focused on baby boys in Egypt. Today, it was focused on baby girls in China. It was wrong, whether it was the elimination of boys or girls or where it appeared on history's timeline.

The leader concluded with, "Whether it is the Son of God or a child of humans, every birth is a miracle of life and every child on earth is a gift from God. God is love. As God loves us, so we should love others, regardless of who they are or what they have done in their lives. Love others and treat them as we would have them treat us." It was a sobering sermon that made Heo appreciate how much he had yet to learn about the Christian religion, The Bible, and God's son.

As each visitor left, they welcomed Heo again and encouraged him to attend and not feel shy about asking questions. Then they said a polite goodbye to his aunt and uncle and thanked them for opening their home. In between the casual conversations, Heo noticed Cha-Li gradually making her way back into the meeting room, taking a chair in the corner. He had no intention of staying in the same room with her. He started for the kitchen to say goodbye to his aunt and uncle but realized they were engaged in a deep conversation with his mother. *Should I interrupt?* The concerned look on their faces told him no. They even glanced into the meeting room a couple of times.

An awkward silence settled in the room. Heo picked up a book on the table in front of him, not caring what it was about. Whatever the topic, it had to be better than trying to be polite to his cousin. *Why is it taking my mother so long to say goodbye?*

"I owe you an apology, Heo," came a quiet voice from his nemesis in the corner. "I have not acted in a Christian manner toward you. I was reminded of that today. Can we be friends again?"

Well, *there* was certainly a different attitude! "I never stopped being your friend, Cha-Li. I just don't know what I did to have angered you. Whatever it was, I didn't mean to." Another awkward silence.

"It's nothing you did on purpose, Heo. It's just that . . ." Her voice trailed off as though she was trying to choose the right words or perhaps hesitating about speaking at all. Heo was tired of trying to figure her out and kept looking at his book, until he heard her crying.

Now what, he wondered! "What is the matter with you, Cha-Li? Why are you crying?" he asked, trying to not sound annoyed.

"It's just that. . . when I teach my class at children's school every day, I look into the faces of eighteen boys and six girls. They are all so precious and anxious to learn. And I think about all the little girls who are not there, those adopted out, given away, abandoned on the street, murdered simply because they were born as girls. And I think about you, my cousin, as a doctor. I know that what you do is your job and you have to do it, but I couldn't help the way I was feeling. It made me bitter. I just couldn't grasp in my mind how someone can kill babies during the week and then go to church—*any church!* Now today I heard again what I already knew, that God is love and He loves all of us, no matter who we are or what we do. I'm sorry I have been judgmental. I know it is your job."

"Cha-Li. Please. I had no idea why you were upset with me, but now I understand. And you are right in your thinking about children, and about me. And you're right that it is part of my job—well, at least it *was* part of my job. But it wasn't something that I wanted to do."

"What do you mean it *was* part of your job?" she sniffed through tears.

"Well, for one thing, the government has changed its direction and is no longer mandating gender testing and abortions," he explained, softening his tone. "Perhaps you didn't hear about it. It was big news in the hospital. Even so, something happened to me this week that I really can't explain, but it made me search my brain and my heart about what it means to be a doctor, or what it should mean. I wanted to be a doctor since I was ten years old so I could heal people, take away their pain, not . . ." He couldn't finish the sentence without the obvious words that would upset Cha-Li so he changed the subject. "It also moved me to want to know more about my mother's Christian religion."

"But how did you know about—"

"Well, that's another story for another time," he interrupted, "but I was made aware that she and Mama Shen went to church together, this Christian church, while Jin and I were with Father and Papa Shen. I am totally convinced now that I cannot attend the Three Self Church anymore. My heart is not there.

"As for being a doctor, I want you to know that I am at a crossroads right now, something I haven't even discussed with my parents yet. I have always been focused on being a doctor of general medicine like Papa Shen, which would mean spending time in a private practice or in a hospital environment. It takes in a broad range of duties, which could still include aborting babies if considered medically necessary. I can't do that anymore for any reason. I either need to specialize or change careers entirely. I've got a lot of thinking to do."

Cha-Li's face brightened. "Oh, Heo! I am so glad to hear you say those things, but please don't give up on being a doctor. We need doctors of all kinds, and my actions were strictly selfish. I am so sorry. I was thinking only of my own career and not yours. You are my cousin, my flesh and blood, and I should not have treated you the way I did."

Oh, if she only knew, Heo thought. He felt a pang of remorse with the realization that he knew more about their kinship than she did. *Maybe the serious-looking conversation going on in the kitchen between Mother and my aunt and uncle has something to do with enlightening Cha-Li.*

"Apology not necessary, Cha-Li. I understand. Now quit crying, will you? You're going to make me look bad to your mother and father. There's a tissue on the table over there."

Cha-Li wiped her eyes, and looked at Heo, and they both started laughing. "There! Spoken like the Heo I've always known. Now that we've gotten the attention of the *real* adults, and I do believe we have, let's act surprised when they ask what's going on and why I look like such a mess."

They laughed again, and it felt good!

"Oh, dear. What is the matter?" Yan Wong asked when she looked at Cha-Li and then Heo."

"Oh, nothing, Mother," Heo answered. "We've been talking about life in general and all that's going on in the world, and Cha-Li just got a little emotional." He gave his aunt and uncle a big smile. "She could probably use another cup of tea, though."

He got a repeat grilling from his mother on the way home and decided he had better enlighten her. "Well, I found out what's been bugging my cousin," he answered, "and we got it all ironed out. It's got nothing to do with me personally but, rather, what I do as a doctor, or at least what I used to do. She was having a hard time understanding how I could abort babies as part of my job and then go home and go on about my normal life. I understand where she is coming from. Being a teacher of small children brings her closer to the subject than most people, especially since she has only six girls in her class. I think she has been blaming doctors, the Three Self Church, and who knows what else for the population imbalance instead of the government."

"Well, I'm glad the two of you got at least that much all figured out today. I want you to know that your aunt and uncle know about our family discussion this week. They are going to talk to Cha-Li soon and let her know about you and Jin not really being twins and how you unexpectedly received all this information."

Are they also going to discuss Cha-Li's story, he wondered? He decided not to ask. His mother hinted at the question anyway.

"There is more to what they might be telling Cha-Li," she said cautiously. "It might be time for more truths."

Nothing more was said. He tried to put it all out of his mind and concentrate on finishing the Book of Luke when he got home. Whatever was about to happen was going to happen whether he knew about it or not. Yet he continued to think about Cha-Li. He not only kind of liked her again, he felt sorry for her. If she was going to be told the truth about her real parents and adoption, it was going to be tough, even tougher than what he went through when he found out he was adopted. With Cha-Li, it might be more than Christian love could handle. Although he would never know his real parents, Cha-Li would. She would have to deal with not only finding out who they were, but learning why she was adopted out of their lives and growing up right down the street from them. Yes, it was going to be traumatic for her.

⸻

It happened two days later. The conversation at dinner was pleasant as always, but there was something amiss. Heo felt it. Whatever the issue, he was pretty sure it didn't involve him. He was wrong.

"Do you have anything important to do tonight, Heo?" his father asked.

"No, Father. Is there something you would like me to do?"

Heo realized it was an empty question as soon as he said it. *Of course there is, or he wouldn't have mentioned it!* Being a military person, Bin Wong was never shy about letting his sons know what he wanted them to do and when he expected them to do it. Heo and Jin were pretty good at gauging when they could joke with their father and when they needed to heel to his demands. Bin Wong wasn't a cold person; he just had a way of demanding respect and didn't always share his sons' sense of humor. This was one of those times. The look on his father's face right now told him it was all business, even more so when his mother sat beside him. It had all the makings of another family discussion.

"Son, your mother and I spent most of yesterday at your aunt and uncle's house with Cha-Li. They decided it was time to tell her, first of all, that you and Jin are not twins and how it all came about that we had two sons. Then they told her the truth about herself. It was time for her to know that she also was adopted. When you and your Papa Shen had that truth session before he died, did he happen to mention anything about Cha-Li? Perhaps about her adoption? He and Mama Shen signed papers as witnesses."

Once again, Heo felt himself being pulled into an awkward situation. He wanted to be truthful; Papa Shen did tell him about Cha-Li, and now his new Christian faith pulled him toward the truth. "Yes, he did, Father. He told me that she was your daughter and that Aunt Han and Uncle He adopted her when she was a year old. I didn't mention it when we had our own discussion because it was really none of my business. It only involved you, my aunt and uncle, Jin and Cha-Li. I hope that by my not speaking I didn't add to your sadness. Papa Shen told me how much you both loved Cha-Li and what a difficult decision it was for you and how concerned he was as a friend and doctor about Mother's health."

Heo wanted to reach out and give them both hugs to ease their discomfort, but he knew it wasn't the consolation they needed. He didn't have to look at his mother's face to know she was upset, but he did. He looked back at his father, who was also visibly shaken.

"Well, I am glad you already know the truth, Heo," his father continued, "and why we made the decision we did. If your aunt and uncle had not offered to adopt Cha-Li, we would not have let her go.

The determining factor was that she would not be far away, and we could still watch her grow up and have her in our lives. She is our daughter, and we love her just as much today as we did then. But we all agreed this week it was the time for truth. You and Jin and Cha-Li all have the right to know as much as we can tell you, with the hope that this information will stay within our families. Please remember, the one-child edict is still in place and the consequences of violating it could be severe."

"Yes, Father. I am reminded of those consequences every time we discuss government mandates at our hospital staff meetings." *Drat! That answer didn't sound the way I meant it; it seemed glib. Why am I having such a hard time lately with words?*

"What I mean. Father, is that I know it is dangerous to go against the dictates of our government. It has been drilled into all of us as doctors. You have my promise that nothing we discuss will leave this room."

Bin Wong smiled at his son, no longer a mischievous teenager, but a responsible young adult. He was proud of Heo. "Well, you may have to modify your promise, Heo. Our family discussion is going to continue at your aunt and uncle's house tonight if you are willing."

Oh, yes. This must be the other *truth* his mother mentioned. He thought about his circle of family members, about his aunt and uncle and the pain of having to tell their somewhat emotional daughter the truth. He thought about his own parents having to explain why they gave her up in favor of a son. His heart ached for all of them, but especially for Cha-Li. He remembered his own feeling of rejection after finding out he was adopted and not knowing if his biological parents gave him up willingly, forced, or as a matter of necessity. Cha-Li's situation was worse. It had to be. Not only was she in the throes of finding out she was adopted, she was duped with both sets of parents. He was pulled out of his thoughts as his father continued.

"As you can imagine, Cha-Li was very upset when she was told about being adopted, that her parents were really her aunt and uncle and her aunt and uncle were really her parents. We all tried to explain that what happened over twenty-two years ago was because of the one-child-per-family edict, and parents all over China were trying to adjust, but she was still devastated. Your mother and I repeatedly assured her that we loved her then and still do and would never have given her up to strangers or an uncertain home. Your aunt and uncle tried to tell her how much they loved her as a baby and how thrilled they were when we finally consented to the adoption after a year of indecision. They told her how blessed they were to have her as their daughter. But she is still overwhelmed, and understandably so. It was a lot to absorb all at one time. She has been in her room since yesterday afternoon, insisting she needs time alone to think, but we know she is terribly upset. We are all getting worried. She hasn't eaten anything and the only person she wants to talk to is you, Heo."

"Me? Why me? I have no knowledge to make her feel any better. I am not even a biological member of her family."

"That is probably the reason she wants to talk to you, Heo," his mother interjected. "Maybe she is relating to your being adopted also. We don't know what she is thinking, but if she trusts you enough to be asking to talk to you, it's something to be thankful for. We are hoping that time will heal her heart and her feelings, and she will eventually accept that what was done years ago was done out of love. Please, Heo," his mother asked again, "please go with us and talk to her."

"Of course, Mother. As you wish. When should we go?"

"Now."

⁓ᵥⁱᵥ⁓

Holding a tray with a pot of hot tea and two cups, Heo knocked softly on Cha-Li's bedroom door. "Cha-Li, may I come in?" There was shuffling in the room before the door finally opened and his tear-streaked cousin stood, motioning for him to come in. He set the tray down on the floor and poured a cup of tea for both of them.

"Here, cuz," he said with a smile. "If you looked better, I'd take you out and buy you something stronger, but this is going to have to do for now. Doctor's diagnosis, of course." She smiled.

"I suppose you know everything that's going on," she replied with a raspy voice. "Thank you for coming over. I didn't know until yesterday that you were an adoptee also. I was told you just found out yourself from Papa Shen before he died. And here I was being mean to you for such a long time, judging you, telling you how terrible you were. Now I know how you must have felt about me and maybe still do. Why didn't you just tell me to go take a hike? I was such a blockhead!"

The thought of his older cousin calling herself a blockhead was something he could never have imagined. She was always the big sister figure in his life and Jin's. But right now, she was a friend who needed help.

"No, you are not a blockhead, cuz. You are a got-it-together professional woman with a sympathetic heart for children and, whether or not you know it or believe it, you are an important person in many people's lives, especially in the lives of your parents."

"But who *are* my parents, Heo? Are they the ones who brought me into this world or the ones who raised me? Who should I call mother and father? The ones I have lived with all my life or the ones who didn't want me? The ones who gave me away because they wanted a son? Obviously, I was an inconvenience because I was a girl!"

Deep-chest sobs followed. Although she didn't say it, Cha-Li was brushed aside to make room for Heo and Jin. There was nothing Heo could think of to say that would make that bitter feeling of rejection go away; there was no magic pill to make her feel better. Yes, it was twenty-two years ago, but time didn't matter. It did happen just like she said.

Heo moved beside Cha-Li, wrapped an arm around her shoulder, and let her lay her head against his chest and cry. It took a while for the sobbing to subside, but it gave him time to think. As a family outsider, his mind suddenly cleared and he was viewing the whole scenario like a big puzzle, almost as though he was looking at it from somewhere up above.

Cha-Li was just one of the pieces. She was seeing herself as a problem, an obstacle that had to be dealt with. She was not accepting herself as a person who was loved then and now by four adults.

Her mother and father were piece number two. They had raised Cha-Li as their own without giving much thought to explaining things to her at some time in the future.

Heo saw his own existence as another piece of the puzzle, the catalyst who uncovered the truths and put the puzzle in motion. Something mysterious was going on in Heo's thinking, and he felt it. Perhaps he was remembering something the church leader said earlier in the week that reminded him of God's love. It occurred to him this was more than happenstance. He envisioned God as the owner of the puzzle, bringing all the pieces together in His timing and His love. It gave him a strange, new feeling of peace in knowing and accepting all things happen as God intends.

Yet that realization didn't help Cha-Li. Heo tried to place himself into her mindset, but the more he tried, the more he felt her hurt. There was no way he could mitigate the depth of her despair. He felt helpless.

Suddenly, she sat up with a look of resolve on her face. "Sorry, Heo." she said with a surprisingly clear voice. "It seems like I am saying sorry to you a lot these days, doesn't it? I don't mean to be such a crybaby, but I do feel better. Thanks for listening to me vent and giving me time to think. How about a nice cup of cold tea?"

"I would love a cup of cold tea," he grinned as he pushed his cup toward her. "So nice of you to ask!" *Whew*, he thought. *Everything has settled down and I didn't have to say much at all. Thank you, God!*

The dark cloud lifted; peace settled in as Cha-Li shared her new outlook. "I have decided to keep on living," she announced. "It occurred to me just now how fortunate I am. At least I know who my biological parents are and where they are, which is something most adopted girls in China don't know, and some boys," she added as an obvious afterthought to include Heo. "My problem is within myself, isn't it?"

"Somewhat," Heo answered cautiously, wondering where all this sudden insight was coming from and where it was going.

"I have also decided to better accept the Chinese *tradition* better," she continued. "My real parents didn't just give me up on a whim. They agonized for almost a year before deciding to do what they felt was the best solution for everyone. They told me so yesterday and I believe them. They have been wonderful to me, and I am thankful they are still part of my life. And I could not have asked for better parents to raise me than the ones I call Mother and Father. I have never wanted for anything. I have been a spoiled little princess and never realized it until now. I do have so much to be thankful for, don't I, Heo?"

"Yes, you do, cuz, and so do I. We both need to be thankful for our families, as mixed up as they are. I don't know what turned your thinking around, but I'm glad to hear you are accepting your situation in a positive way. There might still be some things you are going to have to work through in your mind, but I know you can do it. What made you decide to be happy anyway?"

"I said a prayer. I hated the way I was acting and prayed for God to make me a better person, to make me more deserving and appreciative of the people in my life. I purposely turned my thinking around from negative to positive and it was like a light went on. Think about it, Heo. . . regardless of where we were born or to whom, the parents we grew up with *chose* us. They have raised us, clothed us, fed us, and educated us. They gave us everything we have, everything we ever needed. My parents could just as well have adopted a boy instead of adopting me, but they chose me. Your parents—my biological parents—could just as well have kept me and accepted the heartbreaking fact they would never have more than one child, but they were presented with another option and took it. Their gamble worked, and now they've got two additional children plus me just down the street. It was dangerous for them. They could have given you back to the orphanage, but they chose to keep you in spite of the danger. And now look at you, a doctor and cherished child in a good family."

"You are right, cuz. I have had many of those thoughts myself, but hearing them spoken out loud makes them even more meaningful. It's nice to know I'm not alone in my thinking."

"So, my favorite cousin," Cha-Li continued, "you are obviously a step ahead of me in adopting this positive attitude. How did you turn your own turmoil around? Auntie Yan said you usually keep all your feelings inside when something is bothering you. They almost had to pull it out of you. I have never been any good at that. My mother and father usually know when I am upset just by the way I act, even though I do try to chill out. Guess I'm just no good at hiding my feelings."

"No kidding," Heo laughed. "I've been on the receiving end of your trying to chill out. I feel sorry for your parents!"

It felt good to laugh and be happy again.

"Well, since you asked," he continued, "let me tell you what turned me around. Remember when I told you after church last week that I was contemplating a career change because I could not in all good conscience stay in a profession that condoned aborting babies? Well, it came about because of a valuable lesson I learned from a young girl. She was a patient in the clinic while I was on duty, a sixteen-year-old, unwed, expectant mother who wanted desperately to keep her unborn daughter. She even had the blessing of her parents who were willing to help her but, under the terms of our government, she and her child would have been outcasts, placing crushing financial burdens on her family. So, she did what she had to do, and I know you don't want to hear this, but yes, she had to abort. But," he added quickly, "when she realized I was emotional about injecting the drug, *she consoled me* and told me it was alright. She said that when Christians get to Heaven, they will know their children and their children will know them and they will be together forever. Her faith was incredibly strong and very believable. It made me realize my own situation as well, that someday I will meet my real parents in Heaven. I will know them, and they will know me and we will be together.

"One other thing," Heo added. "While you were crying and praying and I was thinking, I decided about my career. Now, this may sound corny, but I mean it. When I had my arm around your shoulder and felt the heat of your body, I realized the importance of you as a living person. Our God created you, and it is not the place of government to deny you the right to live. I don't know how many girls' lives this controversial edict has taken, probably millions, but it is just not right and I don't want to be a part of it anymore. If there is any way to stop this craziness, that's the side I want to be on. I am not going to walk around holding up a sign like Jin did and get thrown into a work camp, but I want to find ways to save lives or at least make them better. Job or no job, I have done my last abortion. How do you feel about pediatrics or geriatrics for my new focus?"

"Wow! I am so proud and happy for you I could just burst. If you need help doing whatever this new career of yours calls you to do, I want to help. Don't forget me, I'm in your corner!"

"How could I ever forget you? You're the best cousin I've got."

"Because I'm the only one, right?"

"Right. And that makes you the best!"

He stood up and reached out his arm to help Cha-Li off the floor. "But right now, we'd better break up this jam session before our parents go off the deep end worrying about us. How about if we go out and ask for a cup of hot tea and spend time with some very special people?"

They walked out arm-in-arm, holding cups, smiling and greeting parents and aunts and uncles with a new-found appreciation for those who loved and cared for them.

Chapter 4

AN INTERNATIONAL CRISIS

IT WAS FEBRUARY 8, 2003 when phones in the Beijing area started lighting up almost overnight with alarming messages about a deadly flu in the city of Guangzhou in Guangdon Province. There had been sporadic rumors for months, but they did not raise a lot of concern in Beijing. No one was particularly worried about an illness 1,900 kilometers (2,200 miles) away. It sounded like a typical seasonal flu outbreak in a distant province. If it was something they should be concerned about, surely their own health officials would tell them. They were wrong.

Messages from friends and relatives in Guangzhou poured in, now including words like *anthrax* and *bird flu.* People were dying. Stories about the strange illness were appearing on websites, but there was still nothing from their government. Two days later, a downplayed admission of a flu-like disease appeared in a local Guangzhou circular, recommending that people take preventative measures by opening windows for fresh air and using vinegar fumes to disinfect inside air. People were reminded to wash their hands frequently, as they would for any normal flu outbreak.

Heo heard the rumors, as did other doctors, but that is all they had—rumors from phone messages. They waited for information from their own health officials in the Beijing-Tianjin-Hubei Province area. There was nothing. They asked but got no response.

What they did not know was that the media in Guangdong Province was in a government-mandated blackout regarding the epidemic in Guangzhou. It was classified as top secret, which meant only certain government officials within that province were allowed to know about it or discuss it. They were forbidden to talk to health officials in other provinces or the general public, and there were severe consequences for anyone who ignored the warning.

As phone alerts escalated, panic increased. On February 11, the blackout was eased, and local media was allowed to inform residents of the disease. A news conference by Guangzhou provincial health officials reported 305 atypical pneumonia cases in the area to date. They also announced that testing was being conducted, but no effective treatment had emerged. It wasn't a lot of information, more of an acknowledgment to hopefully stem the rising tide of misinformation. When health officials started coming under fire about withholding details, the media blackout went back into effect. It stopped the media, but not the people. Cell phones became the nemesis of the government as messages flowed. With nothing in place to halt its progression, the disease spread.

⁓✦⁓

It started in the Beijing area with just a few patients coming into area hospitals with a flu-like illness. Some doctors remembered hearing rumors about a possible flu outbreak in Guangdong Province months earlier, but there was nothing to substantiate them other than the spike in messaging. As hospital admissions began to increase, however, and the incidence of transmission became evident, the Guangzhou disease drew more attention. But it was too late. By March, it was raging in Beijing.

It was not only highly contagious within families and workplaces, but doctors and other healthcare workers were being infected as well. All of Beijing's 175 hospitals, including sixteen military hospitals, were inundated. People were quarantined and deaths spiked. What was this strange disease now described as an Infectious Atypical Pneumonia, or IAP? Why had they not heard anything from the medical officials? Why was the media not picking up on it? Was it the same thing spreading in Guangzhou, or was it unique to Beijing? Answers were not forthcoming. The government chose silence regarding the epidemic.

Chinese military hospitals were finally informed of the crisis in early March and were working to identify the core of the disease but were prohibited from sharing their findings with civilian hospitals or the general public until they received permission from the government. Communications between China and the World Health Organization were purposely delayed. When World Health Organization delegates visited China in early April, they were initially kept from visiting Guangzhou and the military hospitals.

Hesitation by government officials to inform the public and the rest of the world was a deadly mistake. The disease continued to spread, especially by unsuspecting travelers to and from Hong Kong. By June, the disease had been dubbed SARS, (Severe Acute Respiratory Syndrome) a coronavirus that had spread to twenty-five other countries.

—◦—

Dr. Heo Wong was one of the first doctors in his hospital to promote extensive sanitation measures and caution when encountering infected SARS patients. He knew a lot about epidemics infecting China in the past—the 1918 Spanish flu, 1957 Asian flu, 1968 Hong Kong flu, and the 1977 Russian flu. All but one of them (the Spanish flu) originated in China. Then there was the bird flu on a lesser scale, but also originating in China. Wanting to know more about their origins and how they spread led Heo to do extensive research as a medical student and to publish numerous articles on medical crises in China as well as other countries. Knowing about and recognizing symptoms of each one was an interest instilled in him by Papa Shen when they first talked seriously about Heo pursuing a medical career.

"Be prepared, Heo," Papa Shen told him. "Always be prepared. Forget what Chairman Mao said about farewell to the god of plagues after he thought he conquered snail fever. It was not true. He did not conquer it. It is still a problem in many regions of China. There will always be plagues and, unfortunately, healthcare workers will always be among the first to suffer. Some plagues will be easy to contain and others will not. Here is what you need to do. First, it is important to discern whether it is a resurgence of a known plague or a new one, and yes, there *will be* new ones. If it is not already known, then it is imperative to collect samples, do labs, and identify it quickly so you will know what medicines might have an impact. And don't keep your findings to yourself. Share, share, share with other doctors every day if you are able. And most importantly, make sure you practice sanitation to the extreme and insist everyone around you do the same thing. Protect yourselves first. Sick doctors cannot help sick people."

Dr. Shen's advice resonated with Heo after just a couple of days of the IAP appearing in Beijing and now showing up in his hospital. His forte was not in chemistry or disease identification labs, but he did recognize the possibility of an unknown plague earlier than most. He strongly urged extreme sanitation among his co-workers and led by example. He knew some of them were doing eye-rolling at his insistence and offering apathetic smiles, but after several doctors and nurses got sick, his recommendations were taken seriously. The incidence of medical personnel infections went down and stayed down.

In the absence of official information about the disease, lab personnel worked around the clock in his hospital, examining patient specimens. It took two intense weeks, but they were finally able to identify the class or family of the viral culprit. Even though they couldn't pinpoint the exact virus, it gave them something to go on. It gave them an idea of what medicines might be effective.

The head of medicine at his hospital was enraged when he learned via unofficial means (text messages and *hearsay*) that medical facilities in Guangzhou had been doing lab tests for months. "Why have we not been informed of this?" he bellowed. "Why have they not shared their lab test results? Why are we having to hear about an outbreak from private telephone users? What in blazes is going on?" When he contacted the medical agency responsible for disseminating information in the Beijing area, he was quickly hushed, but defiantly chose to ignore the rules regarding who was allowed to share *top secret* medical information.

As unofficial reports of the escalating disease were now coming in from Hong Kong, and despite government-mandated silence, staff members from Heo's hospital were instructed to share their lab results and sanitation practices with other hospitals. They worked quietly, doctor to doctor, hospital to hospital, discussing which treatments worked and which ones didn't. They couldn't inform the general public to help prevent infection, but they could at least provide patients with effective treatment.

Heo did the same thing at home, instructing his parents on sanitation and using caution when out in public. He was still personally under the silence mandate just like all other doctors. All he could safely tell them was that there was a pneumonia-like illness in the area and it was important to avoid close contact with other people.

"Become a chronic hand-washer," he told them. "If someone is coughing or sneezing or feeling ill, keep your distance. Don't let anyone cough or sneeze on you."

They agreed, but it still worried him, especially his mother. Yan Wong was out in public just about every day. She shopped, met her friends for lunch, attended exercise classes, and volunteered in community charities. She went to church with her sister and brother-in-law one night a week. She had a habit of hugging people, especially those she didn't see regularly, perhaps those who had been sick and just getting back in circulation. She had a caring heart, sending cards, making meals, and calling on friends who were ill. It was just something she did.

His father was different. Bin Wong heard about the IAP during his regular military meetings, although he discerned it was being downplayed. They were not informed of details, only that they should practice distancing and sanitation when in large groups. That was not a problem for him. He was not in the habit of handshaking, only saluting when necessary. He was always meticulous in dress and hygiene.

Bin and Heo both stressed the importance of distancing with Yan, avoiding personal contact with people, whether they appeared sick or not. Would she remember their cautions? All they could do was hope.

Bin and Heo discussed the status of the disease often after dinner. It was not for hype or patient count, just updates on any new information that might be of use.

"I know there is a spike in Hubei Province around Beijing and Tianjin, Heo, but that is all I know. I am not allowed to discuss it, even with family, but that is not a problem because I know very little. Only the doctors in our military hospitals know what is really happening and they are not sharing it with regular military. We are not allowed inside."

Sometimes Heo had updates from lab technicians that were meaningful, especially as they discovered ways the disease was being spread and what was effective in containing it. He was not bound by military protocol, only medical, but saw no reason to keep such important information from his own family.

"It is flu season, Mother," Heo told her, "regardless of which kind of flu. I'm sure many of your friends have heard the rumors of a serious flu going around. Everyone seems to be aware of it. You can help people stay safe by being reluctant to give hugs and reminding them of the importance of maintaining a safe distance. Even though you can't share what we talk about within our family, you can offer reminders that are appropriate during any flu season."

His mother agreed. She would lead by example and do what she could to keep everyone safe. Heo and his father also led by example. They kept their vehicles sanitized as well as everything they touched when they walked into the house. Even with all of their precautionary advice and efforts, however, Yan Wong still contracted the disease.

Heo recognized it as soon as he came home and saw his mother sitting in her chair, covered up with a blanket and shivering. Her eyes were glassy, her breathing labored. He took her temperature. It was 38.05 degrees Celsius (100.5 Fahrenheit), the magic number in determining if an ailment might be the IAP. He had seen patients in every stage of the disease and knew without a doubt that his mother needed to be hospitalized. His father was due to be home in an hour, but Heo decided not to wait. He jotted a quick note and placed it where he was sure it would be seen, put his mother on a clean blanket in the back seat of his car, and drove to the emergency room. The doctors on duty were surprised to see him again as he grabbed a gurney and went back out to retrieve his mother, wrapped securely in a blanket.

When Bin Wong arrived, Heo was anxiously waiting for him. His mother was already in quarantine, hooked up to IVs and a respirator. The disease was hitting her hard—body aches, escalating temperature, chest pain, pneumonia. An hour later, she became comatose. There was nothing more Heo and his father could do except wait while hospital personnel kept her breathing, sedated, and cooled to help bring her temperature down. It was now up to her own body to fight the invading disease. Heo knew the danger as he and his father peered through the window at his mother and the lights of her monitor. Thoughts of Papa Shen surfaced. It had been a little over a year ago when he and his parents were taking turns sitting with their dying neighbor. The difference was that Papa Shen was terminal; this time there was hope.

They went back to the waiting room; the next twenty-four hours were going to be critical. As Heo handed his father a cup of coffee, his heart sank. He couldn't help but notice the look on his father's face, the military stoicism he always knew as a reflection of strength and confidence. Tonight it betrayed despair. From the way his father's jaw was clenched, Heo sensed rising anger mixed with the helplessness he was undoubtedly feeling for his wife, and he knew why. Bin Wong was caught between loyalties. Being true to his military discipline to obey government rules may have cost him his wife's health, perhaps her life. She was a victim of the disease he knew was being ignored for political reasons—a cover up.

Heo sat next to his father and put a comforting hand on his arm. It brought Bin Wong out of his distant thoughts. "Let's say a prayer for Mother," Heo said without waiting for permission. He closed his eyes and bowed his head, not knowing if his father did the same, and said a prayer for his mother's strength and healing. There was no response from his father other than a pat on top of the hand that held his arm.

Yan Wong's downward spiral leveled off and improved slightly during the night. Heo and his father put their lives on hold for the days that followed, sleeping when they could, eating when they should, and alternating trips home to shower and change clothes. Nothing else mattered.

Dressed in full protective clothing, Heo was in the isolation room with his mother when she opened her eyes, looking rather confused by her surroundings. Her temperature was approaching normal, as was her breathing. It was a day for relief and rejoicing as Yan looked over at the small window and waved at her grinning husband on the other side. Even though she was still weak, Yan just wanted to go home! The disease was at its peak in the outside world and beds were needed, so no one argued with her. After all, she had her very own family doctor, plus her husband would be with her. Bin asked for and was granted a leave of absence to stay with her as long as she needed him.

Chapter 5

ANOTHER OUTBREAK AND THE LAOGAI

MONTHS LATER, WITH SARS under control and routines back to normal, Heo was leaving the hospital to go to the medical school administration building. Even though he had a degree to practice general medicine, he decided it was not his ultimate calling. He wanted to specialize in pediatrics. With a new curriculum application in hand, he was feeling good about his decision, even though it meant additional years of study. He was looking forward to working with children and keeping them healthy.

"Heo! Wait. I have been looking for you," a hospital supervisor called. "We have an emergency at the prison and they need doctors—lots of doctors—quickly. We've got a meeting in the large conference room in a half-hour. Whatever you've got on your schedule for today, change it!"

"Will do. What kind of emergency?"

"TB."

An administrative assistant at the reception desk was already on the telephone and making changes on her computer. Heo added his schedule to the pile in front of her, which she acknowledged with a nod. He went to the doctors' lounge, put the med school application back in his briefcase, grabbed a bottle of water, and headed to the conference room. It was filling up with doctors and interns. Nurses were meeting in another room.

Heo already knew a lot about tuberculosis. Diagnosing and treating TB was part of his internship. Since the SARS outbreak, most doctors received additional training on containing contagious diseases, TB included. His recent research into pediatrics also dealt with the prevention and cure of tuberculosis in children. He knew *in theory* what needed to be done to treat an outbreak, but this sounded real.

"We've got a crucial situation on our hands," the head of medicine announced, "an outbreak of tuberculosis at the prison. From what we are hearing, it is widespread among the inmates plus others—prison guards and military, even some of the medical and administration staffs. Inmates who exhibited symptoms and tested positive are currently quarantined in a building within the complex, but we don't know how many more might be in an early stage without exhibiting symptoms. We must assume there will be more. The only way we can stop it is to test everyone.

"We also must assume that prison personnel and guards may have inadvertently spread it to people outside the prison, but that is not our focus, at least not yet. *Our* job right now is twofold—help get it under control within the prison and, secondly, help identify healthy inmates so they can continue to work, and the prison can keep operating.

"If there is any such thing as good news in all of this, it is that we are not the only hospital supplying medical personnel. Time is crucial, and we are approaching this situation as a combined effort to provide around-the-clock assistance. Our plan is to treat administrative personnel, guards, and military first. They have all had the tuberculin skin test. Confirmed cases are quarantined in rooms in the main building. We just have to get them started on the TB cocktail. Then we will tackle the inmate population, starting with those already in quarantine.

"The last part is going to be tough. We're going to have to go into the prisoner barracks and administer the test to each prisoner. There's no other way to truly get it under control. I have never personally been in any of those buildings, but I'm told by those who have that it's not pretty. As we identify inmates in the barracks who test positive, they will be moved to an additional quarantine building—a warehouse that is being cleared out and sanitized. The prison staff is taking care of what to do with the negative inmates to keep them healthy so they can continue to work. They are doing the necessary sanitizing and relocating. We just have to identify the positives and negatives. We will do that by assigning each inmate a case number with their personal information and test result. That should enable us to keep track of everyone.

"As far as people outside the prison who may have come in contact with TB positive personnel, other healthcare workers are quietly getting in touch with them. If it turns out to be more widespread than we think, we may have to set up separate testing stations in the hospitals. Hopefully, however, we can squelch this outbreak before it turns into a full-blown epidemic.

"Bottom line, we may or may not need all of you, but we do need to know your availability. There are two lists at the back of the room indicating whether you are available and willing to be part of this assignment or not. Right now, it is voluntary. For those of you who cannot or do not wish to be involved, you will resume your regular rounds here plus take up the slack for those on assignment.

"For those of you who *are* willing, we will meet here at six tomorrow morning and be bussed into the prison as a group. Supplies are being loaded in a van tonight and will be ready to go in with us. So go home, get a good night's sleep, and let your families know you are going to be working odd hours outside the hospital for the next few days. It is permitted to tell them you will be in the prison doing health checkups. That's all they need to know for now. By mandate of our provincial government, nothing else can be shared. They don't want misinformation circulating with the public like what happened with SARS. We need to get a better handle on the scope of this thing ourselves before we inform the public, and yes, they will be informed as soon as we know more.

"Oh, one more thing. Bring a change of clothes with you tomorrow. We will be coming back here to shower and change before going home. Do this every day. See you in the morning."

Adrenalin was high as the doctors filed to the back of the room to put their signatures on a list. Heo signed the *available* list. As he drove home, his mind was filled with a myriad of thoughts about tuberculosis, plus the rare opportunity to actually enter a laogai prison. He had another reason to participate—his brother, Jin.

∗

Heo thought about Jin a lot. It was over six years—almost seven since he was arrested and sent to a labor camp to await trial. They were still waiting for Jin's trial date. "There are many people ahead of your son," his parents were told each time they inquired. "His day in court might not come up for a long time, perhaps four years, which is allowed by law. Jin Wong is accused of subversion against the Chinese government. He will wait for his case to be heard while proving himself useful in a labor camp where he can adjust his thinking and review his loyalties."

The four years came and went with no news of Jin's trial date. Their inquiries got no further response.

Because of Jin, Heo made it his personal responsibility to know everything possible about the Chinese labor camps. It was a softened description of the prison system. It consisted of two different channels—the *laogai* and the *laojiao*. He knew their history, when they started, and how they operated.

Laogai was a common abbreviation for *laodong gaizao,* meaning *reform through labor.* It was for serious offenders, including those who committed crimes against the state. Its version of reform was reportedly brutal, the labor intense.

Laojiao, was an abbreviation for *laodong jiaoyang,* meaning *re-education through labor.* It was for those who committed lesser offenses and were more likely to become law-abiding citizens at some time in the future. Re-education was less brutal than reform, the labor less strenuous. Laojiao inmates were usually, but not always, kept separate from laogai inmates and the rougher prisons. However, they often worked side-by-side in the same fields, mines, and factories.

Because Jin was accused of subversion against the Chinese government, Heo and his parents knew he was in the laogai, although they didn't know which one. There were more than a thousand spread out across the country. Everything Heo read and heard about laogai smacked of cruelty. He read as much as he was allowed to read, engaged in hushed conversations with dissidents, and saw emaciated and scarred bodies of inmates who were fortunate enough to have been released.

For the laogai, personal rights meant nothing. *Reform* was another word for brainwashing—breaking the body and spirit into submissiveness. Laogai prisoners were considered reformed only when they willingly and totally submitted themselves to the tenets of the country's government. The laogai provided the Chinese government with slave labor, creating goods for export.

Heo had never discussed what he learned about Chinese prison life with his parents. It was preferable for them to hold onto the hope of Jin returning home someday rather than sharing his own gnawing feeling that they would never see him alive again. As a dissident, he would most likely die in the laogai.

Guilt lingered among Jin's parents and Heo since Jin's arrest. Down deep, Heo felt he might have been able to prevent it. *Why didn't I do something?* he agonized so often. *I knew what Jin was planning to do. Why didn't I try harder to talk him out of it? Why didn't I say something to Father? It didn't have to happen the way it did! If only I had known the consequences!*

How many times he had relived that pivotal day when he overheard Jin and a classmate talking about a march, protest signs, and what they intended to accomplish.

"It's going to be peaceful, Heo," Jin assured him. "We just want our government to know we have not forgotten those who died at Tiananmen Square, or their cause. Please don't tell Father. Knowing our plans would force him to choose loyalties between his military life and family. It would cause him pain. The march is going to happen whether I participate or not, and I want to do this!"

Heo remembered how Jin and his friend tried to talk him into joining them, but Heo wavered, not feeling particularly good about the scenario. Loyalty to his twin brother was one thing. It was strong. He was sympathetic for their cause, but Heo thought public demonstrations of government defiance was too risky and radical. Everyone knew the government would crack down on protesters or their causes, no matter what they were. "But it is just a reminder," Jin argued, "a remembrance of the protesters at Tiananmen Square and why they were there."

What Jin and his friend did not comprehend, however, was that the massacre at Tiananmen Square remained a blot on China's image to the rest of the world. China was heavily criticized by the Western world, in particular. The massacre was still a hot-button issue, and the government did not take a reminder lightly.

The peaceful protest had been met with brutal force, cameras confiscated, and the crowd dispersed with tear gas. From distant sidelines, Heo watched as Jin and hundreds of others were arrested. Their pictures flashed across television screens. They were pointed to as examples of what happens to traitors.

It was the beginning of a painful nightmare for families. No one was allowed to visit; letters were not permitted. All that parents could hope for was to be notified when trials were coming up. Year after year, they waited for news of Jin. And year after year, Heo continued to blame himself for Jin's incarceration. He kept hearing Jin's voice in his head, *"Please don't tell Father."* The words were followed by an image of students being gassed, pulled back up to their feet, and shoved into the back of military trucks. Over and over, it played relentlessly through Heo's mind. His failure to act was a bad decision, one he would live with for the rest of his life.

Bin Wong tried to alleviate his son's guilt by telling him that everyone must accept responsibility for their own actions. "It was not your inaction that landed Jin in prison," his father consoled. "It was Jin's choice." Heo knew his father meant well and his words were sincere, but it didn't make him feel any better. Whether they were biologically related or adoption related, Heo and Jin were joined at the heart. Heo wanted to find his brother.

⁓

There was a chill in the early morning air as Heo's group boarded a bus, winding their way through busy streets and into the countryside behind an equipment van. They were waved through the main prison gate and through the barbed wire perimeter to a parking area next to a loading dock. Security guards stood on the dock and pointed to an area inside where they could put their equipment and supplies. There were buses and vans from two other hospitals at the docks next to them that were also in the process of unloading. Everyone was wearing masks, even the dock workers.

When they were finished, a member of the prison medical team welcomed the hospital groups and thanked them for coming. He gave a brief overview, explaining that TB was only recently identified as the strange illness which had been on the increase among inmates for months. By the time TB was suspected and they procured skin tests, it was spreading faster than could be contained, not only with the inmate population, but with administrative, medical, and security personnel as well.

"We are now totally out of testing supplies and medicine. Our supplier cannot give us a date when to expect a new shipment, so we appreciate the supplies you are bringing with you today. Now here is where we are. Our entire medical staff has been tested. About half are positive and are quarantined in a conference room awaiting medication. Please take care of them first. The negatives are taking all precautions to stay safe and are ready to work with you.

"The same applies to our administrative staff. They have all been tested, and the positives are quarantined in a separate room waiting for meds. The negatives are staying safe and are at their workstations. They will assist you in any way they can.

"Our prison guards have been hit pretty hard. They have all been tested. The negatives remain on duty, masked and practicing sanitary procedures as much as possible. I say *as much as possible,* because they are our front line, the ones in close contact with inmates in the work areas and barracks. The positives are lined up in hallways in the main building. Some have received meds and some haven't, and we've tried to keep them separated from each other.

"The Army personnel have also been hit hard, particularly the ones who accompany the inmates on work details outside the buildings. But we tested all of them. As we expected, the ones who secure the perimeter of the complex were negative and remain on duty. The positives are on cots in the cafeteria, which is closed off from the kitchen for now. We are not sure if or when they will be returning to their military barracks or to their own hospital. Right now, they are waiting for meds, which we are told should be delivered from the Army supply depot sometime today. The Army will be sending replacements for them as soon as this outbreak is under control.

"Regarding the inmates. When we were finally able to identify the root of the sickness we were dealing with, we did TB tests on some of the sickest ones, those who first exhibited suspicious symptoms. We did this until we ran out of solutions. There were a lot of positives who have been moved to the upper floor of an equipment building near the front gate, but we know there are more. The ones who tested negative remain in their barracks and are still on work duty. Unfortunately, more inmates are complaining of illness. There is a good chance you will find more positives when you do your testing.

"So that is where we are. Whenever you are ready, I will lead you to the areas where our medical and administrative people are waiting for meds. Again, thank you for being here."

They distributed face masks for protective gear to guard against TB microbes in the air and separated into pairs—a doctor and a nurse. Pushing carts of supplies, half went into the conference room to tend to medical personnel; the other half were led to the administrative staff quarantine area. Heo and his nurse were with the administrative group. While doctors examined and dispensed medicine, nurses filled out information sheets and assigned case numbers. It turned out to be an efficient system and went along at a brisk pace. By early afternoon, both groups were started on medication and given recuperation instruction sheets. They were told to rest and quarantine for two weeks before they could be considered non-contagious. They were given breathing exercises to help their lungs heal. They were informed that medication would be needed for six months and would be available at the prison.

It was two o'clock when Heo and his nurse gratefully accepted a prepared lunch outside the building. It felt good to be outside! As they removed their headgear, they had a chance to introduce themselves. His nurse was someone he had not seen before at the hospital, but she was obviously a tireless worker. Her name was Meili Gei from the pediatric section. It made good sense for nurses and doctors from pediatrics to be involved, Heo acknowledged, because children were especially susceptible to contracting and spreading the disease. He also noticed that Meili Gei was rather attractive.

After replenishing supplies, the doctor and nurse teams from Heo's hospital moved their equipment into one of the hallways where infected prison guards were waiting. The other doctor-nurse teams started with the second and third hallways. It was a closer working environment than the spacious rooms they had been in. They were about halfway down their respective hallways when the night shift arrived. Meili turned her records over to a collection desk so the night team could continue where they left off.

Once again, it felt good to be outside in the fresh air. Heo and Meili shed their protective suits into a bin in the back of their van and boarded the bus. Traffic was heavy during the commute back to the hospital, but they made good use of the time to assess the day and agree on changes for tomorrow.

Back at the hospital, everything was in order. Their fresh clothing waited on racks inside a private back door from the parking lot. Arrows pointed the way to either men's or women's dressing rooms where they could shower and change before returning to their cars.

⸘

The night shift on day two finished checking and treating the prison guards in the hallways and started on the military in the cafeteria. There were many rows of soldiers on military-issue cots, some sitting up, some lying down. An abundant supply of testing solution and meds arrived from the Army hospital mid-morning. Doctors examined each soldier, dispensing medicine, and nurses filled out information sheets and assigned case numbers. They learned that an agreement had been reached between the prison and the military that positive-tested soldiers would remain at the prison until they received medication and were either no longer contagious or until a dedicated area could be made available for them at the military hospital. The goal for the doctor-nurse teams was for the day group to finish treating the soldiers in the cafeteria so the night crew could start with inmates in the quarantine building.

By late morning, they were half finished. The temperature outside was much warmer than the previous day. Doors and windows were opened. The breeze was refreshing as it expelled the muggy indoor air. The prison doctor who had greeted them yesterday came by to assess their progress and make an announcement to the soldiers.

"Your commanding officer has asked me to inform you that you are all going to be staying right where you are for now, under the care of these very capable civilian doctors. Your own military doctors will be coming by in a few days to evaluate your progress and give you further instructions regarding when you will be returning to your base or other locations for recuperation. Meanwhile, if you have any special needs, there will be military personnel stationed here with you starting this afternoon."

Then he addressed the doctors and nurses. "Please feel free to remove your head coverings if you wish. I know they are cumbersome and warm. As long as you have safety masks and your patients are masked, I see no reason why you have to swelter under head coverings."

The doctors agreed; head coverings came off and regular medical face masks went on, then they immediately got back to work; the end of this area was in sight. As they moved through the room going from patient to patient, a soldier one row away from where Heo and Meili were working suddenly shouted out *"Qiang! Qiang! It's me, Zhang!"* He was waving and trying to lift his head. They glanced around, but no one responded. He hollered a second time and a third; it looked like he was pointing and waving in their direction.

"Poor fellow," Meili commented. "He is probably feverish. He is in our section. Do you want me to try to calm him down?"

"Sure. As soon as we get this man finished, I'll get us some water while you talk to him."

While Heo went over to the ice tub for water, Meili talked with the disruptive soldier. He wondered what she told him that caused him to suddenly quiet down. Whatever it was, it worked.

"What was he hollering about, Meili?"

"Oh, he was actually calling you. He had you confused with someone he knows in Beijing named Qiang. He insisted your name was Qiang because he recognized your hair. He said your hair was like Qiang's, and Qiang was a friend who saved his life. I told him your name was Dr. Heo Wong. Then he apologized, saying Qiang wouldn't be here anyway because there are no pianos here. I felt his forehead. It did seem a little warm, so he probably is feverish and maybe a little delirious. I told him we would be over to take care of him in a little while."

He recognized my hair? Chills engulfed Heo. "Let's take care of him next, Meili. If he is delirious, we should make him a priority." They moved over to the soldier.

"I'm sorry, Dr. Wong. I didn't mean to annoy you. It's just that your hair—" I know this sounds foolish, but I have a friend who has hair exactly like yours—exactly. I never met anyone else with that white swatch of hair other than Qiang."

His words hit Heo like a cold, wet towel in the face! "Your name is Zhang?"

"Yes sir."

"I am going to remove my mask for just a few seconds, Zhang. Tell me if I look anything like your friend. Don't worry, Meili, I have to do this. It will only be for a few seconds, and I won't breathe." He removed his mask and looked squarely into the soldier's face, then put it back on.

"Doctor, you look enough like my friend to be his brother, face, hair and all. You might be just a bit taller than he is."

"Please tell me how to find this person, Zhang. Where is he in Beijing?"

"I don't know exactly. He got married and moved a couple years ago, and I lost track of him. I only know that he had a business fixing pianos and making musical instruments in the village we lived in, so he most likely opened a shop in Beijing as well. I heard that his mother lives in Beijing now also and she apparently has hair just like his. I guess it must run in their family. That is all I know. Are you thinking it might be a relative?"

"Perhaps. Your observation is interesting. But for now, let's see what we can do to make you feel better." He looked at Meili who had been sitting quietly through the conversation but ready with her clipboard and pencil. "I will explain later," he told her apologetically. "Thank you for your patience."

They took care of Zhang, gave him medications and instructions, and moved back to their previous row and the next patient waiting in line.

By the time Heo was showered, dressed, and in his car driving home, his mind was crowded with emotions. He knew the possibility of ever finding his biological family was slim at best, but he couldn't help thinking it just might be happening. *Is it actually possible?* Whether it was possible or not though, it would have to wait. The prison project was top priority. Finding Jin was next.

Riding the bus into the prison the next morning was not conducive to a private conversation, so Heo made sure he had a few minutes alone with Meili before going into the building.

"Meili, I apologize for yesterday. The encounter we had with Zhang took me by surprise and I needed time to think. I am adopted and was raised by two wonderful people, but they have no knowledge of my biological family. I couldn't imagine there would ever be a way of finding out who they were or where they were but, all of a sudden, there might be. Whoever would have thought I might be recognized because of something crazy like my hair. Maybe I will have time to go to Beijing someday and look up piano repair shops."

"I understand, Dr. Wong. I really do. I am adopted also and for sure will never know my biological family. I envy you for having that opportunity. I will pray it goes well for you. And your hair *is* very distinctive," she smiled.

"Well then, I guess we have more in common than just our medical passions, and please call me Heo."

"I am honored to call you by your first name, and I will do so when we are not on duty. Your invitation makes me feel very special, though." She smiled again.

What a nice smile, he thought. *How fortunate I am to have such an understanding person by my side.* "You *are* a special lady, Meili, and a very hard worker. I appreciate you."

⁓⁂⁓

The next day started with a deadly glitch. One of their patients on the administration staff, a middle-aged woman who previously had pneumonia, took a turn for the worse during the night. The TB medicine and breathing tube weren't enough to compensate for her compromised lungs. She was rushed to a hospital and put on oxygen but passed away before morning.

Both the nighttime and daytime teams of doctors plus the prison doctors agreed it was necessary to take a step back. It was time to re-examine the patients who were already on meds and make sure they were responding well. It was a wise decision. Two of the guards and three soldiers needed extra attention. All the others were stabilizing, including Zhang, whose temperature was coming back down.

"We're just checking up on you, Zhang. How are you feeling today? You appear to be a little more comfortable."

"I am better, Dr. Wong. Apparently, our hospital has changed its mind. We are all going to be moved back to the military base in a day or two so the prison can have its cafeteria back. They've got a special place for us. I guess we're going to be there until they're sure we're not contagious anymore. Then we can go home to recuperate."

"Are you looking forward to going home?"

"Yes and no. It won't be for a while anyway. My home is far away – a good day's drive, so they're trying to find a place nearby where I can stay until I get my strength back. I shouldn't have to be there too long, though; I feel better already. Thank you and your lovely nurse for all you did."

"Rest is important, regardless of where it is. Just be careful. It is not wise to push yourself too soon."

"I hope you find Qiang," he added as Heo checked his vital signs. "And if you do, I would like to know where he is. He is a nice guy in spite of what he does, but we didn't have much of a chance to get to know each other. I hope to see him again."

"In spite of what he does?" Heo asked quizzically. "I thought he fixed pianos."

"Well, that also, but—" He glanced over at Meili, "That's a story for another time."

"Very well, Zhang. I will let you know if I find him. In the meantime, be careful, wear your mask and continue your meds, even if you are feeling better. If you need anything, contact me at the hospital. Here is my card. Just leave me a message and how to reach you and I will return your call."

"Or would you care to give us your contact information now so we can check on you?" Meili offered.

"Sure." He dictated his phone number to Meili and she put it in her pocket.

Doing checks took the entire day, but all agreed it was time well spent. The night shift would be the first ones to go into the building housing TB-positive prisoners.

∼⁄⁄∼

As the night shift crossed paths with the day shift entering the building, their supervisor issued a few cautious words to incoming doctors. "You will need lots of sanitary supplies, especially wipes. It's pretty rough in there. We opened the windows for you."

It was crowded. The inmates were sitting or lying on the floor with very little room between them. Each had a pillow and a blanket and nothing more except the clothes they had on, which were dirty, and so were they, almost as if they just returned from an outdoor work detail. Empty food bowls were piled next to the door. The room was as clean as an equipment storage building upper floor could be, but a stench of sickness and body odor hung heavy in the air. A make-shift latrine was in the corner. The windows were opened, for which they were thankful.

It was easy to determine where the previous crew left off. The treated men had cleaner faces and arms. *No wonder the night crew told us to bring lots of wipes!* Heo thought. They weren't much, but they were better than nothing. It didn't take long to realize that these men were at a much more advanced stage of the disease than their previous patients.

It was slow going. Some inmates were able to sit up; others were not. Some were able to understand the oral and written instructions; others seemed confused. These men were obviously going to need multiple re-exams!

Heo did a silent assessment. He knew from his research that there were approximately nine hundred inmates in this facility. He guessed there were about a hundred in this particular building. Judging from the condition they were in, plus the need for multiple exams, it was going to take a lot longer to treat them than his own hospital staff anticipated. These men needed much more help. That added up to a lot of time, and time was a luxury they did not have. Without more help, there could be a serious death toll, Heo surmised.

Cleanliness was another issue that had to be addressed. These men desperately needed showers, wherever showers were. Probably not in a storage building. Regardless of how close or far away they were, how would these men get there? Most of them couldn't even sit up, let alone stand and walk somewhere.

The doctors decided among themselves that there needed to be a conversation with prison officials. But who was going to be their spokesperson? The answer to that question was easy— the head of medicine at their hospital, the person who was brave enough to be vocal about the lack of information during SARS and was not afraid of voicing his displeasure. They would suggest an early morning meeting with him.

By the end of the next day, more hospitals were brought into the effort. Preparations were made to transport the affected inmates to dedicated areas at each of the hospitals where they could receive proper treatment. Aides were on hand to help the prisoners get down the narrow stairs of the storage building and into waiting vans and ambulances.

Every inmate in every barracks was to receive the TB skin test, whether they had one before or not. The positives would have to be separated and checked as often as necessary to assess their progress. Additional doctors and nurses were assigned to the prison project; they would all be starting the next day.

Meanwhile, Heo kept checking the summary sheets. Jin Wong was not on any of them. The cold truth was that even if Jin was there, it would be hard to recognize him. So many were lying in beds, on the floor, or huddled against a wall, covered with their blankets. All Heo could do was keep checking the summary sheets.

~☆~

There were enough doctors and nurses now for a dedicated team to work in each of the barracks. While it was good from a patient treatment standpoint, the chances of finding Jin diminished, Heo admitted grimly. He focused instead on identifying the TB positive prisoners and getting them out of there. If his brother did have TB, there was still a chance of locating him later at one of the hospitals.

The level of sickness in the barracks was staggering and exacerbated by the appalling living conditions—filth, rodents, insects, stagnant water, contamination. Many of the inmates had multiple illnesses. As medical people, it was hard to keep focused on just TB. It's what they were there for. By the time they administered the skin tests to all the inmates in their assigned barracks, it was time to go back for the re-evaluations. Patients were relocated to area hospitals. Their work was finished.

When they shed their haz-mat suits and boarded the bus on their last day, everyone was exhausted. The prison experience had been a rude awaking for all of them. To Heo, it was an affirmation that Jin was right to protest government suppression. Tiananmen Square *was* important. It was a desperate attempt to gain free speech, basic freedoms, and human dignity. He now saw his brother as brave and righteous.

Heo also knew he could never discuss what he saw with his parents. The truth about the laogai would not come from him. It would be up to Jin—if they ever found him. All Heo could do was report to his parents that Jin was not in the buildings that he and his nurse worked in or on any of the lists he was able to examine. Perhaps he was not even at that facility or, if he was, he did not have TB. *Deceased* was another possibility, but one Heo didn't feel necessary to mention. They already knew that. He would try checking with the other hospitals.

When they drove through the barbed wire bales for the last time, they were all ready for a rest, physically and mentally. Some of them looked back at the laogai camp as it disappeared behind them; others just looked straight ahead or closed their eyes. There were no words spoken, but the quiet thoughts were loud. As medical people, there was deep empathy for the ones left behind, those who were also sick but not with TB; those unforgettable faces with non-focusing stares who looked like empty shells. It was emotionally disturbing.

Looking inconspicuously at Meili, the tough little woman who worked alongside of him since it all began, Heo saw her wipe away tears. She was hurting too.

Chapter 6

FRIENDS

DOCTORS AND NURSES on the prison project were given a couple of days off to rest. It felt wonderful. Heo told his parents as much as he could to assure them that Jin was either not in that particular laogai or, if he was, did not test positive for tuberculosis. It was all he was allowed to share with his family. He was still under government-mandated silence to keep the outbreak quiet. His father and mother both knew about it anyway – his father from military meetings, his mother from rumors circulating in the public sector. People who were in contact with infected prison personnel and were requested to go to their local hospital for testing could not be silenced. The fact that there were quarantine sections in all the hospitals could not be hidden. SARS was still fresh in people's minds, but this time it gradually got better. There was nothing to talk about except a contained outbreak that the laogai had under control. Inmates who healed well were reclaimed for work duty at the prison. Those diagnosed with permanent lung damage and unable to work were exonerated; their cases closed. Several died.

Heo was not able to access patient records from other hospitals, so he turned his attention to the soldier Zhang and the possibility of finding a brother—a *real* brother. He wanted to talk to his parents about his encounter with the feverish soldier but didn't want to cause them any more anxiety; they had been through enough. For the second time in his life, he agonized over keeping silent.

But I want to know! he argued with himself. *Is it really possible that I have a biological brother and he's only 200 kilometers (124 miles) away in Beijing? What if I go there and find him and he turns out to be just another guy with a swatch of white hair? But what if it really is him? What does he do besides fix pianos that caused a strange comment from Zhang? It couldn't be anything illegal or he would be in prison, especially if a government soldier knows about it. What could it possibly be? Well, there's only one way to find out—talk some more to Zhang. Should I tell my parents first? How much should I tell them? Anything? Nothing?*

Heo couldn't make up his mind. What he really needed, he decided, was a confidante, a person who might be able to offer good advice. There was no one he could think of. He tried praying. Praying worked for Cha-Li, maybe it would work for him. He asked God for wisdom, guidance, someone to talk to. Nothing happened. Coincidentally, this was the afternoon of their church meeting. Maybe praying during a church service would be more appropriate.

Yes, that's what I'll do, try praying again this afternoon.

⁓⁖⁓

The service was at the home of a couple he had met recently. They were nice people, but surely not the ones God would put in his path to talk to. What did resonate with him, however, was the sermon, Jesus's own words about "whatever you did for the least of these, you did for me." He had certainly been with the least of people for the last couple of weeks and did what he could, but it felt like an unfinished project. He had a restless feeling that more could be done for them. But what? And how?

One of their members started playing a beautiful hymn on the piano and some were quietly singing along or humming. They always had to be quiet in their underground church because of neighbors. He closed his eyes, listening, and giving his thoughts permission to wander.

Heo loved his new church; it was a happy place, no matter where it was in any given week. There was so much to learn, and everything was positive. He appreciated that Christianity was all about good—being good, doing good, good characteristics a person should have. It was about love, forgiveness, sharing and caring. Why did such a religion have to be illegal? What was wrong with people being happy? *It doesn't make sense. Well, actually it does,* he reasoned. *Christianity glorifies God, not a government. In this country, government comes first.* Heo didn't see that changing anytime soon.

As the soothing music continued, Meili popped into his mind—sweet, hardworking Meili with the beautiful smile. He really wanted to see her again. *I actually miss her.* Admitting that to himself was scary. It made his heart flutter. *But what if she's married? She probably is, although she never mentioned a husband, children, or family other than she was adopted. A lot of women her age are adopted because of the edict. How can I find out?*

Heo considered himself socially awkward when it came to women. He did go on a couple of dates in college; they weren't anything earth-shaking, just dates. He never had much time for socializing. Whatever spare time he did have was usually spent with Papa Shen talking about theories and ideas, exciting things. Up until now, the only female he ever spent time with was his cousin Cha-Li. Now there was Meili from pediatrics. *She has Zhang's phone number,* Heo suddenly remembered! His mind wandered to another pressing thought: *Should I become a prison doctor instead of a pediatrician? Maybe I can find my brother that way? I could certainly do some good helping those suffering prisoners.* The music stopped and people stood to pray, jarring Heo back to the present. *Maybe God is listening now.* His prayer was short: *"God, please help me with all these decisions. I can't do this by myself. I need help. Amen."*

As he turned to leave, Cha-Li, his straight-talking, no-nonsense but sometimes emotional cousin, was walking toward him. *Really, God?* he said silently. *Cha-Li is my help?* He had to squelch a grin as she approached. *Why not? If anyone is going to tell me straight out what I need to know, whether I like it or not, it would definitely be Cha-Li!*

"Heo. I missed you the last few weeks. Auntie Yan said you were on special duty in the laogai with a team of doctors. I heard something about tuberculosis. Is that true? Were you part of all that?"

"Well, kind of. But remember when you said if I ever needed someone to talk to about anything to let you know? Well, I need someone to talk to. Do you have an hour maybe later today or tomorrow?"

"Of course. What's up? You look pretty serious."

"I've got lots of things on my mind, decisions to make, and I value your opinion."

Cha-Li's curiosity piqued. "Why don't you take Auntie Yan home and come back? I don't have anything to do that can't wait."

"Thanks. I will. Try to think of someplace we can go, though, someplace quiet and private. Think of some reason to go off by ourselves that will sound normal to your parents if you can. I'll see you in a little while."

"Alright. I'll come up with something. This does sound serious."

"It is. Believe me, it is!"

⁓⋎⋍

It was a muggy evening as they engaged in deep conversation on a park bench. Heo poured out all of his concerns to Cha-Li—except for the horrible living conditions of the laogai and his concern for the prisoners. *There's nothing she could help with there,* he decided. A half-hour went by as if it were a minute. Only twice did Cha-Li interrupt to ask for more clarification. Heo felt like the weight of the world was slowly lifting just by talking.

"Wow, Heo. I was trying to decide while you were talking what was going to be the most important issue to tackle first, but they all seem equally major. No wonder you looked so serious!"

"Yeah, I don't know myself what is the most important. After mulling things over for days, the main conclusion I've reached is that I don't know where to start. So, what's your diagnosis?"

Cha-Li looked pensive. "Well, my first thought is that you should start with your parents. Remember how devastated you were when you found out the truth about your birth by accident? I would say don't do that to your parents. Be up front with them. Even though they might be jolted at first to hear about the possibility of finding your biological sibling, I am sure they will appreciate your honesty. Then take it from there.

"About Jin, you need to be realistic. Sure, you want to find him. We all do. But wherever he is, and whatever condition he is in, there is nothing you or anyone can do to change it. Your father has done the right thing by inquiring about him from time to time through normal channels but, until he hears something, there is nothing any of us can do. You must accept that. He is in God's hands.

"Same thing with the laogai. I noticed you didn't go into detail about the conditions in there, Heo, but I know more about those places than you think. There are hundreds more in our country just like the one you were in, and probably a thousand teachers in there who are being punished because they spoke out against our government, especially dictating what we can teach and what we can't. It's not a penal system to try to make criminals shape up and fly right. It's an economic system that is using dissidents for free labor. Free labor enables our country to undercut the rest of the world in cost of goods. You are not going to change that no matter how good a doctor you are or how good your intentions are. As far as changing your medical focus to work in the prison system, that's something only you can figure out. But please look at it logically with your head, not your heart. It's a good intention, but are you really going to make any kind of a difference by being there? Are you going to clean it up somehow?"

As expected, Cha-Li's words hit hard. "I didn't realize you knew so much about the laogai," Heo said. "You are right. My being in the prison system isn't going to change anything. I knew it was bad from research I did on my own because of Jin, but it turned out to be worse than I thought. Truly, it is just plain inhumane. Knowing what I know now, and knowing that Jin has been in there for almost seven years, is tearing my heart out. Why didn't I realize the truth earlier, especially when we were being blatantly ignored by the authorities? How could I have been so blind?"

"Maybe because you were never exposed to it before now. You spent your education years talking and listening to your father and Papa Shen and the leaders of the Three Self Church. They are all government. How could you possibly know anything else? I'm not saying that to be critical, Heo. I loved Papa Shen as much as you did, and I love your father, who is also my father, but it is true. If they didn't know what was going on, how could you be expected to know? Dealing with prison brutality is not exactly something they can teach you in med school."

"Thank you, Cha-Li. Thank you for helping me see a bigger picture."

"Well, you did the same for me when I was all wrapped up in my personal little pity party without considering the times and the reasons for what happened. Sometimes we just need to say out loud what we're thinking to someone who can see the bigger picture for us. That's where friends come in, and I'm glad you chose me to talk to because I care about you.

"Oh, and speaking of special friends, tell me more about this lady love in your life. What is her name? Meili?"

"Yeah. I guess I'm in love but, for all I know, it might be with a married woman. I don't even know how to go about finding out her status without overstepping my boundary as a doctor and co-worker. I can't just blurt out, 'Are you married or engaged? And if not, do you want to go out to dinner?'"

Cha-Li laughed. "You are so funny, Heo. I can't tell you how to handle a lady friend, but you might try something a little less personal than a romantic dinner to start out with. How about lunch in the hospital cafeteria, talk about Zhang, get his phone number, and then casually ask her to talk about herself? If she's not married, then you can pursue that path. If she is, then just be thankful for a good friend and co-worker. Be yourself, that's the best advice I can give you. You really are a pretty neat guy, cuz, but don't let my opinion go to your head. I don't speak for all women. We can be pretty weird sometimes."

That brought a chuckle of agreement from Heo. "Yeah, that's what I'm afraid of. I've known you all my life and couldn't figure you out for a while. But right now, I am thankful for you. You've made good sense out of a scrambled mess. I needed this talk to get my head on straight and my priorities in order, and I think we've accomplished that much. You are a good friend. Ready to go back home?"

"Yup. It's getting chilly out here and I'm ready for a hot cup of tea!"

⁓⁕⁓

First things first, Heo told himself the next day. *I must know about Meili.* His schedule showed he had a half-hour of free time at ten. He walked over to the pediatric ward to find Meili. "She's helping with a birth in the delivery room, Dr. Wong," he was told by the receptionist. "Do you want me to give her a message or can I have her call you?"

"No, I'll just leave her a note." He tore off a sheet of paper from the telephone message pad and scribbled. *Hi Meili, Please give me a call when you have time. I want to talk about the soldier Zhang. Heo Wong.* He handed it to the receptionist. "Please give this to Nurse Gei. I will wait for her call."

He was just getting ready to see his next patient when she called back. "Hi, Meili. How's the new baby? Do we have a boy or a girl?"

"We have a healthy little boy with a fantastic set of lungs!"

"Ha ha! That is great! Second question. What are you doing for lunch? Would you have any time to chat for a bit? The best I can offer right now is a cozy corner in the hospital cafeteria." *Oh please say yes.*

"Of course. My lunch time is at noon. I'll meet you there."

Yes! He felt like a school kid with a crush on the teacher, but he didn't care. At least he was going to see her again, or so he thought. Their schedules did not mesh. She called back with an apology. "I'm so sorry Dr. Wong. We had an emergency here. Want to try for tomorrow?"

"How about tonight after work instead? Do you have to get home to family or can you join me for dinner?"

"Yes and no. I don't have to go home to family per se, but Thursday is date night with my daughter. She always looks forward to our mother-daughter night out, and I can't disappoint her. We missed the last two weeks because of our assignment. But you are welcome to join us if you'd like. I let her choose the place but, as a three-year-old, she always chooses Maidanglao (translated: McDonald's®)."

"Maidanglao it is," Heo laughed. "Which one are we going to?"

"It's near where my parents live. Why don't you follow me when we leave here, and you can park your car in front of their house and then ride with us if you don't mind. It's only a couple blocks away. We won't have to wait long for Molly. She's always ready to go on our date as soon as my car pulls up."

⋰⋱

A little girl with black springy curls bounded out of the house and ran to Meili with a hug, then stopped and looked over at Heo. "Molly, this is Dr. Wong. We work together at the hospital, and he is going to dinner with us tonight. Where would you like to go, our usual place?" She nodded. "But first, let's take a few minutes and let Dr. Wong meet Nana and Papa. Alright?" Another head nod.

Mr. and Mrs. Gei were a typically hospitable Chinese couple. Heo was invited to stay for tea, but Meili politely excused themselves so they could take Molly to McDonald's. They understood; it was Thursday.

As they waited in line with a half-dozen other families with small children, Heo didn't feel out of place. It had been a long time since he visited the fast-food restaurant, but it all came back to him when he smelled the french fries. It was a feel-good place. Molly marched up to the counter and announced her order: a Happy Meal® with chocolate milk. Meili: a chicken salad and water. "I'll have the same," Heo ordered and, of course, insisted on buying.

Heo noticed the dissimilarity between Meili and her daughter. Meili was a beautiful Chinese lady with rather long, dark brown wavy hair and brown eyes. Molly's hair was black with tightly wound curls pushed back with a hair band. Her eyes were deep blue; her skin tone a pale pink. While she looked different from other Chinese children on the outside, she was a typical child on the inside; two bites of her Happy Meal, a sip of chocolate milk, and she was off to the play area.

"She's good in there for a half-hour, on and off," Meili smiled as Molly ran back several times for more of her dinner and milk. It's nice to have an adult to talk to. Thank you for dinner. May I buy you a cup of coffee or tea?"

Heo kept an eye on Molly while Meili fetched coffee. "I think you want this, right" she said as she pulled a piece of paper out of her pocket with Zhang's phone number. "I've been thinking about Zhang and you and perhaps your missing brother, and I think I can help."

"Really? I would love to hear it."

"Well, I attended nursing school in Beijing and still have a good friend who lives there. I was thinking that I could contact her and ask if she would find information on piano repair places in Beijing and the outskirts. Beijing is more than just the big city. There are a lot of small towns surrounding it in Hubei Province that might not pop up on a phone search. It would be easier for her to do a search from where she is rather than us trying to do it from here."

Heo didn't know what made him happier, the possibility of finding a biological brother or knowing that he and Meili were sharing a project again together. "That would be absolutely wonderful if you could do that, Meili. You are not only a top-notch nurse, you are a good friend. Thank you!"

Meili smiled, and Heo's heart melted. It was a magic moment, interrupted by a quick visit from Molly for a french fry and a sip of milk. Then she was off again to the play area contraption with a new friend.

"There are other things I would like to talk to you about also, Meili, when we have more time. Probably another evening would be better than during the day, though, unless you have family commitments. Would you be able. . . is there anyone—" He was stuck. Where were the words he needed?

Meili smiled briefly but then turned sullen. "No, there is no one at home, Heo. Just my daughter and me. My husband passed away before Molly was born. But that's a long story that I'm not going to bore you with. My parents are always willing to watch Molly if I have an evening commitment. I just have to give them a little advance notice. What is it you want to talk about?"

"First of all, Meili, I could not possibly be bored with anything that has to do with you. I hope you know that. For almost two weeks you were my right arm. And now you are continuing to help me. You are obviously a compassionate person, and you have no idea how much that means to me. Other than one cousin, I have no one in my life that I feel comfortable talking with."

"You are not married?"

"Huh?" It took only a few seconds to sink in before Heo laughed out loud. "No, I am not married. I was thinking you might be, though, and I didn't want to tread on your personal life if you were."

The mood instantly changed. Meili was no longer distant; she was more engaging, comfortable with being herself. "Here's to good friends," he toasted, holding out his cup of coffee. "Amen," Meili replied as she joined the toast! It was a relaxing time as they rode back to pick up his car. "Could I have a date night soon?" Heo asked as he got into his car. They agreed on Tuesday evening so Heo would have time to talk to his mother and father over the weekend and give them an opportunity to adjust to the new issues at hand.

⁓⁎⁓

Bin and Yan Wong were very understanding when Heo told them about this surprise twist in his life. "It was nothing I sought to do. It just presented itself," he explained.

"There is no way you cannot pursue this opportunity to find your biological family," his father told him. "If you don't, you will regret not knowing. As for us, you will always be our son, no matter what happens."

His mother agreed. "I don't blame you for wanting to know if you have brothers or sisters. If it were me, I would want to know. You have my blessing as well."

It was followed by an unexpected turn of conversation with his father. "Heo, tell me more about this soldier Zhang. What is his condition? Was he able to go home to recuperate?"

"His case was not severe, Father, mostly fever and intestinal symptoms rather than a cough. The last time I saw him, he was recovering well but was very tired. What he should be dealing with now would mostly be fatigue and getting his appetite back. TB has a way of affecting taste buds. It is not unusual for someone with TB to lose weight, which only makes a person weaker. All military personnel were moved back to their base to quarantine for a couple of weeks, so he should not be contagious if he has been taking his antibiotics, and I'm sure he has. If I understood him correctly, I don't think he was planning to go home to recuperate. He is not from this area. His home is apparently a good day's drive from here and he was too weak to make the trip. I'm sure he will be fine with more time to rest, but it's going to be weeks, perhaps months."

"If he is not able to go home and is staying alone somewhere to recuperate, maybe we should invite him to come here until he is better. He is a soldier, and perhaps a special one. I feel an obligation to help him if we can, that is, if it is alright with your mother." He looked at Yan, who nodded in agreement. "Yes, a comfortable bed and a little home cooking might help him recover faster," his father continued. "He can have Jin's room, although I realize we cannot discuss Jin with him. Please feel free to bring him here if it is agreeable with you."

Bin was a devoted father and husband, but never one to be taken for granted. Surprises were common. "Sure. I will do that," Heo agreed." I will call him tomorrow."

⸎

No one was more surprised by the invitation than Zhang, who was convalescing at an Army infirmary. "Really, Dr. Wong? Your parents want me to come and stay at your house until I am better? Why?"

"Because my father is also military and feels empathy for you as a soldier, and, secondly, because you were kind enough to tell me about a person who might be my biological brother. They understand my curiosity and are supportive. My parents would like to repay your kindness. That's just the way they are. So, if you would like to accept my family's invitation and can get permission to stay off-premises until you recuperate, let me know and I will pick you up."

A few days later, Zhang was released to the care of Dr. Heo Wong. His room at the Wong home was cleared of everything belonging to Jin, the pseudo-twin who would not be mentioned.

Bin was impressed with his young guest's military acumen; they spent many hours engaged in military conversations. Yan made special meals for him, his favorites, and was pleased that his appetite improved. Heo found himself enjoying the company of a person his own age once again, something he missed since Jin was gone. They shared the music of young adults, worked out with Heo's gym equipment, and even engaged in an occasional board game. Resting in a home atmosphere felt good; Zhang's strength was slowly returning.

They were a week into the recuperation process when Heo and Zhang talked about Qiang once again and the possibility of Meili's friend in Beijing finding him. Heo was especially interested to know what Zhang meant by "in spite of what he did." It was puzzling.

"I probably should not have said what I did," Zhang apologized, "because I do not know his whole story. I can only tell you what I do know. He is a person from our village who had a job other than fixing pianos. It was a strange job, and it was certainly not enviable. It was disposing of illegal children in compliance with the one-child-per-family edict. The rumor was that he threw illegal children off a cliff to their demise. The only reason we got to know each other was because I was carrying out my military assignment, which was to determine his method and motives. It was not something authorized by our governor, so I was instructed to follow him, which I did."

"One night, when he was carrying a newborn out of the village toward a hill, we confronted him and I informed him I would be accompanying him to determine his method of disposal. I followed him all the way up the hill, but I never got to the top. I stepped too close to the edge and lost my footing. I was about to slide off to my doom, but Qiang reached out and pulled me back. He saved my life.

"My arm was torn up pretty bad from a rock near the edge, and Qiang used the baby's blanket to make a tourniquet for my arm. Then he made me wait there while he finished the journey alone. We weren't that far from the top and he was only gone for a few minutes. Then he walked me back down the hill and got me to the hospital. He was given a commendation a few weeks later from our governor. It included lunch, at which time I did get to know him a little better. He didn't talk much about himself, but I did come to appreciate his sense of humor. When I asked him why he pulled me back from the edge, his only comment was, 'Well, it wasn't because I really liked you.'

"I never saw Qiang actually dispose of a child, and certainly not toss them off a cliff. I always suspected there was more to his story. When I asked him about what he did and why he did it, all he would say is that it was a self-appointed job to help his people comply with the government edict. There's a disconnect there. However, I owe him my life, and if I am able to help him and you reunite, that is if you really are brothers, I would feel grateful to be able to repay that debt. Still, I would like to know more about him someday, to find out what he was really up to."

The opportunity for Heo to meet Qiang came when Meili called his office with encouraging news. "We have found Qiang," she said excitedly. "My friend in Beijing found his store. It's actually just outside of Beijing. She called a whole bunch of music stores like she was a customer looking for a used piano and trying to find a recommended piano refurbisher named Qiang. So she made an appointment to go over and look at pianos. She even took his picture, rather slyly of course, standing over one of the pianos. I have it on my phone. Want to see it?"

"I'll be right there." Five minutes later, Heo was in the pediatric ward looking at a picture of Qiang, donning a swatch of white hair very much like his own, plus similar facial features. There was also a picture of Qiang's business card. It read *Ming's Music Shop, Qiang Ming, Owner.*

"Want to take a day off work and go to Beijing? I'll go with you if you want me to. I'm very familiar with that area and can drive us right to it, but only if you want me to. If you want to go alone, I will understand. It's a personal thing."

"I would love to have you come with me. As a matter of fact, I can't think of anyone I'd rather spend a day with. How about next Friday? That will give you Thursday for your date with Molly and give me time to clear my calendar."

"Next Friday. It's a date," Meili said. "Meanwhile, I'll see you tomorrow at your house. I look forward to meeting your family."

⋯⋇⋯

Cha-Li came to Heo's house the next day to meet Meili and Molly and talk about getting Molly into children's school, but was not sure about the Wongs' house guest.

She heard about Zhang and was not particularly looking forward to meeting a government soldier who was most likely a member of the distasteful Three Self Church. However, she promised Heo she would treat Zhang kindly. Molly took an instant liking to Cha-Li and eagerly listened to her future teacher's description of school. Then she was off to the kitchen for a sweet treat while Cha-Li and Meili got down to business.

"Do you have Molly's birth certificate?" Cha-Li asked. "That is all I need to get her into my class."

"Yes, I do. Her full name is Molly McIntyre. My full name is Meili Gei McIntyre, but I don't use the McIntyre anymore since my husband died. It takes too much explaining."

"How did your husband die? I hope it is not too personal a question."

"That is fine. It was a motorcycle accident. We met at the university in Beijing where he was studying for a degree in physics and I was taking nursing classes. We got married and he went back to Ireland when he graduated because his visa had expired. I was supposed to join him after Molly was born, and we were going to live in Ireland, but he died two months before she was born. Then I had second thoughts about relocating. I had no reason to move to Ireland without my husband. I had never met his family. My friends encouraged me to put Molly up for adoption because they said no man would want to date me in the future, knowing I had a daughter as an only child. I couldn't do that—I wouldn't. The doctor at the hospital even delayed issuing a birth certificate because he was sure I would listen to the advice of my friends and give Molly up. It took a while for him to accept the fact that I was not going to change my mind. I had a legal marriage license and the legal right to have a birth certificate for my child. Keeping my daughter and staying in China was the right decision."

Cha-Li was rattled by the story, internalizing her own situation, but she handled it inconspicuously with nothing more than an inaudible sigh and a slight smile. "Good for you, Meili. Heo told me quite a bit about you and Molly and I'm so glad to finally have a chance to meet you. Molly is a lovely little girl, and I am looking forward to having her in my classroom."

They walked into the kitchen where Molly was sitting on Bin's lap, munching on a honey rice cake and enjoying lots of attention. Zhang stood as a military courtesy when the ladies entered the room and offered them chairs, while Yan dished out more desserts. It was an enjoyable afternoon. Heo noted that his cousin was not only pleasant to their guest, as she promised to be, but they appeared to be very engaged in conversation. He hesitated to interrupt them, but he was anxious to show Zhang the picture on Meili's phone.

"Yes!" Zhang responded enthusiastically. "Yes, that is my friend Qiang! See the white hair on the side of his head? It is exactly like yours, Heo. You are the only two people I have ever known with such distinct hair."

Heo's anticipation heightened, but he remained realistic. "I am going to call your friend on Monday, Zhang. If a few questions and answers by phone determine there is a possibility we could be related, Meili and I are prepared to go to Beijing to meet him. Is it alright with you if I tell him about how you and I met during your bout with TB? He will certainly want to know how we learned about him."

"Of course, of course! Please do and let me know how he is doing."

"Zhang is really a nice guy, Heo," Cha-Li commented later. "He's not at all like I imagined. Plus, he doesn't belong to the Three Self Church. He doesn't go to any church. Maybe there's hope for him after all."

"Be careful, cuz. I agree he's definitely a nice guy, but he's still government."

Chapter 7

BROTHERS

HEO CALLED FIRST thing Monday morning, hoping Ming's Music Shop would be open.

"Ming's Music Shop," a female voice answered.

"Is Qiang Ming there?"

"Yes, he is. Is this about an instrument you have in here for repair?"

"No, this is a personal call."

"One moment please."

"This is Qiang Ming."

"Qiang, my name is Heo Wong and I am calling you because we have a mutual friend, a soldier named Zhang who says you saved his life at one time and he speaks highly of you. Do you remember him?"

"Yes, I do."

Do you have a few minutes to talk?"

"Of course. Is Zhang alright?"

"Well, he is now. I am a doctor and tended to him in the laogai near where I live. He was one of the soldiers on duty there and took ill. When he was very ill and feverish he kept calling me by your name, Qiang. I thought he was delusional, but we eventually found out it was because I apparently have hair similar to yours, a white swatch on the right side of my head. Because of that, he is convinced we are related, possibly even brothers. He also said we look alike."

There was dumbfounded silence as Qiang digested the news. "I do. . . or I did have a brother," he answered. "But he was an illegal child and was taken away as soon as he was born. When were *you* born? Do you know your actual birth date?"

"It was in 1980. The birth certificate my adoptive parents have says I was born on November 19, but that might be a day or so off."

Qiang froze. He couldn't believe he was actually having this conversation. "My brother was born on that date."

"Then I think perhaps we should meet, if you are agreeable. I live two hundred kilometers away from Beijing and can be there around noon on Friday. I have a friend who used to live in Beijing and said she knows the area where your store is. She is willing to bring me there if you are available."

"I will make myself available."

"Wonderful," Heo managed, his voice nervously cracking. "Needless to say, I am looking forward to meeting you!"

He hurried to the pediatric ward to leave a note for Meili: *The trip to Beijing is a go!*

⁓∖⁄⁓

Qiang was in a state of disbelief as he turned to talk to his wife, Guo. She only heard one side of the conversation, but it wasn't hard to piece together what it was about. They just stared at each other.

"I'm not sure, Guo, but I think we've just found Syaran, or he found us, thanks to Zhang. Remember Zhang, the soldier I told you about who followed me up the hill to watch me dispose of an illegal child? The soldier who I saved?"

She nodded.

"This doctor, he said his name was Heo Wong, apparently looks like me, or at least his hair does. His birth date is the same as Syaran's."

Later in the day, when they had time to think and talk, Qiang and

Guo had decisions to make. The most important one was whether or not they should tell Qiang's mother, Su-Li. She suffered through many years of emotional trauma when Syaran was taken from her, and again four years later when her daughter was taken. They decided to be vague to ensure that she would be home on Friday *if* they determined that Dr. Heo Wong could actually be her lost son.

The only thing that kept Qiang's sanity intact for the rest of the week was business, customers, package deliveries, orders. Nighttime was different. Sleep was elusive as hurtful memories surfaced.

He was four years old when Syaran was born and immediately taken away to be delivered to an orphanage. Qiang never forgot his mother's cries that night. It gave him nightmares for many years.

He was eight when his newborn sister, Xiu-Su, was forcibly pulled out of his mother's arms and turned over to a man named Guang, the most hated man in the village, the child executioner. Everyone assumed he worked for the governor of their province, but no one knew for sure. Guang's job was to take illegal children away from parents to comply with the one-child-per-family edict. If they were boys, he took them to the hospital clinic to be delivered to an orphanage for adoption. There was a waiting list for boy babies and a quick turnaround time. But orphanages were overflowing with baby girls waiting for adoption. Some found homes, but most didn't. They lingered, often in less-than-ideal conditions where only the strongest survived. *Disposal* was easier, and widely accepted as the answer to illegal female children. Even if it was a legal, first-born child, disposal was acceptable if the parents preferred a son.

It was Guang who took Xiu-Su from the village to a cliff and, in plain sight of everyone in the village, presumably threw her over the edge to her death. It was intended to maintain the integrity of the edict plus teach the villagers a lesson—illegal children would not be allowed.

Oh, the piercing scream and sobbing from his mother as Guang left with Xiu-Su in his arms, headed for the cliff. He remembered running into his mother's room, determined to help her somehow, but was stopped at the doorway by his distraught father. He remembered the fear he felt when his mother slipped into fevered unconsciousness for days; he thought she was going to die.

Qiang never talked about those emotional times with anyone. He kept his childhood trauma pent up, but never forgot the terror. It eventually changed his life.

When he was thirteen, Qiang saw Guang heading for the infamous cliff with a child. Anger rushed through his veins as he followed Guang, with the hope of ambushing him and pulling the child away. He stayed in the shadows, darting from tree to tree, from rock to rock, crossing the open expanse between the village and the bottom of the hill. Unexpectedly, Guang stepped out of a shadow, and they came face to face. Qiang didn't realize how big Guang was but, at that point, he didn't care. He was going to put a stop to this monster of a person once and for all! He started swinging at Guang, trying to grab the baby, but Guang held him at arm's length until he cooled down.

What happened next was something Qiang never could have anticipated. Guang talked to him in a normal, almost friendly voice as he balanced the baby on his shoulder, his long arm holding her out of Qiang's reach.

"I am not doing what you think I am doing," he said. "I am not going to kill this child. I am going to save her life. And if you promise to take an oath of secrecy from me, I will tell you how. It is a serious oath, not to be taken lightly. If you don't agree, then I can tell you nothing and you will actually be putting this child's life in danger."

Qiang backed off and agreed to the oath of secrecy and, yes, it *was* serious. Qiang never forgot Guang's words.

"I am taking this child to safety, to be delivered to parents who want to adopt her. What you and others see me throw over the cliff is no more than a baby blanket filled with rocks. It is a long way to the bottom of the ravine, and impossible to get to without scaling down a cliff, so no one can actually see what is at the bottom. I do this because orphanages are full of baby girls. If she is taken to an orphanage, no one will adopt her. She will die there. But right now, there is someone waiting for this child, probably in another country. I cannot tell you anything more. You have to believe me and let me finish my journey without any further delay."

Qiang agreed and went back home, but wasn't totally convinced of Guang's bizarre story. He decided to climb down the cliff to the ravine and see for himself what was at the bottom. He remembered being scared to death as he descended, hanging onto a rope tied to a tree. What Guang told him was true. A clutter of blankets, thin cloths, stones, and wood were strewn everywhere, but no bones. Doubt turned to admiration for Guang and for whoever else was involved with this cause.

Now all he had to do was get himself out of there! As scared as he was going down the cliff, it was even scarier going back up. If he slipped and lost his grip, there would definitely be bones down there—his! By the time he got to the top, his hands were rubbed raw; his arms and legs ached for a week. An apology was in order.

⸙

Qiang found out Guang lived with his mother at the edge of the village. He rode his bicycle there and confessed his foolhardy venture into the ravine, expecting to be chastised by the giant of a man standing before him. Guang stared into Qiang's face all the while he was talking, reached down and examined his bloodied hands, and threw his head back and laughed. Qiang felt like the biggest fool in the world during those few short minutes, but he ultimately gained a friend and credibility.

"You have been watched ever since the night you followed me," Guang told him. "We don't blindly trust someone just because he or she accepts our oath of secrecy. We know you went back up the path to the cliff, and we also know you found nothing that might expose our operation. That is good news for us, and for you. It means we are covering our tracks well and we don't have to decide what to do with you. We also know you have not spoken with anyone about what you were told. We are very alert to rumors or unwanted attention, and there has been none. You are proving to be a person of your word. You are also showing us you are very brave—or foolish!" he added with a grin. "Would you like to come in and meet my mother? She wants to meet you."

He met Mulan, Guang's mother, another person involved with what was simply referred to as *the cause*. He became the youngest person to be included in the closely guarded group, learning more and more over the next few years as appropriate. Their mission had one goal—to save the lives of Chinese baby girls who otherwise would most likely perish. He also learned the cause extended far beyond his village, even into Beijing and other large cities.

There were good memories, too, especially the day he was shown proof that his sister, Xiu-Su, had not died. She was delivered into the *baby tunnel* where adoptive parents waited at the other end for her. The knowledge was bittersweet. How he longed to tell his parents, but he could not! An oath was an oath. To expose their operation meant death—not only for future at-risk children, but most likely for all those involved with saving them, including himself. What they were doing was considered treason against the government.

It was only after Guang became ill years later and eventually died of heart failure that Qiang was given permission to share the truth about Xiu-Su with his parents. The reason—he took Guang's job. He became the *new* child executioner, the *new* most hated man in the village, which would affect his parents.

Guang's mother, Mulan, was shunned by people in the village because of her son and Qiang did not want his own parents to be treated that way. He agreed to assume Guang's job only if his parents were allowed to know about the operation up front, agreed to his involvement as well as their own, and supported the cause. They agreed and took the solemn oath of secrecy. It was a joyous day when he was finally able to tell them that their daughter, Xiu-Su, was alive—somewhere.

Knowing he was saving the lives of countless baby girls brought happiness. Qiang would kiss each one on the cheek as he turned her over to the caregiver at the entrance to a hidden cave at the top of the hill. The ceremonial tossing of a bundle of debris was like a release at the end of a perilous journey, an unspoken permission for the child to live.

Qiang insisted on living apart from his parents, creating the impression he was disowned. It was for their own well-being. Although he lived alone at the edge of the village, he was never truly alone. He was amid a new circle of friends, protective, watchful friends who lived close by, all involved in the same cause. It's how he met Guo, owner of a safety house many kilometers away, the first stop-over point for transporters who were moving newborns through the baby tunnel.

⁓⁓⁓

It was over six years now since Qiang and Guo married and moved to Beijing. Moving away was an easy decision. His father was deceased. His mother, a music teacher, was preparing to move to Beijing for a new position at a school of higher learning. Guo's family lived not far from Beijing. It was a good time to leave the past behind and transition to big city living.

Qiang was happier now than he had ever been. He was enjoying a busy life with Guo and their five-year-old daughter, Lian. He was the owner of his own business that allowed him to do the things he loved, breathing new life into old musical instruments, especially pianos, and offering modern ones for sale. It was all about making people smile with music.

They had found Xiu-Su, Qiang's sister, although quite by accident. Oddly enough, it was also because of their distinctive family hair feature. Her name was now Emily Thornton, and she was part of an international tour of student musicians playing at the opera house in Beijing. Qiang recalled the strange circumstances involved in finding her and the joy of meeting her plus her adoptive Canadian parents. She was a gifted pianist, and they were able to hear her play. Oh, they were so proud. It was a wonderful reunion, but short, leaving a bittersweet memory for Qiang to cherish forever. They had each other's addresses, phone numbers, and email addresses. They would communicate, albeit cautiously. Communication of any kind in China was always subject to government scrutiny.

Emily was not told anything about how she was brought to safety, even though she had asked. Of necessity, answers were vague. She did not need to know about the baby tunnel; nor did her Canadian parents.

Now they were on the doorstep of possibly discovering Qiang's other sibling. Would finding Syaran be another joyous occasion like finding Emily, or would it bring danger?

Qiang felt comfortable in Beijing. He was just an obscure face here, the owner of a small music store on the outskirts of a big city. Only a few people knew who he was or where he came from, and those were friends involved with the same cause and belonging to the same underground Christian church. Anyone else who knew about his past still lived in his home village—except for the soldier Zhang, a person from his past who seemed to be looming on the horizon of his future.

How much did Zhang tell Heo Wong about me? Qiang wondered. *Did Zhang tell him how we met and our treacherous night on the cliff? Probably,* he reasoned. *He would have to have explained how we knew each other. Will he know about my being called the child executioner? Even if Heo Wong is my biological brother, he is still a stranger. He said he's a doctor, which means he has strong ties with the government.*

It was the second time Qiang sensed danger that had to do with the soldier Zhang.

‑‑‑

It was an anxious ride to Beijing. While it was enjoyable to have Meili's company as well as her directions along the route, Heo's thoughts were filled with something he couldn't describe—anticipation, excitement, foreboding? He didn't know. He looked over at Meili. She was so full of enthusiasm it made him smile. Heo just wished he could share it.

What am I so worried about? he chastised himself. *This guy is either my brother or he isn't. We'll soon find out. And what if he is? From what Zhang described, we are from two very different backgrounds. We are total strangers. Perhaps we never will identify as brothers!*

They pulled up in front of Ming's Music Shop. It was in an historic section of Hubei Province. The aromatic smell from a nearby bush of olive flowers greeted them as they got out of the car. The building was charmingly antique, neat looking and inviting. The front window displayed an impressive array of musical instruments, used and new, antique and modern, Chinese and Western.

They walked through the front door where Qiang and Guo were anxiously awaiting their arrival. The two men stared at each other. Zhang was right. Except for Qiang being slightly shorter and having a heavier swatch of white hair, Heo was looking at a very close image of himself. They shook hands. It was a long handshake, and with that personal contact, there was no denying their own flesh and blood. They were brothers and they knew it! Nervousness dissipated. Heo the doctor *wanted* to know more about his mysterious brother. Qiang the businessman hoped to be able to trust this new person in his life.

Guo walked over to the front door, put the *Closed* sign facing out, and invited their guests to a private back room for lunch. Phones were silenced; the ignored answering machine occasionally clicked on and off with messages. Nothing was more important for the next hour as two brothers and women got to know each other—until a school bus stopped in front. "Oh, my gosh, Lian is here," Guo announced as she rushed to unlock the front door. Heo met the first member of his family's next generation, a bubbly five-year-old with almost fluorescent knee-high socks, purple and red sneakers, and an orange backpack. "She dresses herself," Guo explained, tongue-in-cheek.

While Guo and Lian gave Meili a tour of the music shop, Heo and Qiang spent more time together. The main topic was Zhang, his bout with TB, and his feverish insistence that Heo was Qiang.

"I am assuming he told you how we met," Qiang said, now feeling more comfortable with conversation.

"Not at first, but eventually yes, he did. He described himself as a brash young soldier, brandishing a pistol and exercising his authority, and ending up in your debt for saving his life. He is hoping that by bringing the two of us together, he can repay his debt."

"Did he tell you why he was following me?"

"Yes, but he is convinced there is more to your story than he knows."

"He could be right," Qiang smiled, "and maybe someday when we are old and gray I might tell him. Until then, it is permissible for him to wonder. The government is not the only one with secrets! By the way, Heo, is your hospital government-run? Are you involved with the government in your job?"

"Yes and no. It is not a military hospital, but we do get government funding. We are obliged to abide by government edicts as they affect the medical sector, but other than that, we are a separate entity. The government can annoy doctors just as they do everyone else. We are not exempt. My home life, on the other hand, is definitely run by government. My adoptive father is career military. He's a good dad and I respect him and his choice of a career, but I'm glad he didn't try to talk me into following in his footsteps. Military is definitely not for me."

There. The sticking points about Qiang's past and Heo's possible government loyalties were out in the open. Now they could get on with the business of family.

"So, now that you know all about your biological mother and

father and sister and where you were born, would you like to meet your mother?"

"Definitely. It is sad that I will never know my real father, but I certainly do want to meet my mother. Does she know I am here?"

"Not yet. She agreed to be home today but doesn't know why Guo asked her to be. She has been through a lot, Heo. We didn't want to get her hopes up until we were certain you were actually our Syaran. Let's call her and give her the good news."

With the four of them gathered around, Qiang talked with his mother on the phone. His grin told them they were going to be seeing a very surprised and excited parent. "Yes, Mother, it really is Syaran. Wait until you see him, he's almost as handsome as me."

That brought chuckles from everyone. "I think we just put our mother into a state of shock," he laughed as he hung up. "We're only a few minutes away from her apartment, so we should probably give her a little time to compose herself."

"This is so unreal," he said as he looked at Heo and shook his head. "We never thought there would be any hope of finding you—ever. It seemed impossible, which is the way it is supposed to be with adoptions. And now here you are. Are you ready to say hello to the person who has never stopped praying for you?"

Su-Li met them at the door, bubbling with enthusiasm. She cared nothing about protocol, appearance, or social grace, and an introduction was not necessary. She looked intently into Heo's face for all of five seconds, then acknowledged her son with a tight hug and tears, which made everyone else cry, too. Any doubts Heo had about her love for him dissipated. He was totally enveloped with acceptance and affection from this rather short lady with a distinctive swatch of white brushed back into the right side of her otherwise salt-and-pepper hair.

It was the best day of Su-Li Ming's life, a day she never anticipated having but always prayed for. Both of her sons were together, alive and well, and in her home. Even though her daughter lived thousands of miles away, it was comforting to know she was also alive and well with her adoptive parents. For the first time in her life, Su-Li Ming knew all three of her children. For a moment, she thought about Cheng, her husband, deceased eight years ago. Having him here would have been the ultimate family reunion, but knowing he was in Heaven and smiling down on them added to her sheer joy.

The hours went by so quickly. The conversation was mostly about Heo, where he grew up, all about his adoptive parents, how he found out about his adoption, and even about his pseudo-twin brother, Jin. It was a truth he suddenly felt he could share with the special people around him, including Meili. They all understood the extreme circumstances the one-child-per-family edict created. Heo told them about Mama Shen and Papa Shen and their encouragement to become a doctor. It was also time to introduce Meili as more than just a friend from work.

"Meili is the person I have to thank for getting us together, by the way. I didn't introduce her sufficiently and I should have. We didn't know each other until just a short time ago when we were part of a project at the laogai and worked side-by-side. She is a tireless worker in addition to being an excellent pediatric nurse. She is the person who was instrumental in finding you, Qiang." He looked over at Meili. "Show Qiang the picture you have of him on your phone, Meili." Qiang looked puzzled at first when she handed it to him, then burst out laughing. He remembered the woman who wanted to see the inside of a piano so she could take a picture. And there was his head in the picture, white streak and all.

"Does this mean she doesn't really want to buy my piano?"

"Probably not. Sorry about that," Meili answered amid laughter as the phone circulated around the room.

It was eventually time for goodbyes, hugs, the exchange of contact information, and promises to meet again. Su-Li's hug for her son lingered. "Please come back soon," she said quietly. "I have waited a long time for you."

"I will, Mother." That sounded so strange but yet so natural.

As Heo watched his family showering Meili with all the attention of a new but dear friend, he had one thought. *She is the person I want to spend the rest of my life with. Life! How quickly it can change,* he reflected. *It was only a short time ago I felt totally alone in the world— an outsider with no real family to call my own. Now I have two families, plus a future one standing at my side. And each one is special.*

He recalled Cha-Li's words about choosing to think positive. *She's right. Life is wonderful if you let it be!*

Chapter 8

TRUTHS

THEY GOT TO Meili's parents' house just as it was getting dark. It was Molly's bedtime. There were sleepy, good night hugs all around, including one for Heo, before climbing into her mother's car to go home. Receiving hugs from a child was something new for Heo, and he cherished every one of them. It was a special relationship he felt privileged to be a part of.

When Heo got home, Zhang was gone. It was determined by his military doctor that he was sufficiently recuperated from his bout with TB. He was given a week's leave before his next assignment and chose to go home for a visit with his family.

The house felt quiet, almost empty, without Zhang. Heo was looking forward to telling him about the visit with Qiang and thanking him. He wondered how Cha-Li felt about Zhang leaving; they spent a lot of time together. He didn't have to wonder very long. His mother handed him a note. *Heo, please call me when you have time. Cha-Li.*

He definitely wanted to talk to Cha-Li, but first he wanted to talk to his parents. He wanted them to know about the events of the day.

"Father, Mother, can I tell you about my trip to Beijing?"

"Yes, yes! Please tell us, Heo," his father replied anxiously. "Did it go well?

"Yes, Father. There is no question that the person I went there to meet, Qiang Ming, is my biological brother. The birthdays were the same, his missing brother's and mine, but the physical resemblance confirmed it. We definitely look alike. With that established, Qiang told me all about my birth family and why they gave me up. It was as we anticipated. I was the illegal second child, forcibly taken from my parents at birth. I found out that my father, Cheng Ming, was in the import-export business and died eight years ago from a dock accident in Tianjin, but I did get to meet my birth mother. Her name is Su-Li Ming, and she is a music teacher in Beijing.

"I also have a biological sister who is the youngest child, four years younger than me, who lives in Canada. My brother and mother had a chance to meet Xiu-Su—Emily—a couple of years ago when she was in Beijing with her adoptive parents and a group of international musicians. She is an accomplished pianist. The only reason they found her was just like my situation—her distinctive swatch of white hair. It is so crazy, so unbelievable, that something like a genetic hair feature can reunite family members.

"Anyway, Qiang is the oldest child, four years older than me, and owns a music store and instrument repair shop, specializing in pianos. He is married and he and his wife, Guo, have a five-year-old daughter.

"That whole family, my birth family, used to live in a village not far from where Zhang's family lives. It's apparently not very big, but it is where Qiang first started his music business and near where his mother started teaching. Then when Qiang got married, he and his wife decided it made good business sense to move to Beijing. It was around the same time that his mother was offered an opportunity to teach music at a higher level in Beijing, so she also moved. That is what I found out. At least now I know where I was born and to whom and why I was in an orphanage."

"Well, son," his father said, "where do you anticipate going from here, now that you have all this information? Are you going to move to Beijing also?"

"No, Father. As much as I wondered about my biological family, my roots are here. Even though I may have occasion to visit them from time to time, I could never leave you and Mother. This is my home. You are my parents. You always have been and you always will be. Jin will always be my brother. This is where I intend to stay, if you will allow me."

He stood as his mother rose from her chair, walked over and hugged him. "I am glad you have all your questions answered, Heo, and I am very thankful you are not leaving us. You are my son and always will be, no matter where you are. I love you so much."

Yan stepped aside so Heo could get a hug from his father as well. It was a special time for the Wong family, a renewed appreciation for the love and respect they felt for each other.

"But there is one more thing I want to talk to you about," Heo continued. "Well, maybe a couple of things. As we discussed a while ago, I was having thoughts about changing my medical focus to specialize in pediatrics, even before I met Meili. Last week I submitted my application to med school for additional courses and it has been approved. It will mean a couple more years of school, but it is something I can do while working in the practice. How do you feel about my change from general medicine? Are you in agreement?"

"The change is your decision," his father assured him. "It is your future. If taking care of children is your choice, then your mother and I are behind you totally. We will help you all we can. Now you said there were a couple of things you wanted to talk to us about. What else?"

"Well, I am going to ask Meili to marry me."

"Oh! Oh!" his mother exclaimed as she jumped up and hugged him again. "That is wonderful news! She is a lovely person, and little Molly is so sweet. I love them both!"

"Yeah, me too," Heo said with a big grin. "Of course, I haven't asked her yet, but I guess the first step is to pick out a ring and hope she accepts it, right?"

It was one of those special times when Heo heard a hearty laugh from his father. "Congratulations, my son. I also hope she accepts it! I've become fond of her and that little girl!"

Heo was ready to call it a day. He was emotionally exhausted, and his body was tired. It felt good to get everything off his chest – the truth about his biological family, agreement for his new medical direction, and the truth about his feelings for Meili and Molly. He had no energy left to talk to Cha-Li. He would call her tomorrow, then he would call Zhang.

~⁄⁄~

The conversation with Cha-Li was not very different from the cousin-to-cousin session they had weeks before, except this time Cha-Li was burdened.

"I just don't know what to do, Heo! I didn't think I was going to like Zhang even before I met him just because of who he was—a soldier. I am a teacher and anti-government, always having to be careful about what I teach. But there I was judging someone I hadn't even met. Then I got to know him and, the more we were together, the more I liked him—*really* liked him. In less than two months, we were even discussing marriage, and it scared me. I don't want to marry a soldier, Heo! I always viewed them as cookie-cutter human beings with processed minds, standing in a row, all doing as they are told with no thoughts of their own, just blindly obeying a government that oppresses its people. I know I shouldn't put any group of people into a general category, but I can't help it. It's the truth about the way I feel! As a soldier, I can't marry him, but as a person I want to. I really do. He asked me just before he left, and as much as I wanted to say yes, I told him no. Now I wish I had said yes. But I can't have it both ways. I am so confused I don't trust myself. What should I do?"

Once again, Heo sat with his arm around his cousin's shoulder as she wept. *Why is it whenever Cha-Li asks me an emotional question, it's never one I can answer?* He decided to say a prayer *first* this time instead of last. *A prayer worked for me before. Maybe God is still listening and will help me again.* He prayed silently. *Dear God, please give me the right words. Please help Cha-Li and Zhang.*

His thoughts turned to himself and how he would feel if Meili turned him down. It would be crushing. He felt more empathy for Zhang than he did Cha-Li. Then it occurred to him that Cha-Li was doing the same thing she did before when she was upset with her parents—viewing things only from her own negative perspective.

While Cha-Li cried with her head down, Heo spoke. "Cha-Li," he began cautiously, "you've told me how you feel about Zhang, but how does Zhang feel about you? Obviously, he cares enough about you to ask you to marry him, but how does he feel about your future as a couple, as parents? How does he view himself as a soldier? Is he truly intending to make the Army his life-long career, or is it only until he decides on something different? Remember, my father, your biological father, is also a soldier. The image you described of a typical soldier doesn't fit Father. Maybe it did initially, but not anymore. Time and ability have earned him rank plus respect from his peers and from others. He and Zhang both chose military careers, although the length of time served may be different. But think about it, if our country ever goes to war, who is going to protect you? Who is going to protect your family?"

She sat up. There was silence as she contemplated Heo's response. "Now that you mention it, we never really talked about the military as a life-long career, per se. Zhang has been in the Army for seven years, so I am assuming he intends for it to be a career. But I don't know that for sure. He visited my class one time and allowed the children to ask him questions about being a soldier. His answers were not like *rah, rah,* being a soldier is great. They were informative, and some were personal. He did tell them the one thing he didn't care for as a soldier was being away from home so much.

"As far as family, there wasn't much to talk about. He is an only child, of course. We all are. Well, except for you. But he wants at least the one child we would be allowed to have. I'm sure he would prefer a son, although he didn't really say so. I'm assuming that. He talked about families having more children someday when the edict is lifted, but I don't know if he was referring to us or to couples in general.

"As for our future together as a couple, he said he loves me. . . or at least he did. Maybe he doesn't anymore." She looked back down at the floor.

Heo sat in silence and then said, "It sounds to me, cuz, that the two of you might benefit from talking some more. My guess is that he is hurting as much as you are, maybe also angry at being rejected. I am going to call him tonight to thank him for helping me find my brother. If he mentions you, and I have a feeling he might, should I suggest he call you? That you want to talk to him? In a round-about way, of course."

"Oh, Heo! Yes! Please! Oh, crud! There I go again! I've been so wrapped up in myself and my own problems that I totally forgot about your trip to Beijing. You really did find your brother then?"

"Yes. Zhang was right. I met my brother, sister-in-law, and a niece, plus my mother. They are all very nice, hospitable people. My father is deceased but, as our religion teaches us, we will all be together someday in Heaven, and we will all know each other. I will meet him then. It was a good day and I'll tell you all about it a little later, but right now, let's get you back to thinking positive. Do you want me to say anything about you to Zhang?"

"Just that I am miserable without him, but not those exact words. I don't want it to sound like an apology, even though it is. Just somehow let him know that I wish we could talk some more. You know what to say, right?"

"I'll think of something," Heo offered, silently thanking God for the right words once again. "I'll talk to you after I get hold of Zhang."

-\\\'/-

It was late afternoon when Zhang arrived in his village. It hadn't changed much during his two-year absence, but it still felt good to be home. His parents didn't have a telephone so he couldn't give them advanced notice, but it didn't make any difference. His parents were always happy to see him. His mother fussed with enthusiasm, quickly going about making her son's favorite dinner while he spent time with his father.

"What do you think about this, son?" his father asked proudly as he unrolled a drawing of a new archery range he designed for the school. "You were always good at archery. I wish we had this years ago for you to enjoy. It should be completed in a couple of weeks, though. You can try it out the next time you come home."

Zhang always admired his father's devotion to sports, whether rooting at local games or in his capacity as the school's only coach. As the son of the school's coach, Zhang spent a lot of his growing up years in locker rooms after school, cleaning, repainting, refurbishing benches, and whatever other assignments his father provided. He was familiar with all the sports and gym equipment and worked out continually. He grew up very physically fit.

Although being an athlete didn't necessarily appeal to him, the rigorous military regimen did. His physique and strength enabled him to handle even the largest pieces of combat equipment with ease. Within a year, he was an instructor; after two years, an officer, a low-level one, but an officer nonetheless. Now, after seven years and gradually moving up in rank, he was on the doorstep of yet another promotion. While he didn't care much for the changing regimes and mandates of the Chinese government, they usually didn't affect him personally. He was not a member of the high-ranking military echelon, nor did he want to be. He was comfortable where he was. He knew how to accept assignments and carry them out to the satisfaction of his superiors.

Being home was supposed to be a time of relaxation before his next assignment, and he certainly needed it, as he was reeling emotionally. Cha-Li stole his heart as no woman had before, and then crushed it with her rejection of marriage. She said it wasn't because of him personally, she just couldn't marry a soldier. He was angry at first, but if that was how she really felt about soldiers, then going their separate ways was probably for the best. It would not be a good marriage, he convinced himself. It was time to forget her and move on. He looked forward to getting back to work.

Zhang's commanding officer hinted at overseeing another laogai military detachment, perhaps one closer to Beijing. He liked the big city atmosphere, plus it would be a chance to reconnect with his friend Qiang. He wondered how the meeting went between Qiang and Heo. Were they really brothers? But the more he thought about Qiang, the more his old questions kept coming back. There were things about Qiang that didn't make sense. Why had Qiang saved Zhang's life when he knew that Zhang was investigating him? And how could this same person not care about the life of an infant he was supposedly going to throw over a cliff? It didn't add up.

Supposedly! That was the key word, Zhang suddenly realized. Qiang took the baby out of his sight and *supposedly* threw her over the edge. He saw nothing and heard nothing other than the faint sound of something falling to the ravine floor far below. . . not even crying. That was it! The baby had been crying. She was shivering, cold and crying and then suddenly stopped, well before she was thrown over the cliff! Why?

There was only one way to find out, so Zhang decided to make another trip to the top of the hill. Tomorrow. Alone.

~\!/~

"I'm going for a long walk," Zhang announced to his parents the next morning. "It's a beautiful day and I need some exercise. I've been sitting around too long."

It was the weekend and Zhang knew there would not be many villagers out working, so his trip to the infamous hill of death would likely go unnoticed.

Dressed in civilian clothes and with good rubber-soled sneakers, he drove to the bottom of the hill and looked up at the path looming above him. It was wide at the bottom, but he could see halfway up where it narrowed. He just hoped it hadn't eroded since he was last there. He took a walking stick and remembered Qiang saying it was a twenty-minute walk to the top.

It was an uneventful climb to the area he remembered. There was the jagged rock that he tried to grab onto to avert his fall, but it didn't help. All it did was tear his arm open on the way by. And there was the flat area where he and Qiang landed after he was pulled back from the edge. He kept going, paying close attention to his footing.

The top was nothing more than the crest of a hill. He looked over the edge with his binoculars into the ravine below. There was a lot of brush growing out of the side of the hill, but he could see through it somewhat. It looked like remnants of cloth amid piles of rocks below. He remembered Qiang taking the blanket off the baby he was carrying, laying the naked baby on the ground and using the blanket as a tourniquet for his arm. So yes, there would be remnants of baby blankets down there.

It was disappointing. He didn't know what he expected to find – perhaps some kind of clue to shed light on the mysterious Qiang Ming, but it was just as Qiang said it was. He didn't know any more now than he did before.

What he did discover, however, was a spectacular view from this lofty perch above the village. After not exercising his leg muscles for months, the uphill hike had been strenuous, and the day was warm. He chose a rocky ledge to sit on for a few minutes before descending. A gentle breeze felt good as he enjoyed the vista before him.

Then it hit him! The breeze he was feeling was against his back. How could a breeze be coming out of a rock? He turned and looked at the side of the hill. There was nothing there but a big flat rock and more overgrown brush. Or was there? He picked up his walking stick and carefully pushed the brush aside, following the direction of the cool breeze, discovering an entrance to a cave.

There were a lot of caves in the hilly terrain; finding one was not uncommon. But Zhang felt this one was worth investigating. He stepped in cautiously, walking stick at the ready in case he should meet a cave denizen. There was daylight coming through a few crevices in the rock ceiling and walls that enabled him to see slightly. He stood still, allowing his eyes to adjust. Three lanterns took shape on his right, sitting on a crate. He felt the wicks; they were dried up, crumbling at the touch of his fingers.

He was starting to see relatively well now, descending farther into the sloped entrance. He noticed what appeared to be some kind of artwork on the cave wall to his right. He walked closer to examine it and was stunned when he saw what it really was—an array of tiny footprints – probably two hundred or more he estimated as he walked from one end to the other. Each one had a date underneath and some had names. Then he realized they were in chronological order. *Could it possibly be—?*

He looked for the date he had been up on the hill with Qiang. There it was, the exact date. It was also the most recent one on the wall. *So, the baby girl did not die after all!* He was right; there was more to Qiang Ming than child executioner. He was, in fact, a child rescuer.

At this point, Zhang could have turned around and gone back out with suspicions confirmed, but curiosity pulled him further. He continued to the end of the footprint wall where it turned a corner, and he found himself standing in a slightly smaller room. What he saw made him swallow hard.

There were two baby beds, a rocking chair, and an old chest. He lifted the top of the chest. It contained blankets, diapers and baby clothes. A nearby wooden cupboard held baby bottles and a glass jug of powdered milk. He could almost visualize a person sitting in the chair, feeding a baby, and rocking it to sleep.

Against the opposite wall were two single beds, one made up – the other unmade. In the middle of the room was a small table with what looked like powdered paint. Of course! That had to be what was used for making imprints of babies' feet on the cave wall.

As he left the nursery room and turned the corner to go back toward the exit, he noticed another small table with a metal box on it. He lifted the lid and stared down at a pistol. He picked it up; there were bullets in the chamber and more in the bottom of the box. It was a stark message that these people meant business. The other part of the message was that one of the bullets in the chamber could have been for him the night he followed Qiang. Perhaps that was why Qiang didn't object to being followed.

Zhang put the pistol and ammunition in his pocket, left the cave, and headed down the hill, carefully negotiating the narrow parts of the path.

He spent a lot of time that night recalling the encounter he had with Qiang. Vague memories were becoming vivid of what he did, and what was said. He remembered how he and two other soldiers watched Qiang from a distance as he walked from the village with the baby "to be disposed of," letting him get halfway to the hill before driving out and confronting him. He remembered trying to intimidate him, but it didn't work. Qiang was unflinching, stoic, as he stood in the headlights of their truck, with a flashlight shoved in his face. He answered their questions without emotion.

Zhang remembered his own flippant words when the child started crying. "Your bundle of joy is getting anxious to meet her doom. Get in. We will drive you. Then I will accompany you to wherever you are going. I want to see how you handle the disposal."

Oh, how arrogant I must have sounded! he admitted.

"I am going to the path at the bottom of that hill," was Qiang's response. "It is a twenty-minute steep walk from there up to a cliff where she will be dropped into a ravine. That is what everyone knows, and it is very visible on a clear night to those in the village. If you wish to accompany me, I cannot stop you of course. But it is not a good path at night for someone who is not familiar with it."

Being physically fit, Zhang said, "I think I can handle a twenty-minute uphill walk and I can see very well. My instructions are to accompany you."

As Zhang sat alone in his room with the confiscated pistol in his hand, he again contemplated what could have been. A vision of the cave came back to mind. There were crevices in the cave wall where sunlight was coming through. They were probably large enough to see Qiang's approach on a moonlit night. Perhaps there was even a pre-arranged signal. *If the person waiting at the top knew someone was with Qiang, he or she most likely was ready with this pistol. If so, the only reason I might still be alive is because I slipped and got hurt and agreed to stay where I was while Qiang continued to the top!*

Then he remembered something even more incredible. *My gun! My own gun flew out of my hand as I was sliding and trying to grab at that rock. It was lying on the ground. I saw it when we were getting ready to start back down. Qiang picked it up and handed it to me. Why did he do that? Why would anyone return a dropped weapon to his enemy?* He answered his own question. *Because I was no longer a threat. My right arm, the one that carried my gun, was cut deep, wrapped up in a baby blanket. What was I going to do, try to shoot with my left hand?*

Zhang was not a religious person but, thanks to Cha-Li, he did know a little about some of the Christian tenets, one that was now almost staring him in the face. *People live and die according to God's timing, not their own.* While he respected her right to believe in her own religion and politely listened to most of what she said, he didn't buy into it more than any other religion. Now he wished he would have paid more attention. *Maybe she was right. Maybe there really is something to this God of hers being in control of people's lives, things like when they are born and when they die.*

He replayed the events of that night over and over in his mind with different scenarios, trying to imagine the possible outcome of each. He couldn't come up with any, other than the one he experienced, without someone having to die.

I went up the hill to seek the truth about Qiang and I found it. Or did I? What truth did I really find? It was simply not my time to die? It was not meant for the child to die? Or Qiang?

He had more questions now than he did before.

Chapter 9

AN UNLIKELY CONVERT

IN FULL MILITARY uniform, Zhang walked into Ming's Music Shop. "Qiang. It's been a while."

"Hey, Zhang!" said a surprised Qiang Ming as he stood up to shake hands. "It's good to see you! I've been meaning to get your phone number and give you a call, but I see you found me anyway. Thanks for all you did to get my brother and me together."

"You are welcome, my friend. I'm just glad it worked out. I don't remember much when I was ill and sort of delirious, so it must have been fate or something that made me keep calling your name. All I really remember is seeing that swatch of white hair walking up and down the next row and not understanding why you didn't answer me. Have you got a couple of minutes? There's something I have to show you." He glanced over at Guo who was rearranging shelves. "Do you have a place where we can talk? It's confidential."

"Sure. But first, I want you to meet my wife. Guo, this is Zhang, the soldier friend I told you about. Would you mind the store for a while so Zhang and I can go out back?"

Guo responded with a traditional Chinese lady half bow. She was hospitable, of course, but Qiang sensed she was uneasy. She delivered a pot of tea and rice cakes to the back room before tending to the front of the store.

It was a congenial meeting with so much to talk about. Zhang told of his experience with TB, being tended to by Heo, and the surprise invitation to stay with Heo's family while he recuperated. Then it was Qiang's turn to talk about the excitement of meeting Heo, his look-alike brother, and his friend Meili. It was reminiscent of two old school chums at a class reunion.

"So, what is it you want to show me?" Qiang asked.

"I think I have something that might belong to you." Zhang stood and reached into his pocket, pulled out a handful of bullets and placed them on the table. Then he reached around to the back of his belt, retrieved the pistol, and placed it next to the bullets. "If this is yours, you need to do something with it. It's one of two things that can tie you to the cave at the top of the hill."

It only took a couple of seconds for Qiang to recognize the gun. He looked back at Zhang's now serious face and took a deep breath. He felt a hot rush of adrenalin mixed with the cold reality that this person once again held his life in his hands. He used to be an enemy; later a friend, or so he said. *Is he still a friend? Or has his military allegiance pushed him back to being an enemy?* This man he knew only as Zhang stood between him and the laogai—freedom or imprisonment. There was no sense denying his knowledge of the gun or the cave.

"How did you find it, Zhang?" he finally managed to ask.

"Purely by accident," Zhang answered, still with the stance of a soldier. But then he sat and grinned like the friend he said he was. "It has been on my mind since our night on the hill that something didn't seem right. I wondered how you could save my life, a soldier with an obnoxious attitude, and then toss a helpless baby over a cliff without remorse. It didn't add up. I doubted that you would tell me even if I asked, so, I decided the only way I was going to unravel the

Qiang Ming mystery was to go back up the hill alone, in the daylight, and see what I could find. I saw a scattering of colored cloth, maybe baby blankets, at the bottom of the ravine with my binoculars, but no bones. So that was part of the answer. You threw fake bundles over the cliff for the sake of anyone from the village who might be watching, right?"

Qiang decided it was best not to answer.

"That led me to the next question," Zhang continued. "How did you do it? How did you swap the baby for a bundle of whatever you threw down there, and where did the baby go? It meant there had to have been another person up there who made the swap and took the child back down the hill later. So, I had an answer to part of that question—where the baby really went, and it wasn't into the ravine. But the next part was still missing, the details on getting the baby back down. We had been watching you and that hill for quite a while and we never saw anyone coming back down the hill with an infant. It was only when I sat on a rock up there to rest for a few minutes admiring the view that I accidentally discovered the rest of the answer. As I sat there, I felt a breeze, but it was coming from in back of me, from the rock wall. I poked around and found the cave."

Qiang maintained a stoic demeanor, listening.

"I must admit, Qiang," Zhang continued, "whoever set that cave up did a good job. I'm thinking it must have been that guy before you, the previous so-called 'child executioner,' right?"

"Kind of."

"It's alright, Qiang. You can trust me. I know now that you had more than one chance to get rid of me, once by just letting me go flying over the edge of the cliff, which was where I was headed anyway, and again when whoever else was up there probably handed you this gun, or at least could have. I owe you my life at least twice. I still can't believe you handed my own gun back to me when you saw it on the path. You could have simply kicked it over the edge, and I never would have known.

"So those are my observations after seeing your rescue cave. And I am calling it a *rescue* cave because all those little footprints on the wall tell a story, about two hundred babies are alive today because of you and whoever else was part of that effort."

"Two hundred twelve, to be exact," Qiang said. "All but one were girls. The boy had a deformed arm and was not considered adoptable."

"And the last child you rescued was the one you carried up the night I was with you. I saw the date on the wall. I also figured out why your project is now abandoned, because of the new x-ray machines that show the gender of a child before it is born, right? Your efforts were no longer needed? Unwanted children are now systematically aborted."

"Right. Those machines put me out of a job, for which I am very thankful. Being labeled a child executioner is not exactly something to wear proudly like a badge. Oh, sorry. I didn't mean anything personal by that," Qiang apologized after noticing the emblem on Zhang's shirt.

"That's alright. I still do have to go to work," he chuckled, "and I have to leave pretty soon. But I've got two more questions that I'd really appreciate your answering."

"What are they?"

"How *did* you get the babies out of the cave without being seen?"

"There's more than one entrance. If you would have continued into the cave, you would have come out on the opposite side of the hill. That entrance is also very well hidden. What is your other question?"

"If I hadn't slipped on the path and followed you to the top of the hill, would you have shot me? Or what would you have done?"

It was Qiang's turn to enjoy the upper hand for a few moments. "I really don't know," he answered honestly. "No one ever followed me up the hill before. I had all kinds of thoughts while we were driving to the base of the hill, and I could not imagine any way out of my predicament. It was pretty obvious that someone had to die. I just couldn't figure out who it was going to be. And this may sound crazy to you, but I prayed all the way up for God to show me the way. I put myself totally in His hands. Yes, I am a Christian and that is what we do, we put our trust in the one who holds our destiny, and that is God. So, to answer your question as to whether or not I would have shot you, I can only say that your presence *was* known. I *was* offered the choice of the pistol or a bundle of rocks at the mouth of the cave. That was the procedure for such a situation. But God answered my prayer by taking the matter out of my hands. By having you injured, I didn't have to make that decision. I exchanged the baby for rocks. The caregiver had a bottle of milk and another blanket ready to keep her from crying as she took her into the cave.

"Now you said there were two things that could tie me to the cave. What is the other one?"

"The footprints. They speak for themselves, especially with names and dates. They need to be deleted before someone else discovers the cave and ties your name to it as the so-called child executioner. It might be a good idea to get all that furniture and baby stuff out of there, too."

Qiang was pensive. "I was not aware that the cave was still intact. It was supposed to have been taken down and the footprints deleted by now. I will make sure it happens soon."

Zhang held out his hand as he stood to leave. It was the firm handshake of friends. "By the way," he added with a grin, "thank you for not killing me."

"You're welcome. Thank you for finding my brother. And I *will* dispose of this pistol. Thanks for returning it."

~\/~

With the mystery solved, there was one more person Zhang wanted to talk to eventually—

Cha-Li. She turned down his proposal of marriage and he was crushed, but now he knew why. She was speaking the truth about how she felt. She said she couldn't marry a soldier, a government employee, a non-Christian. She said it didn't make any difference how much they loved each other; it would not be a good marriage and eventually they would both be miserable. Although it made him angry at the time, now he understood. He wanted to tell her she was right. It would not have been a good marriage.

There was something else without answers that had been stirring within him for years and was now reignited after talking with Qiang. It started with the protest in Tiananmen Square back in 1989. He watched it on television and couldn't understand the actions of the students. Why were they standing in front of tanks, willing to get tear-gassed or even killed for their cause? Their signs said *freedom of speech, freedom of religion*, and other freedoms. Those were honorable things, yes, but were they worth dying for? Apparently, they thought so. It was many years ago, but he never stopped thinking about them.

He thought a lot about his own destiny after that. *I only have one life. What cause could there possibly be in my life that I would be willing to die for? My country? My family? The government? And if I died, who would care or ever remember what my cause was?*

Uncovering Qiang Ming's *real* cause stoked Zhang's desire once again to find answers to his own questions about life and death. He remembered impulsively starting to talk to Qiang about those things years ago, the only other time they were alone as friends before today. It was after a special ceremony in Qiang's honor. The governor of their province presented Qiang with a Certificate of Heroism for saving Zhang's life, and he was saluted by a contingent of military personnel. It was followed by lunch. When the other soldiers opted for an after-meal cigar in the smoking lounge, Zhang and Qiang chose to stay in the dining room for dessert. It was an opportunity to ask Qiang the question that was really on his mind. "Why did you do it? You could have died. What prompted you to save my life?"

Just as Zhang was preparing to share his quandary about dying for a cause with Qiang, their conversation was cut short by the return of the soldiers. It was the last time he saw Qiang. But now he understood. It obviously had something to do with Qiang's religion. It was almost as if a light switched on in Zhang's head. *Cha-Li!* His head told him to forget her and move on, but in his heart he missed her. Was their future together a dead issue because his mind was closed to religion? Was he missing something about life, its meaning, and happiness because of something he didn't understand? Was this religion of hers the answer to the *cause* he had been contemplating since Tiananmen? He knew being a Christian was important to Cha-Li—very important. And it was important enough to Qiang to be willing to accept death if it was God's timing for him.

He suddenly wanted to know more, but it couldn't come from Cha-Li. He didn't want his relationship with her to hinge on the acceptance of a religion. In all fairness to himself, he wanted to embrace it or reject it personally. He wanted more information from a neutral source, someone like a mentor or a teacher.

Qiang was the only other person he knew who was Christian. Was finding and returning the gun to Qiang meant to introduce him to another Christian? Maybe. He wasn't sure, but it *did* give him someone to talk to—a tested friend, the perfect confidante. His overall view of Christianity was widening.

Is this Christian God already working in my life? Is this God showing me the path to my future, or is it all just coincidence? Is my future destined to include Cha-Li? He felt a glimmer of hope. *If I decide that Christianity is the right religion for me, will it be enough to change her opinion of me? But what about being a soldier? That was another wall between us.* Then he thought about what Qiang said when he couldn't see a solution to his impossible situation. He turned it over to God. *Well then, if it is meant to be, it will happen. God will make it happen. That's apparently what He does. He finds ways when we cannot see a way.* His mind was spinning until his phone rang. It was his friend Heo—Qiang's brother.

"Hello, Zhang. I'm sorry I missed saying goodbye to you since you were called back to duty while I was in Beijing. I've been meaning to call you all week, but there's just been a lot going on around here. Are you at your new assignment?"

"Yes, just started. I was scheduled for a week's leave before I got TB, so my commanding officer gave me a week off before my next assignment. I decided to go home and get reacquainted with my parents. It's been a couple of years since I've seen them. Meili was kind enough to give me Qiang's address in Beijing before you left, though. I found him this morning and we had a good visit. He's really a great guy, and I'm glad we've reconnected."

"Well, that is why I am calling, to thank you for recognizing our similarities. You were right. We sure do look enough alike to be brothers! It didn't take long for us to figure it out and agree once we had a chance to meet. I even met my biological mother. She is a sweet lady, and I'm looking forward to seeing her again. I think I am going to handle having two families very well. Now tell me how you are feeling. No more problems, I take it. How is your energy level?"

"Oh, I'm alright, doc," Zhang chuckled. "It was kind of nice having my own personal doctor in the same house though. Your mother and father are wonderful people, and I don't blame you for keeping your allegiance to them. Your mother is a good cook, and I've got a few extra pounds to prove it. I also enjoyed spending time with your father. He is quite a historian. I learned things about the military that I didn't know before, plus he's obviously a good family man. I hope you don't mind if I stop by once in a while for a visit."

"Well, that's another reason I called. I do want you to stop by and visit once in a while, we all do. You are like a new member of the family. Plus, there's going to be a wedding in the future and we want you to be here. I'm about to be a husband and a father whenever Meili and I can get all the details worked out. It's what we've been doing all week. Deciding to get married was the easy part. Making arrangements is something else. I'll let you know when we confirm the date.

"And by the way, Zhang, you might want to consider giving Cha-

Li a call sometime. She is not very happy right now. I think the two of you need to talk some more, and perhaps you can figure things out. Just my personal observation."

"Oh. Alright. Thanks for the insight, doc. Maybe we should. But right now, congratulations to you and Meili. I am very happy for both of you and Molly. I will try my best to be at your wedding."

Yes! Zhang's heart was flitting around somewhere up in the sky. *This new God is taking charge of my life and I like what He is doing! It might not be for a while, but I believe He has just opened a door for me!*

Zhang could hardly wait to get back to Ming's Music Store and talk to Qiang until reality brought him back to earth. He still had some serious thinking to do about his military career. How could he be a Christian and remain a soldier? They did not jibe, at least not in Cha-Li's world. He thought about the time he visited her class consisting of mostly little boys. The gender imbalance was obvious. How could he be a Christian and not care about the government's practice of forced abortions? He never thought much about it before he met Cha-Li; it never affected him. Now it did. She made it very clear how much she despised it. Zhang realized that being career military would be an obstacle to two things that were quickly becoming more meaningful in his life—religion and Cha-Li.

He thought about his new friend Heo, Cha-Li's cousin. As a dedicated doctor, how did Heo handle his cousin's aversion to medically induced abortions? As a doctor, Heo was under the jurisdiction of the government when it came to enforcing medical mandates. Was that part of his duties as a doctor? If so, how did he address Cha-Li's concerns? *Surely, she has expressed her opinions to him on that subject,* he thought. For the first time in his military career, Zhang felt a distaste for the edict. Enforcing it was just part of his job before, a small part, but required nonetheless. Now he understood why it was so often referred to as "the hated edict."

Perhaps it really *was* time to start thinking about other career possibilities. Would he be allowed to just quit being a soldier? He didn't know. *Probably not.*

⁓ᵥᵢ⁓

Qiang and Guo were surprised when Zhang returned to the store later that afternoon and asked to know more about being a Christian. Would they be willing to teach him or introduce him to someone who could help him? Of course they would.

Over the next few months, they spent countless hours with him. Guo read from her copy of The New Testament, while Qiang repaired musical instruments and took care of customers. She explained each chapter, who wrote it, and its significance. Then she tended to the store while the two men talked about theology and how teachings from the Bible, written thousands of years ago, still impacted the lives of modern people. Zhang learned about the tenets of Christianity, especially the beliefs in Heaven and everlasting life. He learned about persecution, overcoming it, and the dedication of Christians. They talked about underground churches not only in China, but in many other countries as well where freedom of religion was still suppressed.

Freedom of religion! Once again, Zhang remembered the signs. Freedom of religion was one of the issues at Tiananmen Square. Those kids were protesting government oppression of basic human rights; freedom of religion was just one of them. It didn't mean they were anti-government or anti-law abiding as the government had accused. All they wanted was the right to make their own decisions without fear of persecution. It answered the question that had been on Zhang's mind for years; *freedom* was the cause that those kids were willing to die for. He also realized that being a soldier in his country meant enforcing anti-freedom.

The existence of underground churches was nothing new to Zhang. When one was discovered in his home province, he was often involved with shutting it down. It was usually in back of a store or business, in an abandoned building, or in a private home. Sometimes it was discovered by government patrols, other times turned in by loyal neighbors. Regardless of how it was discovered, the consequences were the same—demolition of the building and contents, arrest and punishment of the leaders. As a soldier, Zhang felt no remorse for its leaders who got what they deserved.

Now it was different. He knew the truth. It affected the lives of devoted people who were willing to be imprisoned or die for their beliefs. As a Christian, would he be willing to take that risk himself? *Maybe. Probably.* What he *really* wanted right now, however, was to personally attend a Christian service. He wanted to find out why worshipping together was so important, what it was all about, what it felt like.

But once again, he had to face reality. He knew it was something he could never experience as a soldier. There was no way an underground church was going to welcome him. He could dress in civilian clothes, of course, but then he would have to lie about who he was and what he did. Somehow lying seemed anti-Christian. He thought about asking Qiang and Guo but decided not to. As friends, having to say no might put them in an awkward position. The fear of being shunned a second time kept him from asking.

That *light* he was seeing lately in his pre-Christian life went on again. But this time he knew what to do—pray. He got down on his knees, clasped his hands together, and said his very own first personal prayer:

Dear God, if it is meant for me to become a Christian and attend your church, please show me how. I really want to attend but don't know how. I know you don't want me to lie about who I am or what I am because you are all about truth, but I also don't want to make my friends uncomfortable by asking them, knowing they will have to say no. Is there any way that a soldier can be a Christian? Amen.

He stayed on his knees for a while. Having a candid talk with God gave him a strangely comfortable feeling of peace. Somehow, he felt

God was listening. His prayer was answered a week later.

"Have you given any thought to actually attending a Christian church service?" Qiang asked. "You don't have to answer right away, just think about it. If you do, let me know."

Zhang was stunned, but only for a few seconds. "Yes! I do want to attend a Christian church. Tell me how!"

"I found out there is an exclusive underground church for just members of the Chinese Army," Qiang explained. "As you can imagine, security is paramount. You cannot just show up there, and I do not know where it is. None of the other church leaders know where it is either. I am told that I can make a personal recommendation on your behalf from my church to theirs, but only if you request me to do so. The process is that you will first meet with a leader of my church before meeting with a leader of that church. Then a decision will be made.

"My personal feeling is," Qiang continued, "that you will be investigated and possibly watched for a while before attendance is granted, but that is only my opinion. How does that sound to you?"

"It sounds like the answer to a prayer!" Zhang answered with a big grin. "Maybe now it is my turn to be watched!" he quipped. "My only concern is that if they investigate me, they will know I stayed at Heo's house for a while when I was recuperating from TB. They will know I was staying at the home of an Army officer and doctor, both of whom attend, or at least used to attend, the government church. I don't know if Heo still does, but I do know that his father does. It might raise suspicion."

"It will be what it will be, Zhang. Don't worry. If it is meant for you to attend this church with your peers, it will happen, regardless of what anyone else says or does. I am comfortable with putting in a recommendation for you to get the process started, whenever you are ready. Then it is in God's hands, not ours."

"I am ready."

Qiang reached over and put his hand on top of Zhang's and

prayed for wisdom and guidance for his friend. A month later, as Zhang stood in a circle with his peers, hands on each other's shoulders, he was officially accepted as a member of an underground Christian church reserved for Chinese soldiers.

Chapter 10

GOING HOME

THERE WAS MORE than the usual motor vehicle noise coming from the direction of the laogai's main entrance. Jin Wong was familiar with the sounds of early morning deliveries at the dock area, but these were off schedule. With what little energy he had, he shuffled over to the small window of his barracks, hung onto the bars for support, and looked out at buses and vans. They were parked at the dock closest to the administration building. He saw men and women putting on masks, piling things on carts, and pushing them up a ramp through an overhead door. He didn't know who they were, what they were bringing in, or why, but he surmised it might have something to do with a lot of inmates being sick. Days earlier, he watched armed guards taking inmates from different barracks to a building near the front gate. Many of them had trouble walking; a couple fell, only to be prodded back up by the guards. Others were carried on stretchers.

Two laogai doctors, covered with protective clothing, came into Jin's barracks two days later. They took everyone's temperature, made each one cough, and asked about pain. They ushered five men out the door, across the courtyard, and into the same building. It was obvious they were sick, as they had been coughing a lot and could hardly stand. He watched from his window as they stumbled away with the guards. What he didn't understand, however, was why they took just those inmates. Why didn't they take some of the others who were even sicker, including himself, and especially his friend Shi. All he knew was that they asked a lot of questions and filled out papers.

Shi was sicker than anyone else in Jin's barracks. He had been getting steadily worse for two years. At first, he was accused by the guards of being lazy when he did not meet his daily quotas. He was mocked, beaten, bloodied, and his food ration was cut. Jin and some of the other inmates tried to help him after the guards left, but they had no bandages or cloths to clean his wounds. All they could do was splash him with water from a common bucket and move him from the floor onto his bedroll. Cut rations devastated Shi, depleting his energy level even further. But rules were rules; if you don't make your quota, you don't eat. Jin and some of the other inmates each gave Shi a spoonful of their own meager rations to make up for what he didn't have. They all knew he tried, but he just couldn't physically do what was expected of him.

One morning, Shi could not stand without falling. After kicking and pulling at him, the guards finally decided it was useless. They acknowledged his condition and let him remain in the barracks. By this time, Shi could hardly breathe. His neck was swollen, his eyes looked spacey. He was covered with raw, bleeding purple spots. Maybe they were from being kicked; they didn't know. Shi remained on the floor while the rest of the inmates went out to work. He never left the barracks after that. People came in occasionally and looked at him, but that was all. One doctor said he was going to recommend Shi be discharged and sent home, but nothing ever happened. His rations were reinstated, and he was left alone after that, apparently to survive the best he could.

Since then, Jin and some of the other inmates began having some of Shi's symptoms— headaches, fatigue, sore throat, rashes on their stomachs and back, sores in their mouths, fever. If they were getting the same thing Shi had, they knew their fate.

When the doctors came in, they hoped it was their chance to get help. Shi just needed to tell them how sick he really was... but he didn't tell them. He was confused, not comprehending what the doctors were asking, maybe afraid of more punishment.

The rest of the prisoners did their best to answer the doctors' questions. Surely the doctors would realize how sick they were and take them away, but it didn't happen. The cold reality was that the doctors were looking for specific symptoms for a particular illness, not illnesses in general. Only five inmates were led away.

One inmate cracked. He screamed in despair, shouting out what the rest of them were only thinking. "I can't work anymore! I just want to lie down and take my punishment. Let them beat me until I die! There is nothing to be gained by working. We're all going to end up like Shi! We are all going to die!" From that day on, they accepted death as their release from the laogai.

Now too weak to work and allowed to stay in the barracks, Jin sat on the floor and thought about the day he was sent to the laogai to wait for his trial date. They had a backlog of about two years, he was told, and they could legally hold him for up to four years before coming to trial. Until then, he was expected to earn his keep by working for the government, doing whatever they told him to do.

He was angry the day he arrived at the laogai. He was angry with the judicial system and angry with himself. He had been a star student of journalism. He even had his own column in the university newspaper and was on the verge of becoming one of its editors. He knew the type of content he was supposed to be contributing, but he considered it rubbish. Defiance got the best of him. Month after month, he included more of his own opinions. He should have known better. Students weren't the only ones who read the newspaper. Professors, school staff, and government personnel read it also.

For quite a while after he started injecting radical notions into his stories, he sensed he was being watched. He was right. His anti-government rhetoric on freedom of speech got him arrested.

His biggest snafu, however, the one that led directly to the laogai, was reviving feelings about Tiananmen Square by encouraging students to press for freedom of speech and freedom of the press. He was only nine years old when the clash between students and the Chinese Army took place at Tiananmen. Jin remembered sitting quietly, doing his homework, and overhearing his father and Papa Shen talk. Papa Shen described the situation as "the foolishness of young people these days," and his father voiced agreement. But the older Jin got, and the more he experienced suppression of speech firsthand, the more he sided with the students. He felt they should not be forgotten, that they should not have died in vain. He became a driving force that sparked a renewed student protest. They carried signs through the campus showing muzzled people. He realized too late why Papa Shen was calling young people foolish. It wasn't because they were wrong to want freedom of speech. It was because they thought they could speak their minds without repercussions.

Jin thought about his own naïve foolishness as a newspaper contributor. Did he really think anyone would act on what he printed? Would anything on campus change? Of course not. The only thing that changed was his place of residence.

Well, that was seven years ago, he reminded himself grimly, seven years of mind reconditioning and loyalty training, and hard labor. His fervor for freedom of speech and freedom of the press amounted to nothing. No one would ever remember his name or what he campaigned against. He was just another student dissident locked away in obscurity. His life would end in the laogai.

A short time after all the doctors left, Shi's lifeless body was put on a stretcher and taken to the death pile. Jin knew about the death pile from his editorial days research. It was a place where bodies of deceased inmates were burned, whether they died from disease, self-inflicted means, or by execution. He also remembered hearing rumors about the government harvesting and selling body organs from deceased prisoners. Wisely, he chose not to share that information with his fellow inmates. It was a moot point anyway. Bodies had to be relatively healthy at the time of death. Theirs would not be.

❧

Meanwhile, another urgent meeting was being called by the hospital's head of medicine. Heo attended with all the other doctors.

"We have a new outbreak at the prison but, as far as we know, all the affected inmates are in one barracks building. When we were there last year for the TB outbreak, a couple of you suspected AIDS in one of the buildings, and you were right. Patient zero from that building just died, and the prison requested an autopsy. AIDS has been confirmed. There are apparently twenty-five or thirty more with probably stage-two, or maybe stage-three symptoms.

"If you were there, you saw the conditions these men are living in. There is no way we can treat these men where they are without endangering the welfare of our own people, and we are not going to do that. Instead, we have offered prison officials an option. If they will let us bring the prisoners here for treatment, we will create a dedicated area for them. They have accepted our offer. The contagious diseases area is being expanded as we speak to include thirty more beds, and the inmates will be brought in tomorrow. I am going to need a dozen doctors initially and as many nurses as we can spare to work it. Volunteers would be appreciated. It's going to be a tough regimen until we get it under control."

Heo once again thought about Jin. Maybe, just maybe, this was the opportunity he had been praying for every day. He raised his hand. "I have had experience in that ward. I will volunteer."

Others doctors quickly volunteered as well, some with previous experience in the contagious diseases area plus others who were involved in the TB outbreak and were empathetic toward the prisoners. Meili was among the nurses who volunteered. Her credentials included treating HIV-infected mothers and newborn babies. She felt compassion for the laogai prisoners, the men she remembered with sunken, hopeless-looking faces. Plus, she knew Heo's heart and the love he had for his brother.

~ ~

It was right after the healthier inmates left for work duty when the door to Jin's building was thrown open. Six armed guards in covered clothing and head masks entered and ordered them to get dressed. They didn't know where they were going or why; most were too sick to care. *Execution* entered Jin's mind. Were they all going to be executed because they were sick and no longer useful? It was difficult to move as quickly as the guards kept insisting. They were all suffering from fatigue. Some had stomach aches, fever, nerve spasms, swollen lumps in their necks. Jin had all those symptoms and barely enough energy to put his clothes on.

Those who could walk left first. Stretchers were brought in for the rest. The men who were closest to the door were loaded next, one by one, as carriers worked their way through the room.

As Jin sat on the floor awaiting his turn to be placed on a stretcher, he didn't care about much of anything anymore. If this was to be the day of his demise, he was mentally and physically ready. Nothing could be worse than lingering in this place day after day. He used the last of his energy to move his body from the floor to the stretcher beside him, thinking about his family as he was carried through the door. The smell of fresh air felt slightly energizing. He was carried to a line of ambulances. *Ambulances!* Relief swept over him; they were not being led away to execution. They were going to get medical attention!

He was transferred from the stretcher to a gurney and pushed inside one of the ambulances alongside another inmate. They started moving. What a euphoric feeling to be looking through the back windows and seeing the laogai gate closing as they passed through. They were going out into the normal world!

They eventually pulled up next to a brick building from what he could see through the little windows. After waiting for what seemed like hours, the ambulance doors opened; it was Jin's turn. His gurney was lifted out and pushed up a ramp as the ambulance moved away and another one pulled up. A large freight elevator door opened, and Jin was rolled inside along with five others. When the doors opened, they were met with a flurry of medical personnel in full protective clothing who pushed them down many hallways and into a large room. Curtains on pulleys soon cordoned him off from the others. Within minutes, he was transferred to a real bed and hooked up to IVs. He didn't know what they were giving him, but it didn't matter; he knew it had to be good. With vague awareness, he felt whatever was in the IV seeping into his body. He floated away and slept.

When he woke up, a nurse was doing something with one of the IVs. She smiled at him through the window of her head covering and offered him a glass of water with a straw—fresh, clean-tasting water. Another nurse came in and they washed him from head to toe with warm water and changed his sheets. It was wonderful. He hadn't felt this clean in years. He gratefully accepted a cup of warm tea with honey and a little bit of soft food.

He tried to stay awake, but the warmth and cleanliness of the bed and having some food in his stomach was tugging at him to sleep some more. He felt a hand on his arm. It was that kind nurse again.

"Are you Jin Wong?" she asked.

"I am," he answered, expecting to see a sheet of paper in her hand with his information.

"Your brother is here," she responded with a smile. "He is going to be in to see you in a few minutes after he finishes with another patient."

My brother? Another patient? Jin's heart almost leaped out of his chest. The last he knew, his brother was taking classes to become a doctor. *Heo did it! He's a doctor, and he's here!* It felt like the second miracle of the day was about to happen. There was no one in the world he wanted to see more than his twin brother.

It was a wonderful reunion. For the first time since he was a child, Jin cried. Heo's headgear with its plastic window wasn't enough to hide his tears, either. Oh, how Heo wanted to hug his brother, but he couldn't—not yet. He just held Jin's hand through his glove and gave it a squeeze.

"Get some more rest, Jin. It's the best thing you can do for yourself right now. I will be here with you every day."

As test results started coming back, patients were being informed of their HIV status. They finally knew what was wrong with them, but it was devastating. HIV was a stigma in their country, associated with prostitution, dangerous sexual activity, illegal drugs, and unclean needles. How could they explain to their families and friends that their exposure was to none of those things? In the days that followed, doctors started gathering information from the patients to figure out how the outbreak started and how it spread so they could prevent it from happening again. They knew about the prisoner Shi's death, but they needed to know a lot more.

Overcrowded quarters was already determined as a catalyst for spreading the disease—any disease. The inmates described drinking foul-tasting water from a common bucket. Bedbugs were rampant in their building, another source of sharing a virus.

Jin told the doctors he felt his infection most likely came from helping his bloodied friend Shi from the floor to his bedroll multiple times. "Do you think Shi knew he was infected with HIV?" they were asked. Jin was pretty sure he didn't. All the others answered the same— probably not. And judging from the marks on prisoners' bodies, the doctors concluded that Shi was not the only one who incurred beatings, especially after they started getting sick and couldn't make their quotas. Beatings were common; so were untreated wounds.

Next was mental counseling—how the patients saw their lives from this point forward; how they were going to be accepted, or not, by family and friends; how they could find jobs if they were granted freedom.

Jin had the same emotions. He asked Heo not to tell their parents or anyone else about his condition. He felt shame. "I would rather die, Heo," he pleaded, "than cause our parents more pain and embarrassment than I already have. I don't want to go back to prison, but I don't want to go home either. If I am freed, I will find someplace else to go. Please don't tell them I am here."

Heo was conflicted. The brother side of him wanted to say everything was going to be alright, that Jin shouldn't worry. The doctor side wanted to tell him the truth. Heo wasn't used to choosing words carefully when talking to his brother, but he had to this time. Jin's mental stability was at stake.

"First of all, Jin, it's too late. Our parents already know. Yeah, I know it's against medical protocol to share patient information with anyone without getting permission, but there was no way I could not tell them. I can also assure you without a doubt that they want you back home any way they can get you, well or sick. They have missed you terribly, more than you can imagine. We all have. So, get those negative thoughts out of your head.

"Second, whether you want to go home or not, I intend to fight with everything in me to keep you from going back to prison. Everyone here feels the same way. You and all the others have suffered enough. You deserve to either be free or at least have your cases heard in court. Seven years of waiting is unconscionable. Some of your fellow inmates have been in prison even longer than that. Our senior hospital staff is going to be talking with prison and government officials on your behalf very soon.

"And third, a lot has happened in our family since you've been gone, and I'll bring you up to date later. But take my word for it, you will not be looked down upon by anyone! Don't even go down that road. It is not true."

Jin looked away for what seemed like an eternity before turning back. "Thank you, my wise brother. I needed to hear that, I really did. You have no idea how I have agonized about letting Mother and Father down after all they've done for me. I was a spoiled, headstrong kid who caused them a lot of pain. If it is possible to make amends, I want to do that more than anything."

Heo smiled inside his headgear at his brother, silently thanking God for bringing them together again and giving him the right words to set Jin's thinking straight. It was a long seven years without him.

"Now let's go over your medical status," Heo continued. "I'm going to tell you like it is—no sugar-coating."

Jin laughed for the first time in years. "Since when have you ever sugar-coated anything with me? If you ever did, I'd know there was something wrong!"

"You are so right, brother, and it's not going to change now. So here it is. There are three stages to an HIV infection. You are well into stage two, but not into stage three yet, which is important. Stage three is where the infection actually becomes AIDS. You are seriously ill but, even at this point, you can be treated with drugs and go on to lead a normal life. You are contagious right now, but you won't be when we get you stabilized on the right mix of drugs. If you do what you are supposed to do, which is taking your meds, eating healthy, and exercising, you can look forward to a long and active life. You can do it, and so can all the rest of these guys. But you have to be positive. Look at your situation as one of steadily improving health, not one of defeat. It's not going to happen overnight, but you know I will be with you every step of the way.

"Right now, however, your doctor says get some rest while these IVs are doing what they are supposed to do, which is getting nutrition and hydration back into your body along with the drugs." As he stood up to leave, Heo looked down at his brother again and, with a big grin and a happy heart, reinforced his feelings and that of their family. "Now that's what your doctor says. Your brother says, it's about time you got home!"

Chapter 11

A TIME OF CHANGE

IT WAS 2006 and China was just two and a half years away from hosting the 2008 Summer Olympic Games. Beijing was the main location and in the throes of getting a complete makeover. Dilapidated houses and buildings were being torn down. Historic areas were being refurbished, buildings renovated, city landmarks repaired. Two new ring roads were built around Beijing and all the city streets were like new. High-tech traffic control systems were almost finished. The subway and light-rail systems were rebuilt and extended. An enormous new terminal at the Beijing Airport had just been completed. Existing roads to the airport were improved; more were added.

Construction of Olympic Park, which included thirty-seven stadiums or venues, was continuing. There were state-of-the-art buildings going up everywhere, the most unusual of which was the National Stadium, more commonly referred to as *The Bird's Nest* because of its bowl-like shape.

Being built were digital and broadband telecommunication systems that included wireless transmission, networking, and intelligent technologies using smart cards. Everything that was being installed was described as cutting edge—television, internet, mobile phones, and clean energy. The entire sports industry in China was growing at an explosive pace. Sports venues were being built everywhere—soccer stadiums, ball fields, golf courses, training centers, and even a sailing center.

It was also a time for increased world criticism of China's human rights abuses—the treatment of Tibetans and Ulygars, forced labor camps, illegal detention with delayed or denied legal representation, the one-child-per-family edict, mandated abortions, genocide of baby girls, denial and ignorance of HIV infections, suppression of religious freedom, and the lack of truth in government-controlled media. It was all thrust into the international spotlight as the country moved toward opening its doors to the world. It was clear that China had to address these issues, and it did so with subtlety.

The Chinese government announced an end to re-education through labor—an eventual goal with no specific timeline, but it was too late. Prisoners who escaped the camps and made their way to free world countries were already making the plight of Chinese prisoners known. The free world media carried their stories. In the United States, a laogai museum was being built in Washington DC as a testimony to China's forced labor camp atrocities.

China was realizing the negative effects of the one-child-per-family edict and the widening gender imbalance it was causing. To correct the increasingly lopsided population, it had banned gender testing and forced abortions, but the one-child edict remained in place. Twenty-six years after the edict went into effect, the country's gender imbalance lingered, forcing Chinese men to seek wives from other Asian countries.

The SARS outbreak in 2003 brought world attention, once again, to health threats originating in China, revealing the country's inability to contain them, and their lack of sharing information with the rest of the world.

The stigma associated with HIV was addressed with increased education about the condition. Instead of covering it up as China had done in the past, it was being talked about openly. Testing for HIV in prisons began sporadically in 2004.

The Chinese government knew they had a lot of negative world press heading into the 2008 Summer Olympics, but the general population of China did not know. Suppression of media communications within the country kept the Chinese people in the dark, unaware of their country's worldwide negative image. They only heard what the government intended for them to hear.

ˑⁱⁱ

On a local level, the Wong family was experiencing change. Jin was coming home. Discussions between senior hospital personnel and prison and government officials resulted in an exoneration for the group of hospitalized HIV-positive inmates. After weeks of treatment, rehab, and medical and mental education, the men were embracing the reality that their HIV could be controlled and that they could lead normal lives. Heo personally escorted his brother home.

If Jin had any reservations about being accepted by family because of his illness, they dissipated immediately after walking through the door. The hugs and tears of joy, the warmth of home, and the love of family enveloped him. He appreciated every little thing— the familiarity of his own room, his bed, his mother's cooking, and all else he remembered about home. It felt precious, almost surreal. Even his usually stoic father hugged him again and again, poured tea for him, sat next to him, and put an arm around him. Jin developed a new appreciation for his father as a real person and loving parent. Life never felt so good or so humbling.

Cha-Li and her parents were the first outsiders to welcome Jin home, soon followed by neighbors and friends. He met Heo's fiancé, Meili, and recognized her as one of the kind nurses at the hospital. Then there was her little daughter Molly. She was adorable and soon to be Jin's niece in a few months when Heo and Meili married.

But the biggest surprise was finding out that he and Heo were not fraternal twins. It was shocking, but Jin eventually accepted the bizarre truth that they were related only by adoption, an illegal one at that. It had to remain a family secret forever. It also pulled him into something he never thought would affect him—the one-child-per-family edict. He knew it existed, but never gave it much thought.

Then he heard about Heo's trip to Beijing with Meili and their success in finding Heo's biological family. *And Heo also has a biological sister who lives in Canada that he has yet to meet? Wow!* His delight for Heo was bittersweet, fearing Heo would abandon his adoptive family for his biological one.

The next shocking revelation was about Cha-Li. She was not his cousin, but his biological sister. "Are you serious?" he asked. The story was incredible, but the more he thought about it, the more he liked the idea of having a big sister . . . as long as Heo was still going to be his brother! One of the biggest emotional bombs was when Jin learned that Heo was a Christian, as well as Meili . . . and so was his mother.

"Father, how do you feel about all this? Are you also a Christian?"

"No, son. I am still a member of the Three Self Church. It is the church I am instructed to attend and to have my family attend if possible. Even though I personally believe everyone should be able to go to their own church and practice their own religion, it is a belief I keep to myself. However, I do worry about my family. We are all aware of the consequences of attending an unsanctioned church."

Jin was pensive. "Can you get in trouble, Father, for knowing you have family members who attend an unsanctioned church and not turning them in to the authorities?"

"Yes."

Jin's head was spinning with surprises. But there was one more for Jin to hear about and it hit home with him in a much different way. It concerned a non-family member, the soldier named Zhang who had connected Heo with his biological family, albeit accidentally during an outbreak of TB at the prison where he was stationed. Jin remembered when many inmates were taken away for medical treatment, but he didn't know why. All he knew was that his symptoms did not match the ones the doctors screened for. He was surprised to learn that many of the guards and soldiers were also infected with TB, including the one named Zhang.

It was jolting to learn that this prison soldier actually stayed at their house while convalescing. The irony was hard to fathom.

Days later, after having time to assimilate all the new information, Jin and his sister, Cha-Li, stood side-by-side, looked in a mirror, and laughed! They compared eyebrows, noses, chins, and cheeks. Yes, there certainly were family resemblances. Unlike Heo's adoption, however, Cha-Li's was legal, so no secrecy was required—just discretion. She would remain Jin's cousin to those outside the family.

Jin agreed to share his own story, what it was like living in the laogai for seven years. It was a conversation he would have preferred not to have, but his family really wanted to know. It was private, discussed only with his parents plus Heo and Meili. His stories of mistreatment evoked gasps and tears. Only Heo and Meili were ever actually inside the barracks and saw the filth and pitiful conditions. They were never exposed to the working conditions in the fields and factories, the methods of punishment, mind-conditioning, brainwashing, or beatings. Jin shared a lot—but not everything. Some of what he witnessed or experienced was too gruesome to recount. When he finally unburdened himself of many of the horrors, Jin felt a sense of release, almost as if he had permission now to let it go. It was over. Now his family knew his story.

Meili was visibly shaken, dabbing at tears with a tissue. His mother came over and hugged him and out-and-out sobbed while his father moved over next to him and put a comforting arm around his shoulders. Heo shook his head, buried his face in his hands, and eventually came over and hugged him when his mother finally let go. Jin almost regretted his honesty, feeling that perhaps he should have softened it more, but it *did* feel good to let it all out, especially knowing he would never have to talk about it again. And he wouldn't, he decided, not to anyone.

Jin was also realistic about his personal expectations. He knew that memories of the atrocities would haunt him, but time was the key to his future. He wanted his past to be just that—his *past*. He wanted to be a part of today and be able to look forward to tomorrow.

_⁓_

As the excitement of having Jin home wound down, Cha-Li's thoughts turned more and more to Zhang. It seemed like an eternity since they went their separate ways. She missed him so much more than she thought she would. She remembered the serious conversation she had with Heo. *Heo was right*, she admitted. *I viewed my relationship with Zhang only from my own perspective, not from his. I only thought about our future together from my point of view. I didn't want to be married to a soldier! It was not what I wanted my husband to be!* She remembered Heo comparing Zhang with his father. "Father is a soldier, too," he had said, "and it never seemed to bother Mother. They are obviously happy together."

Yes, Heo was right. If Zhang wants to be career Army, who am I to insist that he change? He has as much right to determine his future as I do mine. Oh, if only I hadn't been so selfish, so stubborn, so self-centered, so . . . whatever!

Whys and *what ifs* kept running through her head, even when she tried to ignore them. She had Zhang's phone number. Maybe she should call him and apologize. No, she couldn't bring herself to do that; she just couldn't. But maybe she should. Heo said he talked to Zhang and suggested they might want to discuss their future some more. It sounded hopeful, but Zhang never called.

Maybe I should talk to Heo again. No, Heo is spending time with Jin right now plus he's in the middle of wedding plans. She thought about her Christian beliefs, especially the one about trusting in God's timing. *Well, do I really believe in God's timing or don't I?* She decided she did and needed to be patient, but also acknowledged to herself that patience was not something she was particularly good at. So, she prayed for patience, and waited.

–⁓⁄⁓–

Her phone rang. It was Jin. "Hey, Cha-Li. You got any time to spend with your kid brother? I really want to know more about this Christian stuff, and everyone around here is up to their ears in wedding plans."

"Kid brother!" she laughed. How strange and wonderful that sounded. A year ago, she was an only child. Now she had Jin, an honest-to-goodness real brother. Her spirits lifted. "Of course, I have time to spend with you. How about tomorrow afternoon when my class is over? Want me to come there or do you want to come over here?"

"Why don't you come over here if you don't mind. I've got Mother's Bible and I probably shouldn't be walking around the neighborhood with it. Plus, she's making her world-famous mooncakes and I don't want to be too far away in case she needs someone to sample them."

It was so good to hear Jin's voice again. His wacky sense of humor was returning, making her smile.

"But seriously," he continued, "I've been reading her Bible and I've got quite a few questions. Maybe you can explain some things to me. I'm hoping to go to your church next week with Mother, and I don't want to sound like a total dummy."

"I will be there tomorrow."

After finishing the Books of Matthew and Mark, Jin was in the sitting room, engrossed in the Book of Luke when Cha-Li arrived. They quickly settled in for their first home-schooled lesson. Yan brought in a pot of hot tea and a plate of mooncakes and smiled at the beautiful sight of her son and daughter studying together. It was interrupted by a knock at the kitchen door. *Probably a neighbor or one of Mother's friends,* Jin surmised, getting his mind back to the lesson at hand while his mother went to answer it.

Yan was surprised and pleased that the visitor was Zhang who said he had questions about some military regulations and was hoping Papa Wong would have time to discuss them. "He's not home yet, Zhang, but he should be here shortly. Why don't you come in and join me for a cup of tea and a few mooncakes while you wait!" As Zhang removed his hat and sat down, Yan placed a sampling of mooncakes in front of him.

"Do you wish to talk to Cha-Li?" she asked nonchalantly as she poured two cups of tea. "She is in the next room with her cousin."

The mooncake that was on its way to Zhang's mouth never made it. "Maybe, but only if she wants me to," he nervously acknowledged. "She might not want to talk to me."

Yan Wong walked over to the door and poked her head around the corner. "Cha-Li, Zhang is here to see Papa Wong who's not home yet. Would you like to talk to him while he is waiting?" Her eyes betrayed a hint of mischievousness.

"Zhang!" Cha-Li shouted in surprise as she jumped up and ran into the kitchen.

He quickly stood as Cha-Li came charging at him. "Hello, Cha-Li. I didn't mean to interrupt but—"

He never got to finish his sentence as Cha-Li threw abandon aside and rushed over to give him a big hug. "I am so sorry—" she started to say but likewise never got a chance to finish her sentence.

"No, I am the one who should have—"

Jin was following close behind but drew back at the sight of an Army uniform. Suddenly, he felt out of place and started retreating to the door, but Zhang looked over at him and extended his hand. "Hi, I'm Zhang, a friend of Cha-Li's, and you must be Jin." They exchanged a firm and friendly handshake. Jin's jitters eased slightly.

"Why don't we continue the lessons another time, cuz," he smiled. "I have a feeling you two have things to talk about, and I don't mind keeping Mother and the mooncakes company out here in the kitchen. Cha-Li smiled as the happy couple retreated to the sitting room.

Bin Wong was later than usual getting home and received a briefing from his wife before being allowed to exit the kitchen. Zhang and Cha-Li were engaged in discussion when Papa Wong came in to join them. The topic changed to military, mostly officer protocol, and Bin answered each of Zhang's questions. Now it was Cha-Li's turn to feel out of place, deciding it was time to join Auntie Yan in the kitchen while the two men talked. But Zhang took her hand. "Please stay. Some of what I want to talk to Papa Wong about includes you."

He turned back to Bin Wong. "I am at a point in my military career, sir, where I have to make some decisions about my future. For years I considered myself to be career military. The Army has been good to me, as I know it has been for you, and I admire your commitment, but I have different priorities now than I had years ago. My eight-year enlistment is almost up, and I am having new thoughts. I am considering not rejoining for many reasons." He looked over at Cha-Li. "First, at my present rank, I am subject to being transferred almost anywhere, and I don't want that, especially if Cha-Li is part of my future. And yes, we are discussing our future together. . . again," he smiled, "and she says she is not opposed to whatever career I choose. We both want children, however, and I want to be a part of our children's lives. I would want to raise a family with strong bonds, like you have.

"Second, I understand that you are aware of Cha-Li's church affiliation, which is different from our Three Self Church. I have become a believer in her church myself recently and I want us to worship together in the Christian church. As a soldier, I cannot do that."

"How do you intend to support your family if you leave the Army?" Bin interrupted.

"As a young child and up into my teens, I worked with my father in the school's athletic program. I am very familiar with athletic equipment, physical therapy, and sports. I would really like to open my own sports gym for body building, plus a physical therapy center to work with patients who need rehabilitation. Right now, with the Olympics right around the corner, and even after they are over, it seems like an opportune time to be involved in anything that has to do with sports and body building. I'm sure my father would be willing to help me get set up whenever I find a suitable location. Finding a good location is probably going to be the biggest hurdle but, once I find a place and secure funding, I could run the business during the day and study at night to get my degree in physical therapy. Cha-Li said she would be willing to help me with the books and keep the office in order. It is something she could do also in the evening after her classes. We feel we can make it work."

"I see," Bin contemplated. "That all sounds feasible to me, Zhang, and I'm sure your good Army training will serve you well." He looked over at Cha-Li. "Are you really ready to tackle a family business, young lady? It could be stressful in its infancy, especially if you are involved in your own career as well."

"I am ready."

He turned back to Zhang. "I have one other thought. Because of the Olympics coming up the end of next year, you will most likely encounter pressure to re-enlist. From what I am hearing, they are going to need many thousands of workers to make the event successful. That includes military for crowd control, security, communications, and whatever else is needed. Have you discussed this yet with your superior officer?"

"No, sir. I wanted to talk to you first and then to my parents."

"I wish you well, but be prepared. This is an unusual time, and there are different circumstances that might affect your plans. If you run into difficulties, I may or may not be able to help, but hopefully I can at least help you work through it."

"Thank you, sir."

Jin heard pieces of the conversation from the kitchen. He was pretty sure that all was well now between Zhang and Cha-Li. It sounded like Zhang was acknowledging his father as a military superior, a respected elder, and a friend. *Maybe that guy is going to be alright after all*, he decided. *Maybe.*

-ᵥᵥ⁄ᵥ-

Bin Wong was right. Zhang's request to opt out of re-enlistment was declined. A full military presence was needed during the Olympics to assure necessary security. He re-enlisted for two more years and was assigned to continuing duty in Beijing.

He also learned about an opportunity for Cha-Li in Beijing. Teachers and overseers were needed in large numbers for young children whose parents were involved in Olympic activities. It was temporary, but the pay was good. She submitted her application, was accepted, and was offered residency at a female housing unit in Beijing. Zhang and Cha-Li both knew there would not be much free time until the games were over, but at least they would not be far away from each other. Their wedding date was set for six months after the close of the Olympics—no details, just a date.

Unlike Zhang, however, who was used to relocating with the Army, Cha-Li had never left home. It was exciting to be a part of something as big as the Olympics, but somewhat unnerving to leave the familiarity of home, neighborhood, schools, and the teaching job she loved. It was an uneasy morning helping her parents load the family car with clothes, food, and personal belongings, and setting off for Beijing.

-ᵥᵥ⁄ᵥ-

Meanwhile, another event was on the horizon. Heo and Meili's wedding was just a few months away. They decided to have two ceremonies—traditional Chinese in a wedding garden near Heo's home, then a small Christian ceremony at Meili's house church in the country with just family and close friends. Plans were in place. They found their perfect starter home not far from the hospital where they both worked, and a short distance to Molly's new school. It was distressing to Molly that Cha-Li was living in Beijing now and was not going to be her teacher, but she met the new teacher and liked her. A month before the wedding, Meili and Molly moved from their country apartment into the house. All was well. Everything was coming together.

The day of the wedding arrived with ideal weather. As guests started filling the beautifully decorated garden, it came to life with the joyful sounds of people greeting each other and having a good time. Heo joined his parents and Jin in welcoming people coming through the gate. Bin and Yan Wong were gracious hosts. They had already met Meili's parents, so the only strangers were Heo's biological family from Beijing—his mother Su-Li Ming, his brother and sister-in-law Qiang and Guo Ming, and their daughter Lian. If anyone felt uncomfortable, it wasn't for long.

Heo was especially pleased to see how naturally the women in all three families bonded—his bride-to-be, her mother, his two mothers, plus Guo and Cha-li. All were smiling, laughing and greeting each other like old friends.

It was the same with the men, but having Jin as his best man was over-the-top special. How different he looked from months ago when he arrived at the hospital from the laogai. From a sick, emaciated inmate on the doorstep of death, he was healthy again, smiling and mingling with guests.

Meili's family was just her parents plus an aunt and uncle and one cousin. All were busy attending to the bride and making sure Molly was properly dressed and ready for her part in the wedding.

The guests were seated; the garden music was turned off. The ceremony began. Heo's heart felt like it was going to burst with pride as he and Meili held hands and accepted each other as husband and wife. The love of his life was absolutely beautiful in her brocade wedding dress with colorful combs and beads adorning her dark hair.

Molly got a lot of attention as well. She was not the shy little girl Heo met a year ago. As a five-year-old with the benefit of some personal tutoring from Cha-Li, she was now much more outgoing, no longer hesitant to talk to adults. Standing attentively by her mother's side during the ceremony, she was a *happy* child, not only because her mother was happy, but for herself as well. She was going to have a father, a real father, something she was denied since birth. When the music started playing again and someone was singing, she was busy with her own thoughts.

She remembered the day she met Doctor Wong, the stranger who worked with her mother at the hospital. She didn't think much about him at first; he was just another grown-up. But when he went with them to McDonald's, she was pretty sure she was *not* going to like him! He was taking up time that was meant for just her and her mother.

It didn't take long, however, before she developed her own personal affection for the man who was so kind. She recalled a day when the three of them were walking through a park and the weather quickly changed. The wind picked up, the rain came down hard, and it got cold. They were a long way from the car. Doctor Wong took his coat off, put it over her mother's head and shoulders, handed her the keys, and told her to run for the car. She was ready to run behind her mother but was surprised to feel herself suddenly being picked up. Doctor Wong held her close and sheltered her as they made their own way to the car. He put her down in the back seat, shook out a blanket, and covered her up, even though he was standing outside and getting soaking wet. She remembered being very cold and shivering, and the blanket felt good.

She adored Doctor Wong, and today was definitely an exciting day. Next week was going to be exciting, too. She was going to be adopted. Her name was going to change from Molly McIntyre to Molly Wong and she would be calling Doctor Wong *father.*

Chapter 12

UPHEAVAL - CHINA IN THE SPOTLIGHT

IT WAS APRIL 2008, four months before the Summer Olympics, and the headlines in Chinese newspapers were positive and rosy. The government-controlled radio and television stations filled the airwaves with high anticipation of an event that promised to affirm China's role as a world leader. That is what the Chinese people saw and heard. In the outside world, however, headlines were different. There were individuals, groups, and organizations who were against the Olympics being held in China. Dissention, talks of protests, and plans for boycotts threatened to derail the event, or at least damage it, until an act of nature changed everything.

It was the middle of the afternoon on May 12, 2008, when the 7.9 magnitude earthquake shook Sichuan Province in Western China. It was felt thousands of miles away in Russia, Taiwan, and Thailand. It rattled buildings in Beijing and Shanghai, forcing emergency evacuations. Construction projects came to a halt. It was China's worst earthquake in more than fifty years. As the severity was monitored inside and outside the country, there was no denying the devastation.

The statistics were staggering; at least 69,000 fatalities including more than 5,000 school children, another 18,000 missing and presumed dead, 375,000 injured. Entire cities and villages were leveled. Hundreds of thousands of people who lived downstream from compromised dams had to be evacuated. China needed help, and the world came to its rescue. While China deployed tens of thousands of its own soldiers to the stricken areas, other countries sent rescue teams. Money and emergency supplies came in from around the globe. It was an outpouring of human compassion, people helping people in a time of need.

As strong aftershocks continued to shake the topography and hamper rescue efforts, nations and activist organizations put their barrage against China aside. The world's interface with China changed from one of criticism to one of empathy.

~>k~

Zhang was on duty at the Beijing Airport that afternoon conducting training exercises for soldiers assigned to security in preparation for the Olympics. When the earthquake hit, his troops immediately did what they were trained to do in an emergency—get everyone out and away from the building as quickly as possible and stop all others from entering. It was a smooth operation with no harm to passengers, visitors, or the new high-tech building. Although they had no idea of the magnitude or source of the quake, Zhang's troops continued in earthquake mode for the rest of the day. They helped protect anxious passengers during aftershocks and assisted airport personnel in getting planes on and off the ground.

Meanwhile, Zhang received a message to report to his base commander for possible reassignment. Maybe it had something to do with the earthquake, or perhaps there was a change with the Olympics. All he knew for sure was that he had just a short time to get to his base and an even shorter time to contact Cha-Li and let her know he might be gone for a while. He tried calling her, but phone lines were jammed.

Her childcare building was locked. There was a sign on the front door instructing parents to pick their children up in a nearby playground. Zhang assessed the traffic situation and decided to run rather than drive to the playground. He was met with calm chaos as cars were parking anywhere there was a space. Parents were standing in a long line to retrieve their children from the fenced playground. He looked through the fence. Some of the caregivers were tending to infants in small beds; others were sitting on the ground with groups of toddlers. He finally spotted Cha-Li at the gate, signing parents in and checking children out.

He didn't have time to wait in line. He called her name loudly and waved his arms; she heard him and looked up. He motioned to her by pointing to his wrist as an indication of time. She spoke a few words to one of the other workers, then ran to the inside of the fence where Zhang waited on the other side.

"I am being reassigned, Cha-Li," he hollered so she could hear above the traffic, "but I don't know where I'm going or how long I'll be gone. Get hold of Qiang and Guo if you need anything. No. Get hold of them anyway and let them know I will be gone for a while and that I would appreciate it if they would look after you until I get back. I'll contact you as soon as I can."

Cha-Li nodded; there was no time to talk. They exchanged one brief look and a wave before Zhang hurried back to his car and Cha-Li returned to gate duty and the line of impatient parents.

A cadre of Army personnel was updated on the source and severity of the quake. The tremors they felt, although disruptive and scary, were minor compared with the devastation more than a thousand miles away in Sichuan Province. Roads and bridges were out, they were told. Communication lines were down. Dams were holding but in danger of breaking. Homes and buildings were destroyed. Schools had collapsed with children inside. The death toll was quickly mounting and there were more injuries than could be counted. Troops were being assembled from all over China to be sent immediately to the stricken area. Zhang and other officers were to report to the deployment area to take charge of search-and-rescue operations.

Cha-Li's workday ended late. It wasn't until the last child was claimed by a parent that caregivers were allowed to leave. Her mind was a jumble of thoughts as she walked toward the train station, trying to decide what she should do first. Phone access was hit and miss she discovered. *Should I go back to my dorm? Maybe Zhang will be there. Maybe he didn't have to leave Beijing after all. Or should I try to get over to Qiang's music store like he wanted me to? It's late. Qiang and Guo might not even be there. Maybe I should try to get through to my parents and make sure they are alright. I should let them know what is happening here. I wonder if Zhang called his parents. Did he have time? Should I try to contact them?*

A strong aftershock jolted her back to the moment. She decided to do as she always did, take the train to her dorm. But as she turned the corner to the train station, her heart sank. There was a large crowd waiting at the boarding site. *Are the trains late, not running, or are they just inundated?* She assessed how long it would take to walk instead of ride. Then she had a chilling thought. *Even when I do get back to my dorm, will I be able to get in?*

She heard someone shouting her name and looked out at the street. It was Guo stopped in the street and waving for her to get in the car. Her seemingly impossible situation suddenly got better as she hurried to accept the ride from her new friend.

"Thank goodness I've found you!" Guo exclaimed as Cha-Li scrambled inside. "We got a call from Zhang a couple of hours ago and he told us he was being assigned to Sichuan Province to help with the earthquake. I'm surprised he was even able to get through. The phones have been jammed," she chattered on. "Anyway, he was heading back to his barracks to pack a few things and drove by your dorm building. There's a rope across the door. He asked us to find you and let you know where he was going and to look after you. We assured him we would take good care of you. I hope you don't mind hanging out with us for a while!"

"Thank you, Guo! You have no idea what a mess my mind was in trying to figure out what to do!"

"I can only imagine!" Guo continued. "But we've made arrangements for you to stay with Qiang's mother, Su-Li, in her apartment for a while. It's a good sturdy building and apparently a safe one. No one has had to leave. She is a very hospitable lady, Cha-Li, as you may have realized from the wedding. She lives alone and is looking forward to having you there. She has already adjusted her music room into a bedroom for you. It has one of those couches that turns into a bed. She is going to have dinner ready for us whenever we get there."

They pulled up in front of the music store and beeped. Moments later, Lian and Qiang came out and locked the door. Then they were off again, weaving their way through traffic, heading for Su-Li's apartment. Knowing she was going to be staying there for a while, Cha-Li tried to make a mental note of street names and landmarks as they went by, but decided it was useless. Too many turns.

A home-cooked meal and a pleasant mother figure was a welcome respite from the hours of upheaval and tremors. Everyone was tired and ready for sleep. Qiang and Guo were just about to leave when Qiang's phone rang. It was Heo. Qiang's face grew dark as he listened to his brother, then handed the phone to Cha-Li. "Heo wants to talk to you, Cha-Li."

"I am home here with Mother and Father, Cha-Li. We have some sad news regarding your parents."

My parents? Sad news? An icy pang pierced her heart, anticipating they might have been hurt from the tremors. She meant to call them after dinner but forgot. "What is wrong with my parents, Heo? Are they hurt?"

"No, but . . ." he hesitated. "There is no easy way to tell you this, cuz, but your parents were arrested this morning. They are charged with conducting an unregistered church in their house. They are waiting for a trial but, until then, they are sentenced to labor in the laojiao."

What! How can this be? Who could have told them? They were always so careful. Even some of the neighbors are members. "Oh, Heo! What can we do?"

"Nothing. Believe me. Nothing! Father and I went to the Army headquarters to speak for them, but even Father's seniority made no difference. No one could tell us when their trial is going to be. The only good news is that they are in the laojiao and not the laogai. Their treatment should be better. Unfortunately, the anticipated outcome is that they will probably be found guilty and will have to serve out their sentence by doing labor."

Cha-Li swallowed hard as she absorbed the bad news. She knew all about the prisons from fellow teachers who dared to teach anything different than what they were told. She wanted to scream, but she couldn't. Her throat closed. She wanted to cry out loud but knew she shouldn't. All she could do was put her head down and release silent tears. She felt Guo's arm around her shoulders and a tissue pressed into her hand.

Another chilling thought emerged. "What about *your* mother, Heo? Was Auntie Yan arrested too? Were any of the others?"

"No. Thankfully. Apparently, when they do this, they just go for the owners of the house church to teach everyone a lesson. They were most likely being watched for a while, though, so we're assuming they do know who the members of the church are. Father is insisting that Mother stay out of sight for now, that she not even leave the house.

"But there's more," he continued slowly. "Your house is gone, Cha-Li. It was leveled along with everything in it about an hour after your parents were arrested. That is why we are assuming they are going to be found guilty. The message is pretty clear, that unregistered house-churches are not tolerated. In a weird way, the earthquake this afternoon took attention away from all this and the soldiers are gone. Your neighbors are sifting through the rubble, hoping to recover whatever they can for you."

Cha-Li was aware of quiet talk in the room. She was thankful that Qiang was telling Guo and Su-Li what was happening so she didn't have to. "So, whenever Mother and Father get out of prison, they will have no place to go?" she asked Heo. "Will they still own the land and be able to build another house?"

"I don't know the answer to that, but chances are they will not. If the government has the right to destroy your home, they probably confiscated the entire property. That would be my best guess, but it's only a guess."

She took a deep breath. "Thanks for letting me know, Heo. Zhang? Oh, he got reassigned this afternoon. He is apparently heading to Sichuan Province to help with the earthquake effort. That is all we know."

"I am so sorry about all this, cuz. I wish I could be there with you right now, but I'm glad you are with friends. Do you want me to come to Beijing? I can be there tomorrow."

"No, I am alright. Please let me know if you hear anything more." She handed the phone back to Qiang. Her mind was numb. Her parents. In prison. House destroyed. She gratefully accepted a fresh cup of hot tea from Su-Li, noting the tear-streaked faces of everyone else in the room, including Lian, who was obviously scared. Guo was quietly explaining to her what the conversation was about and why people were crying.

Doom and darkness had settled over them like a cloud before a storm. She thought about Heo and some of their past conversations. He was always the sensible one who found something positive in even the worst situations. She knew Heo would have looked at this from the viewpoint of others. She remembered his words: *Think about others and how they feel. When it seems like your world is crashing in, it might not be about you at all."*

But Heo wasn't here. Zhang wasn't here. Right now, she knew

everyone was looking at her, feeling sorry for her and not knowing what to do. She had to pull herself together. Blinking back more tears, she gritted her teeth and took a couple more sips of hot tea while quickly trying to think of what could possibly be positive in all of this. *God, please help me!* Dishes rattled as yet another aftershock shook the apartment.

"Well, at least my parents are both alive," she announced quietly. "There are a lot of people in Sichuan Province who were alive this morning and are not tonight. And yes, our house is gone, but there are a lot of people in Sichuan whose houses are also gone. As for prison, we have dealt with this in our family before and we can do it again. We have much to be thankful for. We have a strong and loving God who will get us through this!"

It was met with nods of agreement, smiles of relief, and sympathetic hugs. "You are one strong lady," Qiang commented as he took his turn at a hug, "and I am heartened by your faith and your positive thinking.

"I learned it from your brother," she smiled. "Heo is the most positive thinking person I know."

⁓⌇⁓

Jin did not handle the situation as well as Cha-Li. He was home alone when he heard heavy trucks going by that morning, and a short time later when he heard the rumbling of heavy machinery and crashing sounds. He couldn't believe what he was seeing; bulldozers razing his aunt and uncle's house. There was nothing he could do except watch in disbelief along with their neighbors. Where were his aunt and uncle? He ran back inside and tried to call his father but there was no answer. He couldn't call his mother; she was at her weekly exercise class and wasn't going to be home for another hour. He left a message at the hospital for Heo, who was with a patient. By the time his mother arrived, his aunt and uncle's house was destroyed and the machinery was being loaded onto trucks. His mother was shaking and crying.

Heo called back, immediately changed his schedule, and arrived a half-hour later. He slipped into the crowd and found a neighbor he recognized from the house church. "Your aunt and uncle were taken away in a police vehicle early this morning," he was told quietly. "We know nothing more." There were other neighbors in the crowd he recognized, but no one was talking. No one wanted to draw the attention of the soldiers.

As they huddled around the table waiting for Bin to come home, Heo and Jin did what they could to console their mother. She was devastated by the arrest of her sister and brother-in-law, plus fearful for herself and for Heo and Jin who had attended her church as well.

Their attention changed abruptly when the house shook. Teacups rattled and fell to the floor. They had felt earthquakes before; they were nothing new. But why now? Why did an earthquake have to happen *now*, in addition to the other grief they were experiencing? Everyone in the neighborhood ran outside until the shocks subsided. Yan was cold, scared, and shaking uncontrollably. Jin ran back inside and grabbed a shawl for her.

Meanwhile, Heo noticed a few of the neighbors starting to walk through the pile of debris. He was annoyed that they were scavenging.

"What are you looking for?" he asked one of them indignantly.

"We are trying to salvage whatever we can for your aunt and uncle, Heo," the neighbor explained. "When the soldiers left, we decided it might be our only chance to see if there was anything we could save for them. The furniture looks like it is pretty much destroyed, but there are some smaller things we found that we can save."

"Thank you, my friend. I am sure my aunt and uncle will appreciate what you are doing."

When Bin came home and found out what was going on down the street, and saw the condition his wife was in, he was livid. He did a quick assessment of earthquake damage, which was very little, then took charge. "Heo, come with me!" he commanded. "We are going to find your aunt and uncle. Jin, stay here with your mother. Call me if any of the soldiers return!"

Heo had never seen his father this angry. He could be stern and gruff, but never like this.

When they got to the Army headquarters, everyone was scurrying about. Orders were being issued for deployment to the earthquake site. Bin Wong did not care. He walked over to the officer in charge and insisted they have an immediate discussion. Heo waited outside the office while the two men went inside. He heard raised voices, mostly his father's. Then more raised voices. When his father emerged, he was looking straight ahead. All he said was "Let's go!" The ride home was silent.

Bin consoled his wife and assured her that neither she nor their sons were in danger of being arrested, nor were any of their neighbors who attended the house church. He told her that the commanding officer had overstepped his authority to order destruction of a house church before a trial found the owners guilty. Yes, it had been done in the past, and perhaps too often, but it was not official protocol.

In typical military manner, Bin summarized their situation. "Their crime is not being Christian, or any other religion. It is the technicality of not registering a house church with the government. Of course, we all know what that means. Nothing. House-churches are proclaimed illegal and it would not have been allowed to exist anyway, registered or not. Freedom of religion in this country are just words. We know that. I would give anything if my family could attend a church of our choice together, but it is not going to happen in our lifetime. However, I have made two personal decisions today. First, I am going to retire next year when my tenure is up. Second, starting now, I will no longer attend the government church."

No one spoke while they waited for whatever was coming next.

"Heo."

"Yes, Father."

"I want you to get in touch with Cha-Li, today if you can get through, and let her know what is happening. You are the best one to do that. Tell her just the facts, not the words I shared with you. Assure her she is in no danger of being arrested, neither is anyone else. Tell her that her parents are in the laojiao, not the laogai so she will understand that their treatment will not be severe. Let her know we will do everything we can to make sure they do not linger waiting for a trial. Try your best not to upset her any more than necessary. If you need to go to Beijing and be with her personally, please go."

"Yes, Father. Is there anything else?"

There was quiet for a few moments as Bin lowered his head. "Yes. Let me know if she and Zhang are alright."

Heo left and Yan Wong busied herself preparing dinner. Jin was quiet throughout the family discussions, but his mind was in turmoil. He wanted to tell his parents what he knew about the laojiao. Treatment was not better in there than in the laogai. Prisoners from the laojiao were doing the same hard labor Jin had been doing. It made him shudder. He couldn't imagine his cherished aunt and uncle trying to survive long days of backbreaking work, scarcity of food if they didn't meet their quotas, profuse sweating with only occasional showers, biting insects, stagnant water, and dirty clothing. Maybe it was better that his father did not know the truth. It would probably provoke him even more, and it might tear his mother apart.

His mother insisted on saying a prayer at dinnertime. She never did that before, and his father did not object. As they held hands and his mother thanked God for the blessings in their lives, Jin suddenly realized what she was doing. She wasn't praying for safety or protection, which was what he would have expected after the day's ordeal. She wasn't asking for anything. She was simply thanking God for what they did have. She thanked Him for all the years her sister and brother-in-law offered their home for the church and for the privilege of attending. The only thing she did ask for eventually was, "Please, God, give them strength and protection. Please let this situation not be any worse than it absolutely must be to fit into your plan for their lives."

It seemed a strange request at first, until Jin thought about it. What his mother actually did, he concluded, was acknowledge and accept God's timing for all things. It was a positive way of addressing a negative situation, handing it over to God. *Timing. God's timing.* He heard those words before, but tonight they were taking on a different meaning. He was starting to understand.

Even though he heard others pray in their house church, he hadn't felt moved to say one of his own—until now. He wanted to know the peace that his mother had from praying. When dinner ended, he went to his room and, for the first time in his life, got down on his knees to say a prayer of his own.

Dear God, he started, but he didn't really know how to pray or what to talk to God about, so he just stayed on his knees and let his thoughts wander. What came to mind first was to ask God for release from the bad dreams of the laogai that continually plagued him at night. But that is not what his mother just did. She prayed for others. He changed his focus.

Dear God, thank you that I was not able to talk Heo into going along with our half-witted plan to demonstrate against the government years ago. Thank you that he had a more sensible mind and refused to go with us. Thank you for his success in life. Even though he is not my biological brother, please let us always be like brothers. Thank you, God, for Heo.

He wondered if God was really listening. How would he know? The answer had to be *trust*, he reasoned, but it was difficult. His prison experience taught him not to trust. He thought about his mother's faith. If he wanted to feel her peace, he had to feel her faith. He had to shed his prison mentality.

He thought about his parents as he resumed his prayer of thanks, apologizing to God for all the hurt he caused them as a teenager and as a prisoner. He thanked God for Mama Shen and Papa Shen and all they did for him and Heo, for his cousin Cha-Li who was really his sister, for his aunt and uncle who raised her as their own child so she could still be near her real family. He prayed for their safety and strength while in prison.

The longer he stayed on his knees, the circle of people and things to be thankful for widened. He thought about Zhang. *He's military, God. We've seen today what military can do to people. Is he really a friend or is he an enemy? Is he good for Cha-Li? Why can't I bring myself to trust him? Is it a sin to not trust someone?*

He thought about his new sister-in-law, Meili, and how much joy she and Molly brought to Heo and to their entire family. Heo's biological family was another blessing to be thankful for; just knowing who they were obviously brought closure for Heo.

Strangely, the more he focused on others and on the positive aspects of his life, the less important his own problems became. He decided that being in prison must have been part of God's overall plan for him. *There must be something positive about it,* he thought, *or maybe it wasn't about me at all. Maybe it's about my aunt and uncle.* He didn't want to dwell on it, but his mind was open to the thought that his experience had meaning. It would help someone someday. Maybe it was now.

Jin was feeling peace. Just before he said amen, he thought about his father. *And please help my father, God. He needs peace too. Amen.*

⋰⋱

Zhang stood on a high knoll with several other officers, surveying the progress in the small rural village below. The scene was the same from village to village, no matter how large or small. Clearing roads was always the first hurdle, as they had to be able to get there. Many villages only had one road in and out. Some were paved, others were dirt or stone. They discovered that modern paved roads were more likely to be sunken or heaved, rendering them unusable. Some were obstructed with tons of fallen rock where they butted up against crumbled hillsides. It took several days to clear a road to this village, but they finally managed to get through. Trucks with food and medical supplies were making their way in. Workers were arriving and tents were going up wherever there was room, some for living, others for medical care and supplies. Crews with machinery were working alongside survivors and soldiers, moving rubble and searching for those who were still missing. As lifeless bodies were being identified and buried, medical personnel were tending to the injured. Women were cooking over outdoor fires, using wood that used to be homes and furniture. While recovery and reconstruction would be ongoing for a long time, this village was considered stabilized by Army standards. That meant it was accessible, the list of missing people was dwindling, most of the rubble was bulldozed out of the way, and land was cleared for rebuilding. More helping hands were on their way. It was time to move on.

Their next assignment was another village, the largest one yet. The roads going in were already cleared by a local Army unit, but the situation was quickly becoming dangerous. There were thousands of people living downstream from a compromised dam. They needed to be evacuated, but the people were not cooperating. Even as aftershocks threatened their safety, survivors were frantically going through debris, refusing to leave until they found their missing family members. That's all Zhang and the others were told.

It was a half-day ride. When they arrived a little after noon, Zhang looked into the faces of exhausted workers, men and women, who obviously needed sleep. Then he learned why. The debris they were going through were school buildings. Roofs were collapsed and walls were still crumbling. There were more than a thousand children trapped inside. Even though bulldozers were available, they couldn't be used. It would be too dangerous. The walls were fragile. No wonder the people were not cooperating. Parents were not about to leave without their children, dam or no dam. Civilian crews were on hand, working alongside the contingent of soldiers, but it was far short of what was needed. It was a job for a thousand more hands, which was just about what Zhang's team had!

The dam was holding, for now. They worked feverishly until dark, then by the light of torches as best they could. Whenever a child was found alive it was cause for excitement and renewed hope. It kept them going. But the deceased bodies far outnumbered the injured. As more and more small bodies were recovered, grief gave way to anger. Zhang felt it and heard it. It was anger against their government and the now-recognized shoddy construction. Zhang knew nothing of school buildings or codes, but he was moved to compassion for the pain of parents. Most of them had just one child, which further stoked their anger. They were now childless.

They worked all night, taking shifts for breaks, sleep and food. No one wanted to give up until the last child was found, or until the dam broke.

Reinforcements arrived early the next afternoon. As rubble was able to be cleared quicker, more and more children and teachers were being accounted for. Lists of the missing were checked off; machinery was put into action. A make-shift village on higher ground was ready to accept its exhausted people, and the entire village was moved.

It was a night for rest and reflection as candles for the victims were lit and people mourned. It was also a time of awakening for many soldiers, including Zhang, to appreciate what if felt like to work very hard, alongside common, everyday people. They were not protectors of the country right now; they were not even law enforcers. These soldiers were simply helpers sitting among real people. Although their efforts were appreciated and they were thanked repeatedly, there was still distrust, even disdain, and they felt it.

~•~

Cha-Li did not expect to feel comfortable staying at the home of someone she barely knew, but Su-Li proved to be more than just a gracious host. She became a good friend and unexpectedly filled in for the mother figure now missing in Cha-Li's life. With her parents in prison, no physical home to return to, and Zhang being gone indefinitely, Cha-Li expected to feel loneliness, and she did for a short time. There were no hardships, just a feeling of being alone amid a lot of people. She went through unfamiliar emotions, starting with despair, knowing she was homeless. She felt lost in an unfamiliar city that was changing daily, and a sense of being thrust into a new level of responsible adulthood before she was ready.

Then she saw the framed, wallet-sized picture of Su-Li's daughter, Xiu-Su, sitting on a shelf next to a tiny vase with a fresh flower. She was a beautiful young lady. Guo already told her a little bit about Xiu-Su, now called Emily and living in Canada with adoptive parents. Remembering Heo's wise words to think outside of her own problems and look at a bigger picture, she asked Su-Li to tell her about Emily. It led to a fascinating story of a mother and daughter torn apart because of the edict. She learned how Emily was unexpectedly discovered twenty years later and located with the help of a friend, name omitted of course. She was drawn into Su-Li's feelings of joy at being reunited, only to experience the heartbreak of separation once again when it was time for Emily and her parents to return to Canada. Yes, this lady she was sitting with most assuredly knew loss and despair. Cha-Li tried to imagine how it must feel to hold a precious child for only a few minutes before it is forcibly taken away, and then lose a husband unexpectedly as a result of an accident. Cha-Li was in awe of her host, this strong woman and survivor, but she detected something more in the depth of her stories—years of loneliness.

Now I know why I am here in this large city of strangers, she concluded. *It's not about me at all. It is to help this lady fill a void in her life!* Instinctively, Cha-Li became a caregiver instead of a care receiver. Life changed.

The months leading up to the Olympics were busy for the two women. Su-Li dropped Cha-Li off every morning on her own way to work in her twelve-year-old Volkswagen. Flexibility was important. They had dinner whenever Cha-Li got home from her train commute;

sometimes early, sometimes late. Non-workdays were also busy, but more fun. Many were spent shopping for clothes for Cha-Li to replace the ones lost in the destruction of her house. There were special personal times, too, when they got their nails done, tried different hairstyles, and enjoyed mother-daughter conversations at a neighborhood tea shop. They got together with Qiang, Guo, and Lian as often as they could.

~\'~

The Olympics were just weeks away when Zhang returned. Relieved of his earthquake duty, he was assigned once again to airport security. He surprised Cha-Li by nonchalantly standing in line with the parents who were waiting to pick up their children. When it was his turn to announce a child's name, he just stood there until she looked up from her clipboard. "Zhang!" she squealed as she jumped to her feet. Her co-workers understood; she was allowed to leave early.

Knowing nothing of the news about Cha-Li's parents and their home, or why Cha-Li was still living with his friend's mother instead of going back to her dorm, the homecoming quickly turned somber. He was grateful to learn how everyone pulled together to make sure his bride-to-be was taken care of.

Su-Li had never met Zhang, only heard about him. He was Cha-Li's fiancé, yes, but even more importantly, he was the one who was responsible for finding her lost son Syaran, now called Heo. As far as she was concerned, Zhang was a hero. She was more than ready to welcome him like the family friend he was. Within minutes, she was on the phone to Qiang and Guo with the good news. "Zhang is home! Come over for dinner."

Pulling a dinner together for unexpected company was something Su-Li did well. It was a time for celebration despite the sadness and turmoil around them. They brought Zhang up to date on all the happenings in Beijing and the status of the Olympics. Surely it was going to be a fantastic event, they agreed.

Zhang, in turn, filled them in on the earthquake situation in Sichuan Province. The reports and telecasts they saw and heard through the media were upbeat, of course, but Zhang assured them there was still a lot to be done. Most of the region was stabilized, but it would be years before it was totally rebuilt. He didn't tell them about the catastrophe with the schools, their shoddy construction, and the loss of thousands of children. It was not an appropriate time for such a grim story. All he shared was that a large village had to be moved to higher ground because a compromised dam mandated evacuation. It burst two days after everyone was relocated.

It was a great evening with family and friends that ended too soon, but tomorrow was a workday. Zhang's day at the airport was going to be especially busy; it was starting to bustle with activity.

～✲～

The disaster in Sichuan Province moved to the background as the Olympics drew near. The outside world turned its focus once again to China's human rights violations. Lack of freedom for the press became another anti-Chinese flash point. The Chinese government countered with promises to provide foreign reporters with free and unregulated access to websites and other media outlets within China during the Olympics, and to issue protest permits and safe protest zones for those who requested them. The promises were especially exciting to the people in China, stoking the fires of hope that their country was changing. Those hopes were bolstered when they learned that the American president was going to attend the opening ceremonies, as were leaders from other countries.

Everyone in China was caught up in the excitement of the Olympics, including those in the earthquake-stricken areas. With communications restored, people gathered wherever there were televisions to watch the games. Some lit candles and placed them in the shape of the Olympic rings in support of their country. Its slogan was "One World, One Dream." Sports became the unifying link between China and the rest of the world.

And so it began. The pageantry was spectacular. The hearts of the Chinese people were filled with pride for their country as the games progressed. Sports achievements were record-breaking. The fact that China did an outstanding job with the Olympics was obvious to the world. However, the scenes at the airports and on the streets of Beijing told a different story, one of promises not kept.

In addition to Beijing's extensive police force and area security forces, the Army had a major presence with more than 34,000 soldiers assigned to Olympics-related security in Beijing and other co-host cities. Zhang's unit was among those stationed at the Beijing Airport.

It didn't take long for trouble to begin, and the airport was a chosen battleground. Requests for permits to stage protests were either denied or ignored. Journalists who arrived with the intention of covering anti-Olympics protests were detained, put back on planes and sent out of the country. When groups arrived to protest without a permit, they were arrested. Human rights activists were also arrested and forcibly removed from the city. Chinese websites remained blocked. Communications were monitored. Boycotts were planned but amounted to nothing of significance. It became evident even before the games began that China was not going to make good on its promises to the International Olympic Committee. Yet, The Games went on.

Chapter 13

NEW BEGINNINGS

AS THE 2008 Olympic Games took their place in history, Beijing was returning to normal. Zhang and Cha-Li's spring wedding plans kicked into full gear. They decided to follow the example of Heo and Meili and other young Christian adults of their time, namely to have two ceremonies: traditional Chinese and Christian. Both were planned for the outskirts of Beijing, their new home of choice. Their guest list for the traditional ceremony was modest, mostly business and Army friends, plus family. A private ceremony was planned for the following evening for members of their underground churches plus family members and friends who were Christian.

With Cha-Li's parents still in prison, her biological parents, Bin and Yan Wong, took their place. Very few knew of their true relationship. Bin learned about Christian weddings and protocol from his wife, especially two very important things: the father of the bride gives the bride away, and his other duty was to pay for the wedding. He was looking forward to this new role in his life.

Cha-Li recalled the tension she felt when agreeing to a meeting with her somewhat estranged father. She didn't know why he wanted to come to Beijing to meet with her. *Did it have something to do with her parents,* she wondered? *Did he have news?* She was even more perplexed when he began by apologizing for all the years they missed by not being together as a family. She didn't understand why he was talking about the past. It was over and she accepted the fact that she was adopted out of the family because of necessity. But when he formally asked her for the privilege of being the father of the bride, she was taken totally by surprise. Overwhelmed with emotion, she couldn't speak. All she could do was nod and hug the man whom she had never hugged in her life. Even though she grew up in a different home with different parents, Bin was there for her now, and she was suddenly her daddy's girl.

The traditional Chinese ceremony was lovely. The weather was still cool, so it was held at an indoor garden rather than outdoors. The Christian ceremony was special and somewhat emotional for Bin as he proudly escorted his daughter to the altar. He was a stately man who always walked erect, even out of uniform. Today was slightly different. Still standing tall, he had the demeanor of a protective father about to turn his daughter's well-being over to her life's chosen partner. He always considered Cha-Li to be pretty, of course, but today she was a beautiful young woman. As he kissed her cheek before placing her hand in Zhang's, she warmed his heart with a smile meant only for him. He hoped it also meant acceptance of the love he and his wife always had for her and the end of wounded feelings.

Before turning to Zhang, Cha-Li glanced at Yan, her biological mother, and noticed her tears. Bin took his seat next to her, reached over and held the hand of the other beautiful lady in his life. It was something a man of his era and stature usually did not do in public, but he didn't care. What no one knew was that Bin had chosen a new path.

Zhang's parents did not attend the Christian ceremony; it was held the day after they returned home. They did not know about it and were not invited. As far as Zhang knew, his parents were not affiliated with any church other than sporadically attending the

Three Self Church. They were country people who still embraced traditional Chinese customs and ceremonies. Zhang wanted to tell his parents about Christianity *someday*, but now was not the time.

Su-Li Ming was filled with excitement and happiness for her young housemate and, of course, cried at both ceremonies. The time they had spent together was a shared blessing. For many months, Su-Li enjoyed the company of this quasi-daughter who was otherwise destined to flounder through wedding preparations alone. She felt privileged to take the place of a missing mother during this important time. During their weeks together, Su-Li and Cha-Li talked often about her jailed parents. Sadly, she could not even send them a wedding invitation as they were not allowed to receive mail.

They talked often about Su-Li's own daughter, Emily, who was also recently married. They were notified via an invitation sent to Qiang and Guo as Owners of Ming's Music Store. To satisfy mail monitors who might question an envelope from Canada, it had to give the impression they were being invited to the wedding as an acknowledgment of past kindness. It included a personal note tucked inside the invitation, thanking them for a tour of the music store when they were in Beijing years earlier with Music Students International. What the invitation really did, however, was to let Emily's Chinese family know she was getting married and to whom. It included a newspaper engagement announcement of Emily and Jorg. They recognized Jorg as the pianist who played a duet with Emily at the opera house.

It was joyful but sad news. Joy for Emily's happiness, and sadness that they could not participate. Oh, how Su-Li would have loved to be present while Emily tried on wedding gowns and experimented with hair styles. It was just one more event in her daughter's life she would never know. Being part of Cha-Li's wedding plans helped fill that void. Su-Li had a special seat of honor at both services, front row next to Bin and Yan Wong.

-\\/-

When Cha-Li and Zhang's weddings were over and their lives were getting established as husband and wife, Zhang decided it was time to give his bride a more detailed tour of his home village. She was there just once a year ago for the purpose of meeting his parents. Now they had more time. As they rode through the narrow streets, he pointed out places of interest—his first Army barracks; the school where his father worked as a physical education teacher; the modest house where Su-Li lived with her husband Cheng and their son Qiang; and Qiang's first music shop. Then he pointed to a very tall hill in the distance that he said overlooked a deep ravine. With Qiang's permission, and with Cha-Li's promise of secrecy, it was time to tell her the real story about where he and Qiang first met and the significance of the hill. He didn't know all the details of the cave or who was involved in setting it up, only what he discovered on his own, what he surmised, and the little bit of additional information Qiang had offered.

"It was put in place before the time of modern technology," he concluded after sharing the story with his wife. "It was before machinery became available that could reveal the gender of an unborn child. It is no longer needed for its intended purpose of moving illegal children."

Cha-Li was fascinated. "This is almost like something out of a mystery book, Zhang!" But he assured her the cave was real and most likely still undiscovered. As she tried to absorb the unbelievable story, people shifted in her mind. Qiang moved up a notch from music store owner to fearless life saver; the same for Guo, who they guessed was also involved in the rescue effort.

She thought about Heo, Qiang's biological brother, and realized the stark differences in their pasts. While Qiang was risking his life to save those of infants, Heo was injecting drugs into expectant mothers to end the lives of infants. She knew it wasn't something he wanted to do; it was part of his job. But it had bothered her to a point where she couldn't be civil to him. What welcomed news it was the day Heo told her he was opting out of general medicine and going into pediatrics. Now he was the father of a beautiful little girl named Molly. Cha-Li thought about Meili and her story, how she refused to give Molly up for adoption when she became a widow with the stigma of having a daughter. Heo, Meili and Molly. What a special family!

"Does Heo know anything about the cave and what went on there?" she asked Zhang.

"No. Even though he is Qiang's brother, he has no need to know. Maybe someday Qiang will tell him, but maybe not. That will be up to him. The fewer people who know, the safer it is for all who were involved. The only reason I know is because I was nosy about something that defied logic and was determined to find answers for myself by climbing up there. You are being told because, as my wife, you are likely to visit this village on occasion and might hear stories about Qiang, the last child executioner. I wanted you to know the truth up front. Qiang, Guo, and I trust you, and you have also agreed to their oath of secrecy. You can tell no one—ever! It has to remain a secret. For everyone's sake, I hope the cave will be cleaned out of any traces of it being an escape portal. Perhaps it has already happened but, from what I saw, there's a lot of stuff up there that has to be removed. It's not going to be easy. As you can see, the path is visible from the village. They can't just send a bunch of people up there to carry things down. The other option is to bring it out of a second entrance on the other side of the hill, which is not in view of the village. I was told it is a tedious climb and there are only a few people left around here who know where it is. Perhaps they should just toss everything over the edge into the ravine and hope no one ever finds it. They've also got to somehow erase all the telltale footprints on the wall. I doubt that the paint will just wash off. It's probably going to have to be scraped off or at least destroyed to a point where no one will be able to tell what it was. There are a lot of them, though, including one that belongs to Emily. It's going to be quite a job."

"Emily? Really? Does Su-Li know that her daughter's footprint is on a wall up there?"

"Oh yes. She and her husband both saw it. Qiang was allowed to tell his parents about Emily when he became involved and was about to become the public face of this diversionary operation. He wanted his parents to know the truth before he took over because they would be affected. When they agreed to support him and the cause, Qiang was allowed to take them to the cave. There's a lot more to it, but that is the bottom line to answer your question. Yes, she does know. It was necessary."

Cha-Li sat quietly, pensively, still staring at the distant hill. "How much of this do your parents know?"

"Nothing. They've heard about Qiang the child executioner of course. Everyone around here has, but they never knew him personally. Qiang is a relatively common name so I am sure they will never connect the Qiang who used to live here with the Qiang they met at our wedding. So that's it, my dear. You have seen our entire village and heard some of its history, and it only took an hour! Are you ready to go back to the house? Dinner is probably going to be ready soon."

There was a second reason Zhang wanted to come back for a visit and talk to his parents. He wanted to have a business discussion with them. With only a few months to go before his tenure with the Army would lapse, he was getting anxious to start a sports gym and physical therapy center. He had a list of courses he wanted to take at the university to obtain the necessary credentials. He had drawings of the space he felt he needed to get started and wanted his father to look at them.

After hearing his ideas and looking over the sketches, his parents agreed that Beijing was a good choice for his sports venue. When they were in Beijing for the wedding, they were impressed with all the modern buildings and how much it had grown. Zhang's father offered to donate exercise equipment. It was used, but still in good condition. His mother had some good ideas about how a gymnasium should be decorated! His parents offered funds to help secure a location.

Cha-Li was just as excited for her husband's career outside of the military. She was ready to start setting up books so Zhang wouldn't have to take accounting courses. She would be their official finance officer. It was quickly becoming their combined dream for the future.

Everything was coming together. It was time to start looking for a building to rent when they got back home, hopefully one that wouldn't need a lot of renovating.

Cha-Li also sensed that her new in-laws were curious to know about their plans for a family. It was definitely in their plans, but not right away. It would be business first, then moving out of their apartment into a home of their own, and then parenthood. What she did *not* share with them was their decision to accept whatever child they were blessed with, whether it was a son or a daughter. They just wanted it to be at the right time in their lives.

⛭

Bin knocked lightly on the door of Jin's bedroom. "May I come in?"

"Of course, Father. What's up?"

"I want to talk to you some more about the laogai, just you and me. I know you told us a lot when we had our family discussion a while ago, and I also know you were careful in choosing words that would not be unnecessarily upsetting to your mother, but I want to know more. I want to know about the brainwashing, punishment methods, and any torturous devices they used—everything. I must know."

Jin was surprised. He couldn't imagine why those things would be so important to his father. He really didn't want to talk about it anymore; he was trying to move on. But his father was right, there was more. Some things were too gruesome and personal to share in the presence of his mother and Meili.

Heo had never questioned the scars on Jin's body when he was in the hospital or how he got them. Even if he had, Jin knew better than to tell the truth. Not knowing for sure if he was going to be freed, he was afraid there might be repercussions for telling the truth. That was part of the brainwashing Jin endured. Pulling the buried truth back to the surface was not only painful, it felt disgusting in Jin's new world of normalcy. Still, he respected his father's wishes.

"Thank you, my son. Please forgive me for not asking for this discussion sooner. I had a feeling you endured more than you were telling us, and I appreciate your sensitivity to the women, but I also wanted to give you time to heal, to let you get used to family life again. I've been thinking about a lot of things lately, including that it might be time for me to retire. I have been military all my adult life, and hopefully I have served my country well, but I've also been guilty of turning a blind side to things I didn't want to see or believe. One of those things is what truly happens in the laogai. I've only been inside there once, and that was many years ago for a tour. What I saw was nothing like what you have described. My eyes have been opened a lot lately, especially about how our government says they treat people and how they actually treat people. Unfortunately, I had to find out by seeing the suffering of my own family—you, most of all, then your aunt and uncle being jailed and losing their home for practicing their choice of a religion. Then Cha-Li was suddenly without a home and parents. Your mother has suffered a lot of emotional trauma through all of this and, quite honestly, I am still worried about her.

"If you are agreeable, my son," he continued, "what we discussed today will stay within this room. I appreciate your willingness to talk and your honesty. It has helped me to make some decisions."

"Of course, father."

Talking with his wife was next. "Yan, I want to talk to you about your church. What do you plan to do about it?"

"What do I plan to do about it?" asked a surprised Yan. "What *can* I do about it? There is nothing any of us can do except wait until things settle down and then perhaps we can start up again in someone else's home. No one wants to volunteer right now, and I don't blame them. No one wants to have their house destroyed and end up in prison."

"Then I have an idea. How do you feel about camping?"

"Camping? I know nothing about camping. What does camping have to do with church?"

"Nothing, and everything. There is nothing illegal about having a neighborhood camping group. There are some nice areas in the country not that far away. How would you feel about buying a tent, some camping gear, and roughing it for a few days once a month? We can have an all-day church service of our own, dinner included, sing songs or whatever, and enjoy our own church right out in the open, not in anyone's house. Think about it. You and I could spearhead the effort in getting everyone together. All anyone has to do is buy their own tent and gear, pack some food, and take turns doing whatever it is you do in your services."

Yan stared at her husband in disbelief! "Bin! Are you saying you want to become a member of my church? My religion?"

"*Our* church. *Our* religion. And why not? I've always wanted to attend church as a family and, if I retire, I can do what I want. I really enjoyed Cha-Li's wedding and the sincerity of the service and the wedding vows. Have you noticed that I've already stopped attending the government church? I have to go somewhere," he smiled mischievously. "You may have to tutor me, though."

Yan didn't know what to say; she didn't know her husband had seriously been contemplating retirement. That alone was exciting, but camping? It was an intriguing idea. Going to church as a family? *An absolutely wonderful idea!* She felt herself falling in love with her husband again.

"I would be honored to tutor such a brilliant student," she smiled. "When do you want to start?"

"Today."

She disappeared into the kitchen and took her copy of The New

Testament out of the cupboard. "Here you are, my husband. Read the Book of Matthew and then we can discuss it."

"I will do that, but first I want to talk to Jin and to Heo and Meili. I want them to be the first invitees to our new out-in-the-open church service. We'll have to make sure we have something special for the children as well. Maybe Meili can help with that."

After the conversation Jin had earlier with his father, he was not surprised to hear the news about retirement, although the thought of camping was certainly unique. Heo, on the other hand, was stunned. "You're not going to believe this," he said to Meili after he hung up. "My father is retiring."

"Why is that unbelievable? He has had an admirable career in the Army. He is certainly entitled to retire."

"Well, hang on my dear. There's more. He no longer attends the Three Self Church and mother is tutoring him on being a Christian. They are going to attend church together."

"What? Hasn't he been a member of that church his entire life? What in the world would make him quit? What made him change now? How can he go to your mother's church? It is gone. Has another house church been found? How can—"

"Whoa," Heo laughed. "You haven't even heard the most interesting piece of news. Mother and Father are starting a traveling outdoor church. They are going to buy a tent and camping gear, round up the neighbors who want to do the same thing, and have a church camp once a month in the country where no one will bother them. They are inviting us to join them if we want to."

Meili sat and stared at her husband while she collected her thoughts. "Well, why not? I've been camping before and so has Molly, although she might not remember much of it. My parents camped a lot. Have you ever been camping?"

"No, but I'm sure I can adjust as long as the weather is decent." He laughed. "I cannot believe my mother has agreed to this. I do not remember my mother ever *roughing* it for any reason. This is a lady who considers her yoga class as roughing it, and that is only before she gets her hair done. Even though it is for a good reason, this whole adventure should be interesting!"

Meili smiled. "Well, maybe I can help her with the adjustment. I'm willing to give it a try if you are. Who knows, maybe we might even like it better than our house church. You must admit, it is a novel idea."

"Yes, it is. By the way, I'm just curious. What do campers do for restrooms?"

He never did get an answer, just laughter.

~•~

Bin retired. The neighborhood camping group was formed, and Christianity gained a new convert. Each leader was allowed to choose a part of the Bible that touched his or her heart, present it as a lesson, and then put it out for discussion. Bin was an eager learner. He listened intently to each presenter, asked questions, and listened some more. Eventually it was his turn to lead, and he did. He chose the topic of slavery. His lesson started at the beginning of the Old Testament, which was new to many as they usually took their lessons from The New Testament. True to Bin's thoroughness at whatever he did, however, he had read it all. He didn't necessarily understand much of it, but he found the parts he was looking for. He also made a mental note to somehow find more copies of the Old Testament for their group.

Bin talked about the days when the Hebrews were slaves of the Egyptians and what it took for them to finally be free. He brought it right up to the present time, using Biblical slavery to make his point that little has changed in thousands of years. Slavery then was a way to use free labor, often pushing captive people to toil beyond their capacity for the sake of the country.

"What we have in our country is modern-day slavery," he emphasized. "I have no issue with people who have committed a crime having to work as restitution, but to abuse that practice to the extent of what my son went through is not only abuse in every sense of the word, it is dehumanizing. The world needs to know what is happening here. I am not suggesting we should all walk around carrying protest signs, but we should pray for change and be alert to opportunities for change. Our government announced publicly three years ago it was going to do away with the laojiao, but it has not happened yet. We need to remind them of their promise and do what we can and whenever we can to keep that flame of hope alive. It does not have to be confrontational. Sometimes a subtle reminder can work wonders if it touches the right ears."

Yan never realized what a powerful speaker her husband was, almost mesmerizing. She looked over at Jin. She was seeing changes in him lately, especially in the way he carried himself. *Almost like his father,* she thought. *He seems to be walking taller and with more confidence. Perhaps it is from knowing that his father is championing the cause of those who are imprisoned for the crime of speaking out for freedom. It's almost as if a weight is lifting from his shoulders. Well, of course it has,* she reasoned. *He was brainwashed for seven years. His mind was saturated with the belief that he did something wrong and it was necessary for him to be punished. I am so glad we can talk about it now, at least out here. Bin is right, our penal system is cruel! It must change!*

The next month was Jin's turn. His entire family was there to hear him—his mother and father, Heo and Meili, and even Cha-Li and Zhang. His father and Zhang were now civilians, but it was difficult to get the vision of uniforms out of his mind as his topic was also anti-imprisonment, anti-government. He tried to not look at them as he led the worship service for the first time. Emboldened by his father's support, Jin stepped out of his comfort zone and talked openly about the plight of prisoners and his own experience. The group listened intently. His final remarks came as a surprise, even to his family:

"So, what is the difference between suppression of religion outside of the prison walls and suppression of religion inside the prison?" he asked.

"The bare truth," he continued, "is like comparing day to night. On the outside, like when my aunt and uncle's home was destroyed and the congregation dispersed and went into hiding, faith still existed. The remnant was still there. The flame didn't go out. You all reorganized, the church was renewed, and here you are again.

"Inside prison there is no place to hide. There is a brainwashing process that continues day after day, week after week, year after year. It never ceases until your mind is erased of everything you used to know and believe in. You write what they tell you to write, and you do it repeatedly. You see it in your sleep. You repeat what you are forced to say, and you say it over and over again. Even if you are strong willed enough to fight it mentally, at least for a while, eventually you internalize it. You cave. The flame goes out. There is no ember to rekindle. You believe the lies about yourself and God. You truly believe that God is fictional and believing in Him is a senseless and evil thing. In a strange way, I was fortunate. I knew very little about Christianity when I went to prison, so I didn't have a problem letting go of it. But you are made to believe that you are a failure and your only hope for survival, the only thing that can possibly save you, is the government. The government, and only the government, is worthy of your worship and support. Your duty is to help the government. If you see or hear of anyone who believes otherwise, it is your duty to report it to the authorities.

"That is the difference," he concluded. "That is what our government calls re-education. My father was right when he said the laogai is a form of slavery. If you survive, and many don't, and are fortunate enough to ever be a free person again, the brainwashing takes a long time to wear off. Talking about it does help, but it takes time. I was fortunate—no, blessed—to have a disease that made me physically unable to work. It got me out of the prison. I was even more blessed to have a brother for a doctor, and an understanding family to welcome me home. Not all the prisoners who were pardoned that day were as fortunate. But right now, religion is the shining light in my life, and I have my family and all of you to thank."

Yan Wong was so proud of her son that she was ready to burst. She looked over at Heo and knew from the look on his face that he felt the same way. He was obviously learning more of the *rest of the story* than what he pulled together from the hospitalized prisoners. Never in her life was she happier than sitting in the midst of all three of her children: Heo, Jin, and Cha-Li.

The camping group grew a little larger every month as more members from their destroyed house church joined. Some eventually bought enclosed campers; others stayed with their tents, but they circled around a beckoning fire and enjoyed a freedom they never imagined would be theirs. No one brought Bibles, just in case they were visited by the area police, and they were from time to time. Instead, they simply took turns being presenters. They listened, taught, and learned.

Chapter 14

A NEW GENERATION

WITH NEW BEGINNINGS, there also must be endings. In 2015, after being in effect for thirty-five years, the controversial one-child-per-family edict was discontinued. Couples were now allowed to have two children, with more exemptions available for a possible third child.

What changed? Many believe it resulted from the 2008 earthquake in Sichuan Province. It was a threefold disaster—widespread destruction of property, a humanitarian crisis, and a population void. With the collapse of school buildings, more than 5,300 school-aged children were lost plus hundreds more injured or maimed. Hard-hit areas were left with a whole generation of people missing, toddlers through college age. Thousands of couples suddenly found themselves childless. It brought glaring attention to yet another downside of the one-child policy—loss or injury of children due to natural causes or disasters.

After the earthquake, the government quickly offered certificates of exemption to childless couples, allowing them to have a second child, but many were too old. They chose monetary compensation in lieu of a certificate of exemption.

The earthquake gave rise to another crisis; middle-aged parents who lost older children (teenagers) and chose to have a second child eventually found themselves having to work longer into their otherwise retirement years. Most of these parents were products of the one-child edict themselves and were already shouldering the burden of being sole caregivers for their aging parents. The earthquake affected three generations.

~\\/~

Zhang's whole concept of family changed during the aftermath of the Sichuan quake. He saw and felt it all firsthand. Being born at the time the edict was in effect, he was an only child. So were all his friends. His school was small, mostly boys with just a few girls. He didn't think much about it back then; it's just the way things were. It was a comfortable childhood. It wasn't until he was an adult and a member of the military on disaster cleanup that he understood closeness of family. As he helped thousands of parents in the rural China countryside who were frantically trying to recover their children, he felt their loss and heartbreak.

He was in places where soldiers ordinarily would not go, places where multiple children were needed to work and help the family survive. They were places where illegal second and third children *did* exist in large numbers and were just as important as firstborns. Hidden from outsiders, the illegal children were educated and cherished. Local authorities understood and did not enforce the one-child edict. As far as they were concerned, it was something for larger cities, not feasible for rural life. It took a while for Zhang to realize why so many people were lighting multiple candles.

No wonder we were treated with suspicion when we arrived, he acknowledged. *Even though they needed us and knew we were there to help, they didn't trust us. We were big government. We were perceived as a threat to their way of life.*

Memories of years ago. Things were different now. Today he was going to be a dad, maybe a double dad. The phone call from Cha-Li as she left the doctor's office an hour ago was just starting to sink in:

"The doctor said she thought there might be two heartbeats, but she couldn't tell for sure. We will know next month when I go back for another checkup. We might be having twins!"

They had names picked out for a boy or a girl. Whether it was going to be a son or a daughter made no difference; it was going to be their very own child. Now there might be two! *Twins! Wouldn't that be something!* he thought excitedly. *We will have to come up with more names.*"

Zhang was never happier, which he attributed to God's timing, his *very own* God that he personally embraced. The chain of events of his life played through his mind like a movie: contracting TB, helping the doctor find his family, meeting and marrying Cha-Li, a career change, a new religion. Now he was the owner of a successful sports gym and rehab facility in Beijing, on the threshold of opening a second location in Tianjin, and possibly a third location next year on the opposite side of Beijing. His life was busy, as was Cha-Li's, but they always saved time for their underground church meetings and especially their monthly church camp outing. Being a Christian was dangerous, yes, and probably always would be, which they accepted. But being part of a Christian community was fulfilling. It was meaningful. It was truthful. The more Zhang learned, the more he wanted to learn.

Their happiness did backslide a couple of years earlier when Cha-Li received the news that her mother passed away in prison. It was a shock to all of them, especially after the government promised before the Olympics to end re-education through labor, the laojiao. The hope they held onto month after month, year after year, amounted to nothing, not even a date for a trial. The letter they finally received from prison authorities said that her mother fell and was recovering from her injuries when she died unexpectedly. She was cremated in their crematorium. A few days later they got a second letter indicating Cha-

Li's father was scheduled to be released and they would be informed regarding a date when he could be transported from the facility. They mourned for her mother and continued to wait for more news of her father. Once again, just like in Sichuan Province, he felt the anxiety of a family waiting for news of a loved one.

While they waited, Bin and Yan Wong refurbished Heo's old bedroom to accommodate their widowed relative. Neighbors prayed for him in their camp church and brought over small personal items pulled out of the rubble of his destroyed house, hoping they would bring him cheer. Cha-Li made several trips back to her home village to help prepare for her father's return. Zhang remembered Cha-Li's sadness when she saw a new house sitting on the land. They knew it was there, but actually seeing it was a chilling reminder of what happens to people who host an unregistered house church.

Bin and Yan were realistic. As it was with Jin, they expected Cha-Li's father would be mentally affected, malnourished, and physically spent. His room was made ready, but if he wasn't strong enough to come home, Heo was prepared to have him treated in a rehab facility until he was stronger. Plans were in place. They waited. More months went by until they heard from the prison again.

We regret to inform you . . . it began. It was over. Both of Cha-Li's parents died in prison.

Cha-Li was different after that, almost as if she was withdrawing into herself, unable or unwilling to participate in enjoyment of any kind. She accepted a job teaching at the school where she worked during the Olympics, and afterward as a substitute teacher. She had been offered a permanent position several times, but faithfully turned them down to focus on their family business. However, the business grew quicker than either of them anticipated. They were able to pay off debt, hire more staff, and buy their house sooner. It allowed Cha-Li to step back from the business and return to her teaching career. Zhang knew she was happiest at the school. It was familiar surroundings, a classroom with small children, a place to keep busy while recuperating from the devastating loss of her parents.

But it also had a downside. Having a child of their own became less important. She said it had nothing to do with the lighter workload of their family business or with her new job or because of her parents. She was just having a change of heart about parenthood. She had a lot of friends in Beijing now and many of them were opting out of parenthood in favor of success in the workplace.

Zhang's road to happiness with Cha-Li was bumpy for sure, but he respected her as an individual who was entitled to make up her own mind. It was the same consideration she had given him with his own career. She had the right to choose whether to be a mother, and he promised to support whatever decision she made. He tried to not let his disappointment show, but hoped she would change her mind. And she did, a year later. Strangely enough, it was because of Jin, Cha-Li's journalism-minded cousin.

Thinking about Jin made Zhang smile. He was so much like Cha-Li, willful and determined. Jin decided he needed a job, but not just any job. He set his sights to get into the business world, specifically into advertising and sales promotion. He took classes, sent out resumes, and didn't despair despite many letters of rejection. His tenacity paid off when he finally landed an entry-level position in a large advertising firm in Tianjin. He learned quickly and made good connections; now all he needed were customers. Zhang and Cha-Li decided to be his first. It was an experiment on their part to see if professional promotion was worth the expense. Cha-Li moved some figures around in their budget and came up with the money. It took a few months, but the effort paid off.

Jin's ideas were not only eye-catching promotions, they showed up in just the right places for businesspeople to notice and remember. It wasn't long before Jin's customer base increased, as did Zhang's own business. It was because of Jin that they decided to open a second location in Tianjin and possibly a third on the other side of Beijing. The image and reputation of the gym and rehab center was spreading, and it was exciting. Cha-Li's personal focus changed again, this time away from her teaching career and back to their own businesses—and parenthood. It also coincided with the government's announcement of easing the one-child edict. *More evidence of God's timing,* she thought. It was time to start their own family.

~\|/~

Twins! Yikes! Cha-Li thought about having two children eventually, but not at the same time. She adjusted her thinking. *Can I really do this, handle two at a time?* Zhang was going to be pretty busy running two businesses. Would he be of much help? He promised he would, and she knew he meant it, but could he really do it without wearing himself out? She tried to think positive like Heo had always encouraged. If she could handle a classroom full of small children, then surely she could handle two at home. But doubt still lurked in the back of her mind, until a family gathering convinced her that no matter what the trial, it would all be worth it. Family was precious. Family was everything.

It was a party to celebrate Su-Li Ming's sixtieth birthday and retirement. Fifty-five was the usual age for a Chinese woman to retire but, because she started her career late in life, she was given permission to teach to age sixty. There were two gatherings to honor Cha-Li, both at Zhang's spacious rehabilitation center. One was a mid-week cake and ice cream reception, open to all her students, faculty, and friends. The second was a weekend affair of fun, food, and music with family and just a few special friends. Qiang convinced his mother that just because she was a music teacher during the day, it didn't mean she couldn't share her music on the weekend with family as well. Perhaps she could play her guitar and they could have a sing-along? She agreed.

Su-Li loved to play her guitar. Although piano was the main instrument in her teaching life, she had a special fondness for the guitar, a strange looking, rather bulky instrument made in a place

called Tennessee that Qiang had given her many years ago as a
birthday gift. She was ready for their sing-along. She supplied song
sheets with traditional Chinese favorites mixed in with some church
selections and even a couple of ditties for the children.

The music began. It was happy, beautiful, and even funny. Qiang's
singing voice was well known for being strong, so he automatically
became the singer-conductor. It was not surprising that his brother,
Heo, also had a strong melodic voice. The two brothers good-
naturedly pulled Zhang, Jin, and Bin Wong in between them as
they sang a men's spoof song that brought gales of laughter from
the women. Then Su-Li started *Khua, Khua, Khua Mai Cheo* (Row,
Row, Row Your Boat), one of her school favorites for children that
brought more laughter, especially from Molly and Lian as they sang
along with their parents.

Time went by quickly and dinner was almost ready, and Cha-Li
was selected to say the blessing. It was a special request made of
her earlier by Su-Li. Would she be willing? Of course she said yes.
She made a mental note of the things she wanted to thank God for
on this wonderful occasion, realizing that the number one thing to
be thankful for was family. It was the positive nudge she needed to
accept that having twins was a double blessing, not something to be
feared. Even if it meant double duty, she and Zhang were going to
have two beautiful children.

After watching Su-Li playing her guitar while everyone sang
along, it reinforced what she already knew. *This joy and laughter
would not be happening tonight without family, and the more the
merrier! I am not a member of Su-Li's actual family, but she treated
me like one of her own, and she has for a long time. She accepted me
as a daughter many years ago when I really needed a mother, and she
never let go of my hand. What a fool I was to think that a career could
be more important than this. What was I thinking? Who did I think
I was going to spend my retirement years with? Friends from work?
Customers from the gym? This lady has juggled a family and a career.*

If she can do both, so can I! Plus I am blessed to have a hard-working, very handsome husband who will undoubtedly be a wonderful father. Yes, family IS important!

Food was on the table as they stood in a circle and held hands. Now it was up to Cha-Li to maintain the celebration through prayer. It was short but meaningful as she thanked God for the special blessing of being together as a family in honor of a person who was dear to all of them.

The entire evening was filled with reflections for Su-Li as well. Bits and pieces of her life played through her mind like a story from an opera. Music! Hearing Qiang sing reminded her how music was such a big part of the early years of her and Cheng's marriage. It was how they met as students at the university. It was during a festival, and she was playing the pipa and chimes with several other female musicians. A group of male students were walking by and stopped to listen, soon adding their impromptu voices to the music. She noticed Cheng right away, especially his beautiful tenor voice.

She thought about Qiang when he was just a toddler, displaying his own propensity for music. She and Cheng laughed at their chubby little son singing nonsensical words of his own as he moved his awkward body to the music, only to fall, get up, and try again. Oh, they were such wonderful years.

She listened to Heo sing, the son pulled out of her arms at birth, the son who brought an end to the sound of music in their home as she dealt with depression. It was even worse four years later when a daughter was pulled from her arms. Two children she wanted so desperately to keep but was not allowed. She lived through many dark years of despair and loneliness until music brought her out of it. It was only when she and Cheng heard Qiang sing in a school play that she realized how unfair she had been to him because of her own sadness. Music slowly moved back into their lives. She revived her musical instruments, playing them at home and in their underground church, until their church building was discovered and destroyed along with everything in it, including her instruments. They were crushed. It was another musical setback.

The importance of music took an unexpected turn after Cheng died. She went back to school to become a teacher. She had a major in music and a minor in economics and could have pursued a career in either one. She chose music. The only drawback was that she had to learn to play the piano. She didn't have to play it well, she was told, just well enough to be able to teach it. With the help of a church musician, she learned how to play, fundamentally at least. And it did bode well for getting a teaching job at an elementary school in a nearby village. She loved that job and her students, but it included a challenge—reviving their long-abandoned music program. The deteriorating instruments she had at her disposal were pitiful; many were beyond repair and had to be thrown away. The piano wasn't much better. It was dried up and lopsided because it was missing a leg. She gained permission to restore it and, with Qiang's help, brought it and the other instruments back to life. She ignited the love of music in many young children as well as their parents and even faculty. As time went on, that old piano became dear to her. The more she played it and taught it, the more she enjoyed it. It was an intriguing instrument, maybe because she knew its history. Pianos were banned by the Chinese government for many years, labeled as evil instruments of Western culture. Thousands were pulled out of homes and destroyed. The one in her school escaped destruction by being stored away in the furnace room along with dozens of other instruments.

It was her dedication to music that brought her to Beijing thirteen years ago. She was recommended by her school administrator for a new position at a school of higher learning, a class created for older students who showed exceptional musical ability, a class that would encourage them to think of the world stage rather than only local venues. Saying goodbye to her precious little ones in the rural village was sad, but it proved to be the right decision. Qiang and Guo were already living in Beijing, which was one more reason to make a change. Now she could see them more often.

Music also led to the accidental discovery of her daughter. Flipping casually through a travel magazine one day while her car was being serviced, she caught a quick glimpse of a piano. She went back to the page. There was a young girl sitting at the piano with a group called Music Students International and Su-Li was startled to see that she had hair exactly like her own. Exactly! It was a slim chance at best that it could possibly be her Xiu-Su, but she proceeded on faith. Their schedule included a performance at the opera house in Beijing. To Su-Li, it was a revelation of God's grace in answer to her prayers that someday, somehow, she would find her children. It allowed her to walk through a door that was never supposed to be open, but it was! Along with Qiang and Guo, they heard the Canadian Emily Thornton play that night, and she was amazing. They had a chance to confirm their relationship and were reunited. Although they knew they might never see each other again, at least they met. She remembered how Emily had so many questions—where she was born, who was her family, why was she given up for adoption. They answered all her questions, but carefully. Her adoptive mother gave Su-Li the wallet-sized graduation picture of Emily that she cherished. It was a seemingly small act of kindness, but a tangible piece of her daughter's life to keep in her sight and in her heart. But the memory she clung to the most was the hug that Emily gave her before leaving.

She could never forget that hug! It was after breakfast on the morning of their departure. Emily stood, walked around the table, gently pulled Su-Li to her feet and, with a hug, quietly whispered in her ear: "Thank you Mother. I love you." They were the sweetest words she ever heard. She never wanted that hug to end.

Her reverie was broken with the announcement that it was time to open presents. Every one of them was special, and she loved them all, but Qiang's and Guo's gift was extra special—a *liuqin*, a four-string Chinese mandolin. She was drawn to the liuqin ever since she saw one in Qiang's music shop. Qiang noticed her interest; now she had one of her own and was excited to start practicing with it. Oh, how she loved trying out new musical instruments.

"It is a little trickier to tune than some of the instruments you are familiar with," Qiang explained. "Do you want me to show you the easiest way to do it?"

She gratefully accepted instructions and played a couple of scales ever so carefully while Qiang beamed with delight, knowing that once again he chose the perfect birthday gift for his mother.

～•～

Heo looked on with interest at the unusual musical instrument, demonstrated so adroitly by his brother and now in the hands of his mother. She was doing surprisingly well for a new endeavor. He had a feeling that her plunking would sound very different the next time he heard her play it. Music was never a part of his formative years, but he suddenly had an urge to try his own hand at something musical. It looked like fun.

"Hey, Qiang, could I come by your music shop sometime and try out a couple of instruments? Maybe you could help me find one that I might be capable of playing. I learned how to read music in school for singing, but not for playing. I wouldn't mind trying my own hand at one. I just don't know which one."

"Of course! Just give me a little notice so I can devote the day to you. First, you must decide if you want to play something with a keyboard, a wind instrument, a percussion instrument, or strings. I've got beginner books for every instrument in the store. We'll have you playing in no time, as long as you can fit practice into your busy schedule. I do know you are a busy guy."

"That's true," he laughed, "especially now."

Heo's pediatric practice was expanding. With parents now allowed to have two children, he suddenly needed more staff and office space. He hired two additional doctors and an office manager plus three nurses to work with Meili. He felt good about the change to pediatrics and loved taking care of children, whether they were sick or healthy.

To his delight, his own family was also expanding. Molly was going to have a sibling. She was in her third year of big children's school, feeling very grown up and eager to help with anything that had to do with her new little brother or sister. She was allowed to paint part of a wall in the baby's bedroom. She went shopping with her parents to pick out furniture and curtains for the nursery. Meili let her help open presents at her baby shower. Her most important job, however, was crossing off days on the calendar as they counted down to when her new brother or sister was supposed to arrive.

Heo had been thinking a lot about Su-Li lately. She was his biological mother, yes, and his unborn child would be her biological grandchild, but there wasn't much of a connection between them. He felt there should be more, but not at the expense of the parents who raised him. How could he make her feel important with the new baby without making the parents he grew up with feel less important? How could he explain all this to his child years from now, or should he, and at what age? He put all these questions out to Meili, his valued confidante.

"Don't do anything for now except make sure Su-Li is included in family events that have to do with the children. Like Molly, have the new baby refer to her as Nana Su. When our child is older, there will be a time for truths about how families were torn apart years ago because of a population-control mandate, and how blessed we are that you were able to find your real mother. By then, the edict will be a part of history and it will be a lot easier for a young person to understand."

Heo zeroed in on the "time for truths" more than Meili realized. He agreed with what she suggested, except he wanted to make sure that the truth came from him, not inadvertently from someone else, like it was with him and Papa Shen. For the present, however, his mind was at ease to accept the best of both worlds—his biological one and his adoptive one. Meili was right; he was truly blessed to have found his family.

No one felt more blessed, however, than Su-Li. Not only were all three of her children alive and well and successful, there were now grandchildren in the picture, a new generation. She would cherish each one.

First, there is Lian, she contemplated as she looked over at her, *Qiang and Guo's little walking rainbow.* It always made her smile to see Lian's unique clothing.

Then along came Molly, grandchild two, she counted. *Meili's shy, curly-haired little daughter adopted by Heo after they got married. Now look at her. She is an outgoing little chatterbox, eagerly awaiting the arrival of her baby sister or brother. She wants to be a nurse someday, just like her mother, and I'm sure she will be a good one! She also wants to learn how to play the piano and the guitar just like Nana Su. How special is that to be admired by a grandchild. Pretty soon she is going to be a big sister and I am going to be a grandmother again. I can't wait to meet this new baby! I just wish they lived closer.*

Frederik came to mind next, Emily and Jorg's four-year-old son. *He's a handsome little boy from what I can see. Light brown hair and light brown eyes like his mom. Oh, my grandchildren all look so beautiful and so different. I hope to meet Frederik someday. Emily and Jorg live in Canada most of the time, but make occasional trips to Jorg's home in Germany. Maybe we could meet there.* She thought about little Frederik speaking both German and English, wondering if they would be able to communicate even if she did have a chance to meet him. *Well, I guess it will be a good reason to brush up on my English,* she decided. *I will do that just for Frederik.*

Babies A and B were next, Cha-Li and Zhang's twins. Not her biological grandchildren, but she was going to adopt them in her heart anyway. She remembered seeing the sizable collection of children's books already waiting for them in their nursery. *Cha-Li will be reading to them before they even know what words mean,* she chuckled. Zhang made her smile, too. He had little shirts made up in graduated sizes with the logo of their gym printed on the front, logo created by Jin, of course.

Her thoughts returned to her oldest grandchild with amusement. Guo told her how Lian pleaded with her to ask Aunt Cha-Li and Uncle Zhang if she could help them decorate the nursery with a mural. They happily agreed, and Zhang gave her a section of wall to see what she could do. She amazed them with her stencil art forest scene—a plaid rabbit playing a red pipa, trees with pink, yellow and green leaves, striped mushrooms, and birds with square feathers.

"Your wall is adorable," Cha-Li had told her, "and definitely colorful. I am sure the children will love it."

Last, but always on her mind, was Cheng, the love of her life through twenty-four years of marriage. She talked to him often, hoping he could hear. In her reverie tonight, she saw his face, heard his beautiful singing voice, and basked in the warmth of his memory. Somehow, she knew he was present.

It was time to make a wish and blow out the candles. "Now remember, Mother, don't tell anyone what you wish for or it won't come true," Guo reminded as she placed a beautiful, over-the-top colorful cake in front of her. She looked over at Lian, who was beaming from ear to ear.

Her wish was threefold but simple: Continued success and happiness for her children; her grandchildren growing up in a safer world; and the one she wished for herself was to someday see Emily again. She accepted the probability that it wouldn't happen, but it didn't hurt to wish.

She blew out the candles amid applause and laughter, only vaguely aware of a ringing phone and Qiang's voice while Guo handed her the first piece of cake.

"Lian, you will have to tell me sometime how you got all these colors on the inside of the cake as well as the outside. It is beautiful," Su-Li assured her. Lian tried to smile back at her Nana Su, but, with a mouthful of cake, wisely decided on a thumbs-up instead.

Su-Li's attention was briefly drawn to the doorway where Qiang was walking in with several people. Assuming it had something to do with business, she didn't pay much attention until they started walking toward her. Su-Li jumped from her chair when the lady in the group removed her scarf. *Emily!* Her most coveted wish was already granted! Emily was here with Jorg and Frederik.

"I am sorry we are late, Mother," Emily was finally able to explain amid the long hug and happiness tears. "I've been wanting to see you again for so long, and I know how important a sixtieth birthday is in your country. It seemed like this was the perfect time for a visit. We just couldn't commit to being here until we knew for sure we could get a flight out of Dusseldorf and clearance through Beijing Customs. We told them our purpose was to visit the opera house again, tour Beijing, and spend some time with our friends at Ming's Music Shop. I am so thankful to Qiang and Guo for helping us work it out."

Qiang took charge of introductions while Su-Li was recovering from her initial shock. He and Guo were the only other ones who knew Emily from a dozen years ago at the opera house concert. Qiang kept in contact with his sister through all the years, albeit discreetly under the pretext of a music store owner and a customer.

Heo was apparently clued in on the pending surprise ahead of time and was anxious to meet his sister. They came face to face, looking intently at each other for only a few moments before offering their arms for a life-long awaited embrace.

While the adults were all busy talking and hugging, Lian and Molly took Frederik's hands and led him to the table where cake was being served. It didn't matter that they spoke different languages. They had no problem communicating. Children were children; holding hands and enjoying birthday cake was universal.

The room was filled with happiness and good wishes for Su-Li, her retirement, and the reunion of her children.

--- ·⁄·⁄· ---

The precious fun-filled days of a family reunited went by all too quickly; it was time to say goodbye once again. As Su-Li, Qiang, Guo, and Lian watched the plane take to the sky, there were unspoken thoughts with those on the ground. Would they ever see Emily and Jorg again or would they eventually get caught up in their own busy lives a half world away? Would little Frederik remember his Chinese cousins? Would the day ever come when they would be able to communicate openly by phone, the internet or by mail? So many questions without answers.

Su-Li felt that familiar emptiness again as they walked toward the airport exit, that lonely spot in her heart reserved for Emily—until Lian took her hand.

"Don't be sad, Nana Su. Aunt Emily will come back. And if she doesn't, we will just get on a plane and go visit her!"

They were simple words spoken with all the innocence and optimism of youth but, for some reason, they resonated deeply with Su-Li today. It was almost like an affirmation that it was alright to accept a release from sorrow through a child unburdened by the past.

"Yes! Of course we will, Lian. Of course we will! Why not!"

As they approached the car, Qiang's phone rang, and he became deeply engrossed. They stayed outside, enjoying the warmth of late morning while they waited for Qiang to finish with his caller. "Thank you," they heard him say. "You have made my day." He looked at Guo and Su-Li with a strange expression, almost like half of a smile or something that wanted to break into a smile. "That was Zhang on the phone," he explained. "He and Cha-Li are visiting his parents for a few days. His message was that he went for a hike and visited my abandoned house. The furnishings have been removed and the wallpaper has been stripped down to the bare walls. It is back to its original condition, so I don't have to worry about it anymore. Neither does anyone else."

Guo and Su-Li knew what the message meant. The cave that could link Qiang with the cause for saving illegal children was now benign. There was no more evidence. It was done.

"We have a change of plans," he announced. "I know where there is a very nice shoe store not too far from the river. What do you say we all buy a new pair of shoes and then go down to the river for lunch?" Guo and Su-Li nodded their agreement. Lian was just excited about getting a new pair of shoes to decorate.

They all bought new shoes, but the only one wearing them out of the store was Lian. She was confused. "Why are you carrying your new shoes instead of wearing them?" she asked. "

"We will wear them later," Guo explained, "after we get to the river."

While Guo explained the centuries-old tradition to Lian of throwing one's shoes in the river when a worrisome burden had been lifted, Qiang was the first to stand at the river's edge and throw his shoes, one at a time, as far as he could out into the water. He was finally able to walk out of the shadow of his past. The lingering evidence of his earlier life was gone.

Lian was still confused. "Is that why Father bought new shoes, mother? So he could have something to wear home?"

"Well, yes and no, Lian. Yes, it would certainly be nice for your father to have shoes to wear home, but no, that is not the only reason. The rest of the tradition is that once you throw your old shoes that carried the burden into the river, you should put new shoes on your feet to carry you into a happier life. That is what your father did. He has worried about that old house of his for many years. Now it is gone, and he doesn't have to think about it anymore. He can have a happy life from now on."

"Oh."

Su-Li was next. She had two burdens to shed. She held up one of her shoes and quietly thanked God for all the infants Qiang saved and for no longer having to worry about his safety. She threw it out into the water. As she picked up her other shoe, Lian's optimistic words touched her again. It was time to let go of pain from the past and embrace the future. Maybe she would see Emily again, and maybe she wouldn't. She would always love her child of the past, but she also loved her children of today. As her second shoe flew through the air, she thought about her grandchildren, a new generation with new thinking. Qiang placed her new shoes of happiness on the ground and she slipped into them.

It was Guo's turn, and Qiang was already unwrapping her new shoes. With the threat of discovering the cave of their operation gone, she was more than ready to seek happiness. Her family was involved with the baby tunnel long before Qiang got involved. Theirs was the first safehouse on the baby tunnel route. She was always fearful that one of the transporters would be followed and her parents would be arrested. There was a Plan B, of course, and that was for the transporter to keep going if he felt he was being watched. When she and Qiang met, he was one of the transporters. They all shared the danger of moving children through the tunnel to safety. When Qiang assumed the public role of child executioner, she worried about him even more. Although the operation for saving the babies had been abandoned for years, the cave and its lingering evidence was still there. Her husband remained in danger. They may never know who took the cave down or when but, thanks to Zhang, they now knew it was over. She could throw her shoes in the river and enjoy a happier life with her family.

Lian watched it all, thankful she didn't have anything serious to worry about so she could keep her old shoes. She liked her old shoes. They were beautifully decorated. She took Nana Su's hand as they walked from the river's edge back to the car; it was time for lunch, and she was getting hungry.

Yes, it was turning out to be a beautiful day for the family of three generations. With new shoes on their feet, and embracing an old tradition, they were ready to step out of the past and into the future. They were ready to go wherever life was meant to take them.

Acknowledgments

THANK YOU TO all those who have contributed to the writing of this book:

Betty Calliham

Michael and Virginia Dickson

Victoria Ingalls

Karen Kunzer

Carole Marks

Dr. Pamela Miller

Jerry and Henrietta Paulsen

Yvette Rooker

Reverend Bradley Scott

William and Beverly Stives

Donald and Genevieve Stone

About the Author

MADELYN ROHRER

BORN IN UPSTATE New York, Madelyn grew up as a "border kid." She spent early years living on both sides of the Canadian border and later years in Southern California where she lived just a few miles from the Mexican border.

In between borders, she spent over two decades in Jonesborough, Tennessee, the home of international storytelling, before returning to her hometown in New York.

Her business career is just as diverse. It includes twenty-eight years in a large New York photographic corporation, partnership in a family-owned business, and owning her own office management company.

Madelyn's tenure in Jonesborough sparked an interest that led to yet another career – professional storyteller, speaker, and published author. Although her portfolio of oral and written stories is diverse, her favorites are those that inspire, strengthen moral values, and bring history to life. Her stories are suitable for all audiences.

MADELYN'S BOOKS

Tiggy Touch Wood, her first book, was published in 2014. It includes ten original short stories composed for the storytelling stage and subsequently converted to written form. The book has received excellent reviews from the storytelling and literary communities, including a five-star award from Red City Review. Several stories have been chosen for writers' guild anthologies.

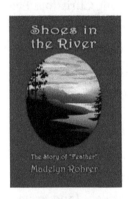

Shoes in the River, a novel, was released in 2015. It presents an insight into real life in China as affected by the one-child-per-family edict that produced a worldwide dilemma still being dealt with today. The characters are fictional, but the issues are real. It has received excellent reviews from Red City Review and Writers Digest.

Touched by Tennessee, Second Edition (copyright 2016; second edition 2020) is a collection of eight true historical stories originally told on stage with the common thread of the State of Tennessee. One of the stories was chosen as a first-place winner by *Storytelling World Awards,* a publication of the National Storytelling Network. It is also available as an audio book.

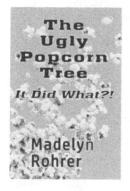

The Ugly Popcorn Tree (2018) is a novella of true-to-life fiction about older orphans ("tweens"), some of the circumstances that would have them lingering in an orphanage at an older age, and the difficulties they encounter while waiting for new homes and parents.

Children's Books

Hobie the Christmas Spider (2017) is the first in "The Critter Series" of children's books. It is created from a bit of Germanic folklore and an Old-World Tradition of sharing Christmas Eve with the animals...only from the perspective of the spiders. It teaches children about the love Jesus has for all living creatures, even the tiniest of all. It is a story of the magic of Christmas.

Bert the Owl Bat (2019) is the second in "The Critter Series" of children's books. Join Bert as he meets a new but unlikely (and scary) friend quite by chance. Bert and his friend are leery of each other at first but soon decide in their minds to be friends. When their lives are interrupted by danger, their bond of friendship becomes one of the heart.

Other Publications

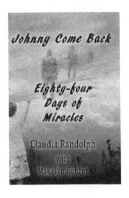

Johnny Come Back (2018) is a novella, the true story of an East Tennessee couple. When Claudia, a seasoned emergency room nurse, takes her husband to the hospital on Christmas Eve 2017 with flu-like symptoms, they don't return home for eighty-four days. This is their amazing story as they lived it. (Written for them by Madelyn Rohrer).

On the Horizon

There's a Ferret in the Neighborhood! The third children's book in The Critter Series.

Eirene the Dove of Peace – The fourth children's book in The Critter Series.

Madelyn's website: **www.storytellermadelynrohrer.com**
YouTube channel: **Stories by Madelyn Rohrer**

Bibliography

Education in China

Medical Degrees in China, Study in China - Undergraduate - List of Undergraduate Courses, https://www.studyinchina.com.my/web/page/medical-degrees-in-china/

Medical Degree and Education in China, http://www.besteduchina.com/medical_degree_in_china.html

Education System in China, https://www.scholaro.com/pro/Countries/china/Education-System

One-Child-Per-Family Edict and Family Planning Laws

Beijing Social Maintenance Fee Collection Management, November 2002, https://www.global-regulation.com/translation/china/168301/beijing-social-maintenance-fee-collection-management.html

Family Planning Law and China's Birth Control Situation, China.org.cn by staff reporter Hu Huiting, October 18, 2002, http://www.china.org.cn/english/2002/Oct/46138.htm

China's two-child policy: Single mothers left out, 2 November 2015, https://www.bbc.com/news/world-asia-china-34695899

One-child policy, Chinese government program, Pletcher, Kenneth. Encyclopedia Britannica, 15 Sep. 2021, https://www.britannica.com/topic/one-child-policy. Accessed 1 April 2022.

Crackdowns show how China's one-child policy keeps the black-market boy business churning, Gwynn Guilford, Reporter, Published March 25, 2013, https:/www.qz.com/66862/crackdowns-show-how-chinas-one-child-policy-keeps-the-black-market-boy-business-churning/

The Effects of China 's One-Child Policy: The Significance for Chinese Women Kristine Sudbeck University of Nebraska, 2012, https://www.digitalcommons.unl.edu/cgi/viewcontent.cgi?article=1178&context=nebanthro

Blood smuggling in China: Why pregnant women are breaking the law to find out their babies' sex, Julie Zaugg, CNN, Updated 3:30 AM EDT, Thu October 17, 2019, https://www.cnn.com/2019/10/13/asia/hong-kong-blood-smuggling-nipt-intl-hnk/index.html

China blood smuggling: Hong Kong used as hub for illegal baby gender tests, Web Desk Updated: October 15, 2019 18:54 IST, https://www.theweek.in/news/world/2019/10/15/china-blood-smuggling-hong-kong-used-as-hub-for-illegal-baby-gender-tests.html

Religion in China

Religious Repression in China, US-China Summit (June 1998) and Human Rights - Campaigns Page, https://www.hrw.org/legacy/campaigns/china-98/religion.htm

Religion in China, Beina Xu and Eleanor Albert, February 17, 2017, https://www.cfr.org/backgrounder/media-censorship-china, Last updated September 25, 2020 8:00 am (EST)

Eleanor Albert and Lindsay Maizland, https://www.cfr.org/backgrounder/religion-china

Christianity: Religious Freedom in China, Sarah Cook, Senior Research Analyst for China, Hong Kong, and Taiwan, 2017, https://www.freedomhouse.org/report/2017/battle-china-spirit-christianity-religious-freedom

Chinese Prisons

Inside a Chinese Prison: An American's Perspective. Stuart B. Foster, June 22, 2014, https://www.prisonlegalnews.org/news/2014/jun/22/inside-chinese-prison-americans-perspective/

The Laogai System, History and Purpose: Laogai Research Foundation, https://www.laogairesearch.org/laogai-system/

China's 'Re-Education Through Labor' System: The View From Within: Minami Funakoshi, February 6, 2013, https://www.theatlantic.com/international/archive/2013/02/chinas-re-education-through-labor-system-the-view-from-within/272913/

Human Rights Watch, Re-education Through Labor in China, US-China Summit and Human Rights - Campaigns Page. June 1998, https://www.hrw.org/legacy/campaigns/china-98/laojiao.htm

China: The World's Biggest Slave Labor Camp, Northstar web radio, http://www.nstarzone.com/CHINA.html

SARS and Other Medical Outbreaks

The SARS Epidemic and its Aftermath in China: A Political Perspective, Yanzhong Huang, Institute of Medicine (US) Forum on Microbial Threats; Knobler S, Mahmoud A, Lemon S, et al., editors, Washington (DC): National Academies Press (US); 2004. https://www.ncbi.nlm.nih.gov/books/NBK92479/

SARS Epidemic: SARS Outbreaks in Inner-land of China, Yichen Lu, Emerging Infections in Asia. 2008 : 75–96, https://www.ncbi.nlm.nih.gov/pmc/articles/PMC7122843/

Severe Acute Respiratory Syndrome, Beijing, 2003 Wannian Liang, Zonghan Zhu, Jiyong Guo, Zejun Liu, Xiong He, Weigong Zhou, Daniel P. Chin, Anne Schuchat, and for the Beijing Joint SARS Expert Group Emerg Infect Dis. 2004 Jan; 10(1): 25–31, doi: 10.3201/eid1001.030553, https://www.ncbi.nlm.nih.gov/pmc/articles/PMC3092360/

SARS, https://www.who.int/health-topics/severe-acute-respiratory-syndrome#tab=tab_1

Severe acute respiratory syndrome (SARS), https://www.mayoclinic.org/diseases-conditions/sars/symptoms-causes/syc-20351765

Learning from SARS: Preparing for the Next Disease Outbreak: Workshop Summary. THE SARS EPIDEMIC AND ITS AFTERMATH IN CHINA: A POLITICAL PERSPECTIVE Yanzhong Huang. https://www.ncbi.nlm.nih.gov/books/NBK92479/

Schistosomiasis Control and Snail Elimination in China Kawai Fan, PhD, Am J Public Health. 2012 December; 102(12): 2231–2232.Published online 2012 December. doi: 10.2105/AJPH.2012.300809, https://www.ncbi.nlm.nih.gov/pmc/articles/PMC3519337/

Schistosomiasis in the People's Republic of China: Prospects and Challenges for the 21st Century, Authors: Allen G. P. Ross, Adrian C. Sleigh, Yuesheng Li, George M. Davis, Gail Williams, Zheng Jiang, Zheng Feng, Donald P. McManus Research Article, 01 April 2001, https://www.journals.asm.org/doi/10.1128/CMR.14.2.270-295.2001

History of influenza pandemics in China during the past century Zhonghua Liu Xing Bing Xue Za Zhi 2018 Aug 10;39(8):1028-1031. doi: 10.3760/cma.j.issn.0254-6450.2018.08.003, https://www.pubmed.ncbi.nlm.nih.gov/30180422/

Tuberculosis and HIV in Chinese Prisons

Tuberculosis/cryptococcosis co-infection in China between 1965 and 2016, Emerg Microbes Infect. 2017 Aug; 6(8): e73., Published online 2017 Aug 23. doi: 10.1038/emi.2017.61, https://www.ncbi.nlm.nih.gov/pmc/articles/PMC5583669/

Epidemic Situation of Tuberculosis in Prisons in the Central Region of China, Am J Trop Med Hyg. 2019 Sep; 101(3): 510–512., Published online 2019 Jul 8. doi: 10.4269/ajtmh.18-0987, https://www.ncbi.nlm.nih.gov/pmc/articles/PMC6726957/

A Preventable Outbreak of Tuberculosis Investigated through an Intricate Social Network, Clinical Infectious Diseases, Volume 33, Issue 11, 1 December 2001, Pages 1801–1806, Published: 01 December 2001. https://www.academic.oup.com/cid/article/33/11/1801/442724

The HIV epidemic in China: history, response, and challenge, November 2005, https://www.nature.com/articles/7290354#Sec2, 5

China to Start HIV Test on Prison Population, (Xinhua News Agency November 26, 2004) http://www.china.org.cn/english/government/113219.htm,

Chinese prisoner who contracted HIV in prison wins US $14,000 payout, 9 November 2019, South China Morning Post, Zhuang Pinghui, https://www.sg.news.yahoo.com/chinese-prisoner-contracted-hiv-prison-101716698.html

Chinese Military

How Censorship Works in China: A Brief Overview, 2006. Includes:
1. The "Great Firewall of China": Censorship at the Internet backbone and ISP level
2. Censorship by Internet Content Providers: Delegating censorship to business
3. Surveillance and censorship in email and web chat
4. Breaching the Great Chinese Firewall
5. Chinese and International Law
https://www.hrw.org/reports/2006/china0806/3.htm

Military Service Law of the People's Republic of China Subject: Military Issuing-Dept: National People's Congress Issue-Date: 05/31/1984 IMPLEMENT-DATE: 10/01/1984 http://www.asianlii.org/cn/legis/cen/laws/mslotproc463/

China's National Defense in 2006, issued by the Information Office of the State Council, People's Republic of China, December 29, 2006, https://www.nuke.fas.org/guide/china/doctrine/wp2006. html

Military Power of the People's Republic of China 2006, https://www. nuke.fas.org/guide/china/dod-2006.pdf

2008 Olympics

The 2008 Olympics was a soft power victory for Beijing. A successful Games in 2022 could validate its authoritarian system; Analysis by James Griffiths, CNN Updated 9:05 PM ET, Sun February 21, 2021, https://www.cnn.com/2021/02/21/asia/beijing-olympics-2008-2022-soft-power-dst-intl-hnk/index.html

The 2008 Olympics' Impact on China, USCBC, July 1, 2008, https:// www.chinabusinessreview.com/the-2008-olympics-impact-on-china/

One question hung over 2008 Games: Would they change China? Stephen Wade; August 16, 2020, https://www.apnews.com/article/beijing-sports-asia-2020-tokyo-olympics-china-olympic-games-73163e1885612915b4742de2bfa3d277

Calls to Boycott China's 2022 Winter Olympics Echo 2008: CHINA NEWS; February 27, 2021 1:26 AM, https://www.voanews. com/a/east-asia-pacific_voa-news-china_calls-boycott-chinas-2022-winter-olympics-echo-2008/6202624.html

China's Olympic press freedom pledges: Worthless in 2008, absent in 2022: Iris Hsu/CPJ China Correspondent, October 25, 2021 10:08 AM EDT, https://www.cpj.org/2021/10/china-olympic-press-freedom-pledges-absent-2022/

How China changed after 2008 Beijing Olympics, https:// www.dw.com/en/how-china-changed-after-2008-beijing-olympics/a-44986744

Sichuan earthquake

Benchmarks: Earthquake devastates western China, May 12, 2008: Sam Lemonick August 31, 2015. https://www.earthmagazine. org/article/benchmarks-may-12-2008-earthquake-devastates-western-china/

China: Focus - the Sichuan earthquake, Posted 30 Jun 2008, https:// www.reliefweb.int/report/china/china-focus-sichuan-earthquake

The Other China: Beyond the Olympic Spotlight in Earthquake Stricken Sichuan: David Muir and Jo Ling Kent, February 18, 2009, https://www.abcnews.go.com/International/China/ story?id=5551894&page=1

New Documentary Revisits Deadly 2008 Earthquake In China,/ February 23, 201012:00 PM ET, Heard on Tell Me More, Lynn Neary, host https://www.npr.org/templates/story/story. php?storyId=124004518

Precious but Precarious: Wenchaun's Second Families, May 10, 2018, Eileen Guo, https://www.sixthtone.com/news/1002232/ precious-but-precarious-wenchuans-second-families

Fallout of the One-Child-Per Family Edict

China's Secret Children Step Out of the Shadows Survivors of the one-child policy recall forced adoptions and derailed careers Bloomberg News, January 8, 2019 at 4:00 PM EST Updated on January 9, 2019 at 7:12 AM, https://www.bloomberg.com/news/ features/2019-01-08/china-s-secret-children-step-out-of-the-shadows

China's Former 1-Child Policy Continues To Haunt Families Updated July 4, 20217:06 AM ET, Heard on Morning Edition, Emily Feng https://www.npr.org/2021/06/21/1008656293/the-legacy-of-the-lasting-effects-of-chinas-1-child-policy

Have three kids! Can China's new edict reverse the fallout from its one-child policy? May 13, 2022, Eryk Bagshaw, https://www.smh.com.au/national/have-three-kids-can-china-s-new-edict-reverse-the-fallout-from-its-one-child-policy-20220408-p5ac3y.html#:~:text=For%20four%20decades%2C%20strict%20family,to%20three%20children%20per%20couple.

Chinese 'one-child policy' an enduring evil Jan 30, 2014, Updated Jan 31, 2014, Blake Seitz @BlakeSeitz https://www.redandblack.com/views/chinese-one-child-policy-an-enduring-evil/article_99b71ba8-89e0-11e3-8566-0017a43b2370.html

Other

The Modern Chinese Wedding Ceremony and Banquet, https://www.thoughtco.com/chinese-wedding-rituals-687490

Traveler's Guide to Camping in China in 2021, May 5, 2021. Josh Summers, https://www.travelchinacheaper.com/4-tips-for-camping-in-china

Into the Wild: Camping in China 101, October 5, 2015. August Hatch, eChinacities.com, https://www.echinacities.com/expat-life/Into-the-Wild-Camping-in-China-101

Retirement Age in China

China is trying to change its problematic retirement age By Tripti Lahiri, PublishedApril 22, 2022, https://qz.com/2149635/china-is-trying-to-change-its-problematic-retirement-age

China to delay retirement ages 'gradually' by 2025, after holding firm for seven decades, Luna Sun in Beijing, Published: 8:30 pm, 22 Feb, 2022, https://www.scmp.com/economy/china-economy/article/3167985/china-delay-retirement-ages-gradually-2025-after-holding-firm

Musical Instruments in China

Classical Music During the Chinese Cultural Revolution, April 16, 2019 by Andy Fein, Luthier at Fein Violins, Ltd. And Ivana Truong, http://blog.feinviolins.com/2019/04/classical-music-during-cultural.html

Beethoven in China: The Dark Years By Georg Predota, June 18th, 2017, https://interlude.hk/beethoven-china-dark-years/

Instruments of the Traditional Chinese Orchestra, https://www.web.northeastern.edu/music-chinese/liuqin/

CPSIA information can be obtained
at www.ICGtesting.com
Printed in the USA
LVHW040352220723
752879LV00001B/196